"WAKE UP, SLEEPING BEAUTY."

Chris leaned over as if to kiss her, then quickly drew back. "Nap time is over. We got here about an hour ago."

"An hour!" Holly cried. She sat up and stretched her cramped muscles. "I'm sorry. How boring for you!"

He grinned. "Not at all. You seemed to be having some mighty interesting dreams."

She felt her cheeks burn. Had she said or done anything to indicate the erotic turn her thoughts had taken? "You could have been a gentleman and left me a little privacy."

"Yes, I could have, but I didn't want to disturb you."

"Meaning?"

"Meaning your embrace was somewhat restrictive, but, I hastily add, very satisfying...."

ABOUT THE AUTHOR

Megan Alexander is a woman of seemingly
boundless energy! Formerly a distinguished
academic, music teacher and newspaper
columnist, Megan, who is also the mother of three
accomplished children, now devotes herself to
writing, and boasts a list of hobbies that include
theatergoing, gourmet cooking, miniatures and
world travel. She recently discovered and fell in
love with Oaxaca, Mexico, where she has set her
third Superromance.

Books by Megan Alexander

HARLEQUIN SUPERROMANCE
17–CONTRACT FOR MARRIAGE
95–BLOSSOMS IN THE SNOW

These books may be available at your local bookseller.

Don't miss any of our special offers. Write to us at the
following address for information on our newest releases.

Harlequin Reader Service
901 Fuhrmann Blvd., P.O. Box 1397, Buffalo, NY 14240
Canadian address: P.O. Box 603,
Fort Erie, Ont. L2A 9Z9

Megan Alexander

ONCE A STRANGER

Harlequin Books

TORONTO • NEW YORK • LONDON
AMSTERDAM • PARIS • SYDNEY • HAMBURG
STOCKHOLM • ATHENS • TOKYO • MILAN

Published October 1986

First printing August 1986

ISBN 0-373-70230-2

To Stephen, James and Deborah, my children.
To dear friend, Ruth Walker, with gratitude,
and to Mary Hallock for introducing me to Oaxaca
and her charming Casa Colonial,
thus providing the inspiration for this book.

CHAPTER ONE

ALTHOUGH THIS WAS the second week that Holly had reported promptly for her new summer job, the shop had yet to open on time. Juana, the manager, would stroll up soon after Holly had arrived and shrug her shoulders in elegant disdain at the compulsive clock-watching American. "Five or ten minutes, what does it matter in the world scheme of things?" she would mutter in Spanish.

The brilliant Oaxacan sun already promised sufficient excuse to indulge later in the midafternoon siesta. But for the moment, Holly basked in the warmth and watched a sleepy shopkeeper across the street pull back the accordion grating and open the door for the day's business.

A few feet away a young boy stood at the curb whittling on a chunk of wood. A chip had lodged rakishly in his hair, giving him a vulnerable look. Something about his earnest concentration arrested her, and she realized it was the same youngster who had been coming into the shop recently, apparently intrigued by some of the wood carvings. Every line of his body seemed geared to his task. She wished she could sketch him.

She glanced into the window of the little jewelry shop next door and caught her breath. The display highlighted a single ring on a raised pedestal. Tiny sapphires were set in a circle of swirling gold and sparkled in the morning sunlight. She bent to examine it more closely.

Yes, the ring looked a lot like hers. Resolutely she straightened and turned away.

She'd adored her wedding ring but had discarded it along with Christopher Brooke's name almost seven years ago. She'd been another person then, and she'd come a long way. Now she was able to feel compassion for that naive nineteen-year-old bride who hadn't had the courage to be herself in the shadow of a brilliant husband, but who had managed to hide her anxieties behind a self-possessed and reserved facade.

Divorce. It had taken all her resolve to put Chris out of her system, to ignore all the hurts that had mended so slowly. But she'd done so, and all on her own. Now she worked in a profession she loved, as a member of the art department in one of California's most prestigious small colleges. Only rarely, as just now, did something or someone touch off those far-off troubled or tender recollections. It meant nothing, she would tell herself. Such memories were natural. They came with the territory. Anyway, Oaxaca was a whole different world and was not likely to incur many such lapses.

Holly had arranged for a year's leave of absence from her job in order to study with various master weavers and ceramicists, mainly hoping to work with Doña Elena, a world-famous potter. Last month when the letter had finally arrived announcing her acceptance in Elena's summer class, she had ecstatically shared the news with Jeff, a colleague whom she'd dated recently.

He pulled an aghast expression. "You're going to Mexico? But we'd talked about going to Hawaii for the summer. I thought your leave didn't start until fall. What brought this on?"

"*You* talked about going to Hawaii. *I'm* going to study with Elena!"

"Elena! Good lord! Who's Elena? Are you saying you'd rather spend the summer in front of some cruddy potter's wheel than languish on the silver sand with a virile, charming fellow like me?"

"Your modesty touches me, but odd as it may seem that's my plan. First of all, Elena doesn't use a potter's wheel. That's just one dimension of her skill, and she works with a unique kind of clay. Her creations are in important museums and galleries all over the world. I still can't believe I've been accepted. It's a dream come true!"

He shook his head morosely. "And all the time I thought I filled your dreams." He picked up her travel folder of the area. "Oaxaca," he said, anglicizing the *x*. "Never heard of it."

"Then it's time you did. It's a marvellous center for artisans, a city of almost two hundred thousand people, mostly Indian. And your pronunciation is terrible. It's *Wah-hawk-a*, and don't waste that hangdog expression on me. You'll whip out your little black book and find some blonde to replace me in less than five minutes."

He grinned. "You know I prefer brunettes."

"Oh, sure, today brunettes, tomorrow blondes, and yesterday redheads. Buzz off!"

The moment the spring semester had ended she had packed her bags and had flown to Mexico. Almost immediately, because of her background as well as her fluency in Spanish, she had found a part-time job in a shop that specialized in the work of the city's finest artisans. Mornings she worked with Juana, the manager, and three afternoons a week she studied with Elena. Thus far it had been a satisfying arrangement.

She even had a new man in her life—Miguel, the owner of the beautiful Casa Avalon where she now stayed. She'd never known anyone quite like him, a man to whom old-fashioned gallantry came naturally. He was an artist, a zealous scholar of Mexican history and an almost too-attentive companion, a refreshing change from Jeff's breezy company. Elena had introduced her to him, and he'd rented her one of the spacious suites in his century-old Spanish colonial home near the center of the city, a sanctuary of high-ceilinged rooms and tranquil gardens surrounded by high walls. The summer loomed ahead full of promise.

Now she watched as Juana walked briskly down the street toward the shop. Probably in her mid-thirties, Juana was a widow. She was pure Spanish, born in Barcelona, with fine-boned aristocratic features and snapping black eyes. She had no children, yet didn't seem to lack for company; she was always quoting various cousins, aunts and uncles. Her lively chatter and vivacity didn't obscure her business acuity, and Holly knew how Juana cut corners in order to save for the cottage she passionately hoped to own some day. At present she lived in a cramped and rather depressing apartment. Now Juana paused at the window of the jewelry shop and, like Holly a few minutes earlier, bent closer, apparently also intrigued by the lovely ring.

It had been like Chris to choose sapphires for her wedding band. "We can't have anything ordinary for you, darling Felicity," he'd said when he'd had it made for her.

Felicity. Perhaps she could blame the entire painful mistake of her marriage on that name. Her mother had insisted that anyone with a last name as commonplace as Jones needed something unusual to distinguish it. The original Felicity had been her red-haired great-grandmother who had suited the name to perfection. According to Holly's mother, the woman had been a saint. From turning out the lightest biscuits in town to raising eight children and becoming a doctor, there was nothing she hadn't been able to do. Holly's mother had made it plain that Holly was expected to follow in her great-grandmother's footsteps, but it had been an impossible chore. The name became a burden, a continual reminder of her great-grandmother's successes that eventually caused her to despise it.

After the divorce she'd shed the name along with her married one. It didn't fit her. She desperately sought new beginnings, and taking a new name underlined her determination.

SHE'D MET HER FUTURE HUSBAND when a classmate at Berkeley had insisted on dragging her to a student rap session with a distinguished visiting lecturer named Christopher Brooke.

"Come on, Felicity," her friend said. "He's already a big name in the field of film documentaries and the author of several books, and he's only twenty-eight."

"Since when are you interested in film documentaries?" Holly asked. "I thought you were a dietetics major."

"Listen, my girl, education is supposed to be broadening. There's more in this world besides vitamins and calories."

They arrived at the hall to find Christopher Brooke sitting on the floor surrounded by students. He was no owl-eyed, bearded professor, as Holly had expected. In jeans, sweatshirt and jogging shoes, he looked more like one of the students, comfortable with his body as well as his clothes. Probably close to six feet and perfectly proportioned, he moved with the controlled grace of a gymnast, and his intense gray eyes, the most attractive feature in his expressive face, focused respectfully on any student who questioned him.

As Felicity joined the group, Chris met her glance. In that instant she knew she'd entered dangerous territory. She'd heard a lot about magnetic personalities, but she'd had no conception of the power they could wield. His one brief look had the force of a shock!

His voice was as modulated as an actor's. Did he use it in the same manner? To persuade? To manipulate? She felt as if she'd turned into a lump of her own clay and desperately wished she could take the feeling and knead it into something beneficial instead of this breathless state in which she'd so unexpectedly found herself.

"Felicity," he said later when someone introduced them, and his tone caressed the name. "I've never met a girl called Felicity." Afterward, when coffee and sandwiches were being served, he elbowed his way through the roomful of people, and she almost froze when he took her arm and found them a place to sit on a stairway. What did a mere college sophomore say to a two-time winner at international film festivals?

When she spoke at all, it was in a breathy monotone that he obviously took as the ultimate in sophistication. How could he have guessed that the reserved dark-haired girl with the steady blue-green eyes, the girl who wore the handwoven djellaba, actually carried the destroying seeds of self-doubt underneath her distinctive exterior. Felicity, the cool sophisticate, appeared to be the perfect mate for a man who moved in worldwide circles. How disappointed he must have been. It was surprising that the marriage had even lasted two years.

Oh, at first it had been a grand adventure. He'd introduced her to her own backyard as she'd never known it; they would bicycle Golden Gate Park's pathways on misty Sunday mornings, tramp through the shaded groves of the Muir Redwoods and drink in the sunset while perched atop Angel Island. What a heady time it was! She fell wildly in love with him at once, and he with her. Or so she believed then, and they were married six weeks later.

Holly promptly set out to find a house, any house, a place where she could settle down and make a home. As an army brat, dragged from post to post for most of her childhood, a permanent home represented heaven. She wanted to live in one place, go to one school and have long-lasting friends. Her parents' marriage had broken up, and Holly suspected that her mother, too, had hated their rootless life. From then on, she'd vowed that when she married she would have a permanent home, even if it were located on a desert island.

With the help of a realtor, she found a house within their means, listed euphemistically as a quaint turn-of-the-century Victorian home. She knew it was her house the moment she saw it; Chris was less enthusiastic.

He cast a dubious eye at the peeling paint and worn shingled roof. "I didn't think you'd be taken in by white gingerbread trim and three-generation magnolias."

"That's what I like about it. We could put down firm foundations in a place like this," she said with an intensity that had been building in her for years. "Look at that staircase. Can't you just see our daughters floating down it at their weddings?"

"Our sons had better be handy with a saw and hammer," he teased, then put his arms around her. "Okay, my darling. I have an offer for a job at the university next fall. That will give us the summer to get settled."

She talked excitedly about how she knew all about refinishing old furniture and how she could sew up a storm.

She even wanted to weave the fabric to cover the chairs. They made love with added excitement, and as always, Christopher, the tender lover, took her to heights that banished all thoughts but the brightest and most promising.

A week later Chris received a call from Marissa Levesque, coauthor of his last book. His face grew radiant during the conversation. "I can't believe it," he cried as he put down the phone. "A publisher has accepted our proposal to write the history of nonfiction film. I'd almost given up on it." He named a generous figure, swooped Holly up in his arms and whirled her around until she was dizzy. "L.A., here we come!"

"Los Angeles? Can't you work here?"

"Good Lord, no. Our research facilities are mainly in that area. Besides, I'll be team-lecturing with Marissa, giving international film workshops at the Davis Institute while we write the book."

"But, Chris, what about your job at Berkeley? And our house? Tomorrow is the day we were to meet with the realtor to give him our down payment."

"I haven't signed a contract yet, and as for that house, let's face it, those old places are pure termite fodder. Come on and help pack. At the risk of sounding like a walking cliché, home, my darling, is where the heart is."

She took in his glowing face, and her throat contracted so that it was hard to speak. Eventually she gave a brilliant performance, pitching in with all the enthusiasm she could muster, making breathless little comments, all positive if not jubilant. After all, she'd had years of training in adjusting to sudden moves. Christopher slept that night wearing a euphoric smile, unaware that his wife wept in her pillow.

In L.A. Chris worked long hours researching and writing, and whenever he was home, their small apartment teemed with people from the institute, an older, sophisticated crowd who intimidated Holly with their brittle, often caustic wit and esoteric chatter. THE INSTITUTE. She always thought of it in capital letters, as an omnivorous menace that was consuming their marriage. She counted the weeks until the year was over.

Then, at a party where the topic focused on wine, she got lost in the unfamiliar jargon. When someone asked her if she didn't think a certain cabernet was a bit flinty, even austere, she answered truthfully, "I have no idea. I guess I'm a peasant about wines. I know what I like, and cabernet is one of my favorites."

Later she overheard a remark by the wife of one of Chris's colleagues. "A pretty little thing, but honestly, isn't it amazing how often brilliant men are attracted to featherbrained women?" Holly knew without a doubt the reference was to her. Now anxieties ballooned as she worried that she'd say or do something that would prove the woman's words beyond all doubt.

A few weeks before they were to return home, an invitation arrived for Chris to conduct a summer seminar at a university in Stockholm. From there they went to New York to fulfill a similar offer at Columbia. Holly happily got settled, enrolled in a night school art class and a month later won a contest for designing a logo for a computer corporation. Chris bought champagne and toasted her talent, then announced that they could also toast his good fortune. Marissa had wangled a grant to do a TV documentary on the political strife in Ireland. She would do the script and he the filming as usual.

Holly felt as if she'd just read her obituary in the paper. Frustration whipped her into a fever. There was to be no dream house. Her life had become a rootless extension of her childhood.

"What about me, Chris? My prize for winning the contest is tuition to the California Academy of Arts and Crafts, one of the best in the country! It means a lot to me to go there. My loom and my pottery tools have been in storage ever since we were married. I feel as if I'm atrophying!"

"It's only for four months. Then I'll come home and take that job at U.C. and you can continue your studies. Darling, I don't want us to be apart."

"I want to be with you, too, Chris, but I've had it with traipsing all over the world. Why can't you accept the university position now?"

"And give up a chance to film in Ireland? My God, every director I know would give his right arm to do that documentary. What brought on this change?"

She hadn't changed. She had merely expressed a little of what had boiled inside for some time. How could she tell him she needed to become her own person instead of languishing forever in his shadow? She looked at his hurt, bewildered expression. *Understand me! Read my mind!* she cried out to him silently.

He looked at her with concern. "You needn't worry. We'll find a good art school for you to attend."

"Be practical. You'll only be gone for four months. I'd barely get started. Anyway, you know very well you'll be on location most of the time and won't even miss me."

"I'll miss you," he said stubbornly.

"I want the scholarship," she said, trying not to weaken. "I've supported you all the other times, haven't I?"

His eyes looked bleak, and he shook his head sadly. "And you haven't wanted to?"

He left finally, bewildered and hurt at her decision. She enrolled in her course at the California Academy and accomplished far more than was required, knowing she was driven, not only by her need for fulfillment, but the need to diminish the very real pain of Chris's absence.

His letters were sparse and filled mainly with descriptions of the contrasts he found: the beauty of the countryside and the warmth of the people against the ugly political realities.

Meanwhile she won an award for an urn at a ceramics exhibition, and an article she'd submitted on blue glazes was accepted for publication in a crafts magazine. She wrote rapturous accounts, sharing her success with him to prove she'd made the right decision.

Then came a letter from Chris saying he would have to stay another month, something about how certain scenes had to be filmed over. The five months stretched to six, then seven as Holly grew desolate worrying that it wasn't only the documentary that was keeping him in Ireland.

Marissa? His co-worker was probably ten years older than Christopher and a decidedly attractive woman. She was no "featherbrained" female, but someone who could communicate with him on his own level. Holly had met her once briefly, but Marissa was someone who left a strong and lasting impression.

On his homecoming day, Holly was so tied up in knots she could hardly speak when she met his plane. Chris hugged her effusively and chattered on about the successful completion of the film and the chilly Irish weather. She answered in nervous monosyllables, but he seemed not to notice.

In their apartment he pulled her into his arms. "At last, my darling. Let's never stay apart again. Do you have any champagne? I have a surprise for you."

Oh, no, surely not another far-flung project! She stiffened, and he released her.

"What's the matter?"

"Out of practice, I guess. It seems as if you've been gone for years."

He spotted a decanter on the hutch and went over to pour them each a sherry. Trying to ignore the strain that was rising like mist and threatening to envelop them, she sat down beside him on the couch. He reached for her hand.

"These things always take longer than expected. I missed you, too, Felicity."

"Really? I seem to recall only two letters in the past three months, and they might as well have been post-cards."

His expression turned rueful. "I know, I'm sorry. We were up against so many deadlines that I let everything go."

"You had plenty of time for Marissa obviously." She couldn't prevent the waspish tone.

"Well, dammit, we were collaborating on this project. You were aware of that."

"And is that all you collaborated on?" she asked softly.

He gave her a measuring look. "You don't mean that, I hope."

"I can't help it, Chris. I was worried. Marissa is an exciting person. You kept extending your stay. You called only a few times and sent only token letters. I felt like the forgotten woman."

He set down his wineglass and enclosed her hand in both of his. "You know how unconscious of time I am when I'm working, and we were at it all day and half the night." She removed her hand.

"Half the night?" she questioned, and fear rose to engulf her. "What about the other half? You still haven't answered me, Chris. Did you spend that with Marissa, too?"

The direct question was obviously unexpected. A deadly silence held the two of them in its vortex and told her all she needed to know. She felt as if she could have heard a leaf fall from one of the potted plants in the room.

He bowed his head, and his voice was low. "Believe me, darling, I never meant it to happen."

"So that was the reason for the extra months?"

"No, dammit! We worked like dogs until the day I left."

"Yet you still found time for a little diversion."

He grabbed her shoulders angrily. "Listen, I slept with her once. That's all. Believe me, she means nothing to me except as a hell of a researcher and a great scriptwriter. It's not important!"

She pulled away and fought for control. "It's important. It tells me something about our marriage."

He reached toward her in a gesture of entreaty. "Oh, God, Felicity, it's you I love!"

"So how could you let it happen?"

"I'm not sure," he said miserably. "I was a fool. It was a crazy mistake. Meaningless, I tell you!"

"But how? I have to know, Chris."

"I don't want to hurt you."

"Tell me."

He threw up his hands. *Why the details?* the gesture asked. "One night we skipped dinner and worked late, reviewing a film sequence and getting the narrative the way we wanted it. We had a few drinks, and well, it just happened. I'd give anything if it hadn't."

Felicity felt as if she were falling into a black abyss and would never touch bottom. Chris got up and paced across the room, then came back and stood before her, his fists clenching and unclenching continuously.

"Why the hell didn't you come with me then?"

She bristled. "Is that your excuse for infidelity?"

"God, no! Call it aberrant behavior, whatever. I swear it will never happen again!"

"How can I trust you?" she cried, knowing if she started weeping it would be as if she'd held back for years.

Suddenly frustration, anger and hurt exploded in both of them at the same moment, and by the time the storm subsided, she and Chris had turned into strangers.

He grabbed his suitcases and took a taxi to a hotel. She forced herself to work with frenzied speed through the night, packing their things and straightening the apartment. If she taxed her strength to the limit, maybe she wouldn't be able to think or reason.

She separated their belongings and stacked all of Chris's things neatly on a table. He had very little except for a few pieces of clothing, an old stereo and the valuable research material—notebooks, taped interviews and such—he'd painstakingly collected for a book he'd always wanted to write. Everything else she put in boxes for the Salvation Army with a note specifically directing them to pick up only the stuff that was boxed.

As early as she dared the next morning, she left the key with the landlady, explaining that she was going back to college and would no longer be able to afford the apartment. She gave her the note for the truck driver and said to help herself before he arrived if she saw something she wanted from those boxes designated for the giveaway.

Holly put her few possessions in a friend's garage and took an afternoon flight to Reno. In the weeks that followed, she refused Chris's calls and threw away his letters without reading them—he had obviously coaxed her whereabouts from a friend. She felt numb and lonely, but a steel core of resolve prevented a sense of defeat. She would finish her education. She would work to develop her talent and skills, strive to reach her unique potential until she became the person she was meant to be. It would have been perfect if Chris had understood and remained at her side to encourage her, but that would not happen now.

She got the divorce and refused all support. It mattered to her that she make her way on her own. The calls and letters eventually stopped, and she found out through the grapevine that Chris had become the head of the film department at the University of Texas. That had been the surprise he'd referred to that stormy night. So he'd finally settled down when it had suited his convenience. Had he bought a home in San Antonio? she wondered.

She enrolled again at U.C. Berkeley, where she'd dropped out when she had got married, supporting herself by working odd shifts in the university library, tutoring, and giving classes in ceramics for the city's adult education program. For months she carried around a nebulous pain in her chest and wondered if she'd ever feel normal again. Then, as she plunged into the creativity her classes demanded, the pain decreased. But the healing process was a slow one.

After graduation, she was accepted as a member of the art department at Rothmoor, a small but prestigious private college on the peninsula. She adored the stimulating climate and the interesting people she met there. There were plenty of dates, almost more than she could handle. Several men had wanted to marry her, but she held back. This time she had to be certain. Her divorce hadn't been the end of the world. She'd proved she could get along without Chris, hadn't she?

Holly jerked herself back to the present and watched with amusement as Juana continued to scan the window of the jewelry store, oblivious to the impatient customers who'd gathered waiting for her shop to open. Eventually she joined them, dissolving their peevishness with a warm smile that brought forth enchanting dimples.

"Buenos días." She spoke the greeting in a low, musical voice and opened a door that was scalloped right out of the facade of the building.

The next hour was a busy one as Holly dusted the cerámic pieces and folded the handwoven goods into neat piles, waiting on customers in between. The shop was no second-rate center for cheap, touristy curios. Embroidered clothing and hand-loomed goods, ceramics of all kinds, wooden sculptures, ornaments, jewelry and baskets were all representative of the city's finest artisans.

She was pleased that the discriminating board of directors had seen fit to accept a growing number of her own creations: some handsome bowls using Elena's technique in black pottery, and her personal favorite, a ceramic quail she'd fired in subtle shades of blue.

As she showed a customer some rugs, she spotted the young whittler who'd been coming into the shop of late. His attention was fixed on a sculptured wooden horse. His dark eyes gleamed, and his attitude was almost worshipful as he ran his hand slowly over the contours of the figure. Then he caught Holly's glance and gave a shy smile. She'd learned that his name was Lee and that he was an American. His eyes gave away a mixed parentage, probably part Asian.

She wrapped the rug the woman had chosen to purchase and bent to find another to replace it on the display rack. As she rummaged underneath the counter, a male voice speaking in English caught her attention.

"Oh, God," she muttered as she recognized the resonant baritone explaining something about the Mixtecs and Zapotecs, the indigenous Indians who were the primary inhabitants of the city. She tried to rise but felt as though she'd been cast in iron. An old gentleman took her elbow.

"You're awfully pale, miss. May I help you into a chair?"

Holly stood with an effort. "I'm okay, just a bit dizzy for some reason," she said, trying to marshal her resources into some vestige of poise. She would need every ounce she could summon in about twenty seconds, just as soon as Christopher Brooke, the man she hadn't seen since their divorce seven years ago, reached the counter to pay for her blue quail.

CHAPTER TWO

HOLLY WATCHED CHRISTOPHER make his way to the counter with her ceramic quail. An entire range of emotions swept through her, and she couldn't identify one of them.

He still moved with well-knit coordination and an economy of motion that allowed him to go twice as far as anyone else.

But there were changes—a toughness in his face that hadn't been there before. Was it doggedness or cynicism? she wondered. Probably both. The squint lines around his eyes had deepened, too, as if he'd studied knotty problems so long the expression had become set. Or maybe the lines were due simply to the days spent filming out-of-doors. But the stray lock of sun-bleached hair that dipped on his forehead still made for an appealing boyishness despite his thirty-seven years.

He handed her the quail, and she saw his instant, shocked recognition. "Felicity! Of all places to run into you! What are you doing way down here in Oaxaca?" His swift glance moved over her dark hair, which fell in soft waves to her shoulders, no longer caught in the severe French knot. For an instant his objective appraisal softened, and she felt a thrust of pain at the brief, familiar expression.

She could usually project a facade of self-possession when nervous, but she couldn't help the way she felt now, as if there were sensors all over her body making her painfully aware of the unexpected confrontation. "I'm here for the summer to study in Doña Elena's master class. I work in this shop part-time," she said, and felt relieved that her voice sounded as though she were waiting on any customer.

"Elena, eh? You must be damn good. I hear she takes only the best."

"Judge for yourself. That quail is my work."

His eyebrows shot up, and he lifted the bird and turned it around slowly as if examining it for the first time. "Little wonder I chose it," he said coolly.

She felt a stab of disappointment. She knew the quail was the best thing she'd done thus far. *Good heavens! I had no idea you had all that talent stored up in you!* he might have said. Did he think she'd been marking time all these years as she'd done during their marriage? It angered her that she should find herself caring.

He turned the quail over and read her signature. "Holly?" he questioned.

"Yes, I go by that name now," she said, and hoped they wouldn't get into any involved Freudian discussions on why she had changed her name. "And you? On a holiday?" she asked, devoting avid attention to the wrapping of his package. Of all the hundreds of items in the shop, how had he happened to select this one?

"I'm doing a documentary on the artisans of the Oaxaca Valley," he said. "I'm hoping for a TV contract by the end of the summer."

"Still globe-trotting then?" She could have bitten her tongue when she saw his desolate smile.

"Actually, this is only my third trip abroad since—" he hesitated "—since I took the position in Texas. I'm on leave now." Did the word *divorce* taste as bitter on his tongue as it did on hers? "I've always wanted to film this area of Mexico. The century-old techniques used by the artisans here aren't well-known to the outside world."

She recalled how a new place became his intoxicant, made his eyes shine, turned him into an ardent explorer. How had he ever been conned into staying in Texas for seven years? He was a Columbus, a Lawrence of Arabia!

"Except for Elena's classes, I haven't had time yet to see any of the other artisans. I've only been here a couple of weeks," she said, and breathed a little easier. At least polite conversation was coming naturally, helping them slip through the first awkward moments.

Lee, the boy who'd been coming into the shop recently, now walked with lagging steps to join them. He was around sixteen, she judged, and the way he stood, head down, shoulders drooping, reminded her of a whipped animal. If ever a child exhibited a lack of confidence, he did. Chris clapped a hand on the boy's shoulder and made the introduction.

"Holly, Lee Manjung Brooke." Holly's eyes widened. Lee Brooke? What on earth did that mean? The boy squirmed away sullenly, and Chris's face grew taut.

"Lee and I have already gotten acquainted," she said kindly, and wondered about the tension evident between boy and man. Lee remained silent.

"Can't you remember your manners?" Chris snapped, prodding a response. "I've just introduced you to..." He paused, and seemed at a loss for words. During their entire marriage, she'd never recalled that happening once.

"Holly Jones," she said. Obviously he hadn't known whether she'd dropped his name.

The boy reluctantly extended his hand. "Hi," he mumbled. He moved a little aside, and pulled out the chunk of wood he'd been working on earlier and whittled intently, allowing the fragments to fall on the floor.

"Cut that out! Can't you see the mess you're making?" Chris said, not curbing his irritation.

The boy took his time picking up the chips, dropping them one at a time into a nearby wastebasket. He turned the block of wood around, observing it critically, then heaved it hard on top of the chips in the basket, shooting Chris such a look of desolation that Holly winced.

"I'll wait for you in the car," he muttered, and ran out of the shop.

Both frustration and anger mingled in Chris's countenance. "He's upset because I'm enrolling him in military school on Monday."

Holly barely considered the information as she tried to swallow the lump or whatever it was that seemed stuck in her throat. Who was this boy? If he was fifteen or sixteen, he surely couldn't be Chris's son. Yes, he could, she realized at once.

She thought of Chris's dalliance with Marissa. Of course there must have been others, and she knew he'd had an assignment in Korea before they had been married. *So what?* Such matters were no longer any concern of hers, she told herself firmly. One had to be either very cynical or extremely forgiving to handle adultery, and she'd been neither.

"Don't count on a military school to solve personal problems," Holly said, hoping she hadn't shown shock at the implied relationship between Chris and Lee.

Chris sighed. "I've gone every other route. There has to be some way to reach him. Colonel Hidalgo's academy is highly recommended."

She thought of the boy's sensitivity to the beautiful things in the shop. In spite of his surly behavior around

Chris, he somehow didn't seem a likely candidate for such a school, but it was none of her business. A customer claimed her attention, asking to look at some of the hand-painted tin Christmas ornaments. With relief, Holly obliged, feeling as if she'd held her breath too long and finally was able to come up for air.

Chris fingered a wool hanging, then with a brief nod in her direction, turned and left the shop. *And that's that,* Holly thought. She supposed it was inevitable that they would eventually run into each other. Thank God it was over. *Please let at least another seven years pass before it happens again!* By then such an occasion would barely cause a wrinkle. Thank goodness there had been no polite mention of future meetings!

The rest of the morning passed quickly, while Holly waited on customers, restocked shelves and answered questions about the shop's merchandise. Holly worked automatically as her mind churned with the morning's incident. She probably wouldn't have to worry about running into Chris again. This was a big city. Anyway, he'd be on location most of the time.

But she couldn't stop thinking about the boy. What was he to Chris? Since his last name was Brooke, he had to be either Chris's adopted or natural son. She recalled the way Chris had laid his arm around the boy's shoulder and the wretchedness in Lee's expression as he had pulled away. They seemed to be caught in a disturbing current, torn between antagonism and some mode of caring.

Suddenly she remembered the chunk of wood the boy had whittled, and rummaged in the wastebasket to retrieve it. She could only gasp at what she saw. A man's head emerged from the block, the neck and shoulders not quite complete, but the likeness was unmistakable. Chris.

But a different Chris, one with a cold and calculating expression. She turned the piece slowly around, examining it, marveling at the talent it showed, even though it had been hewn with a pocketknife.

"Juana, take a look at this," she said as the manager fiddled with something at the cash register.

Juana put on the glasses that were attached to a chain around her neck and looked closely at the little head. "Who did it?" she asked.

"That young boy who was in the shop earlier this morning. I saw him working on it."

"Amazing," she said. "The child has real talent. Who is he? I saw you talking to him."

"He's some relation to the man who bought my quail." It wasn't necessary to reveal Chris's identity now. Juana would chew for days on the information, relishing it like a plate of *antojitos* or snacks.

"A shame he doesn't have the right tools. Even so, the expression comes through." Juana held the piece up to the light. "*¡Madre de Dios!* Deliver me from meeting such a person!"

Holly bit her tongue as she started to explain that the man was not as cruel as Lee had depicted. "Who knows?" she said lightly. "It's probably a product of his imagination."

Juana shook her head. "Not this," she said with assurance. "It takes strong feeling to bring out such emotion from a block of wood."

Holly put the carving in her purse but grappled with the enigma for the rest of the day. The only conclusion that made any sense was that, if there was ever a boy who shouldn't be sent to military school, it was Lee. Here in Oaxaca, a center of fine artisans, he should be given the opportunity to work and develop his talent, not shrivel up in an atmosphere of rigid regulations. Couldn't Chris see that?

No, he probably couldn't, she thought angrily. He hadn't seen her needs, much less understood them. It wasn't that Chris was selfish. In many ways he was the most generous man she'd ever known. He simply had a lot of blind spots.

She tried to stop thinking about it. The affair was none of her business. Still, she couldn't prevent the recollection of the awe in the boy's face when he had run his hand over the sculptured horse, nor the misery in his eyes when Chris had spoken sharply to him concerning his whittling. Even now she felt a pang of tenderness for the young craftsman. His spirit would be broken as well as his self-confidence—whatever was left of it—at the most vulnerable point of his life.

After wrestling with the situation all day, she knew she had to do something about it. Her empathy with the child was too strong to ignore. She would have to call Chris, and of course he'd probably get the crazy notion that she was using Lee as an excuse to renew their relationship. Well, so be it. It wouldn't be difficult to call a halt to that. But he hadn't seemed the least bit interested anyway.

That evening she called the operator to get Chris's number and dialed before she lost her courage. "Chris, this is Holly," she said in a cool businesslike tone when he answered.

"Oh, yes?" he said carefully.

"This probably sounds as if I'm way out in left field, but something has come up that deeply concerns Lee, and I'd very much like to talk it over with you."

"I see," he said coolly. "I had no idea you'd be interested."

She ignored the thrust. "I'm interested. I wouldn't ask you if I didn't think it was important." Her words spilled out quickly, as though she were trying to get them all out before he could stop her. "Could we meet soon, say on the square? I'll explain everything over a cup of coffee. It will only take a few minutes." *Please, Chris, don't argue. Just come.*

"What do you know about adolescents, Holly? Have you had some experience in dealing with a situation like this?"

She bristled. *Plenty,* she could have said, but she kept her temper. Lee's future was at stake here. "Let's just say I think I know what I'm talking about."

"Why can't you tell me now?"

"Because I want to show you something. I feel certain you'd want to see it."

He paused so long she wondered if he were going to hang up. "You were never devious," he said finally. "Okay. How about tomorrow around five at La Posada on the *zócalo*. But I can assure you that nothing is going to change my mind about packing Lee off to Colonel Hidalgo's."

"Thanks, Chris. I know you won't regret it," she said. Changing his mind was precisely what she intended to do, and she knew she'd have to be as persuasive as an expert attorney confronting a jury.

Chris could be stubborn, and she suspected the trait had not lessened. Well, she would show him that she was no longer the reserved young woman who allowed feelings to seethe inside without ever expressing them. She could be every bit as articulate as he.

During the rest of the day she planned convincing arguments that would demolish his resistance. Something approaching exhilaration leaped in her as she waited for their meeting. Winning a chance for Lee had become the most important thing in her life. Some small but piercing voice told her she was correlating the boy's frustrations with those of her own during the time she'd been married. She hadn't known how to cope then, but now she would make up for it.

The next afternoon she dressed with care, brushing her dark hair until it shone with blue-black highlights. Her hair was the same color as that of most of the young women of the area. However, her fair skin, blue-green eyes and height, though average, made her stand out in a city where most people had deep brown skin and were less than five feet tall.

She chose a simple turquoise silk dress and wore a strand of matching beads purchased recently at the shop. She was aware that the color flattered her complexion and accented her eyes, making her appear a quite different young woman than the little gray dove who'd been Chris's wife. Her confidence zoomed, sufficiently, she hoped, to conquer Goliath on the square.

The wide city plaza, the *zócalo* in Spanish, was filled with people. Wrought-iron benches invited them to relax in the shade of the ancient trees. Several children trailed a man tugging at a fistful of balloons. A woman in native Indian costume carried her stock of rebozos on her head and caught Holly's eye, ready to bargain over the shawls at a glimmer of interest.

Celebrating his prosperity, a peddler with an armful of handwoven serapes self-consciously enjoyed a shoeshine in one of the raised chairs nearby. With a great flapping of wings, pigeons scrapped over a piece of bread and refused to scatter, so Holly walked around them to the sidewalk cafés located under the arches of the colonial buildings.

She found a table and was immediately entranced by the street flutist who was playing in the white gazebo in the center of the plaza. His melodies leaped vividly into the air to entertain the well-dressed young couples holding hands, the shoppers, the tourists, and the hordes of others who were sitting at tables sipping mescal, coffee or Coke. The sun poured its late golden light on the scene, making it look like the setting for some colorful light opera.

Holly ordered coffee and looked at her watch. Chris would not be here for another twenty minutes, but in Oaxaca waiters cared not at all if one dawdled the entire afternoon. She wanted to sit quietly for a while, to revel in the charm that surrounded her, and for the hundredth time, test her rebuttals to the arguments she knew she would meet.

"Señorita Jones, I can't allow a lovely lady to sit here alone."

Miguel Avalon, the owner of the spacious old colonial home where she stayed, bowed and pulled a chair over. "Dear lady, may I join you for a few moments?" He spoke in Spanish, as he nearly always did to her, obviously happy not to have to struggle with English, which he'd never wholly mastered. She forced a smile. Miguel was already a good friend, but what an inopportune time for him to appear!

"Of course, Miguel. But I hope you won't mind. I'm meeting a gentleman at five to go over some important business."

He glanced at the clock on the church across the street. "My dear woman, I'll disappear in five minutes, depend on it. I grasp this moment to extend an invitation."

She smiled at the old-fashioned formality of his words. In English they would have sounded stilted and ludicrous, but spoken in the soft Spanish tongue, they flowed gracefully.

Actually Miguel lived in the wrong century, Holly had decided when she had first met him. He belonged back in the mid-1800s, when his family hacienda was first built. As a descendant of the Spanish conquerors living in an Indian environment, he found it his duty to preserve the traditions and manners of his ancestors. Already he had given her a fascinating history of the area and had introduced her to some of the cultural aspects. A slight man, with a handsome fine-featured face, he always seemed far older and more mature than his forty-four years.

He sat down, then reached for her hand and kissed it. "How beautiful you look today. You must allow me to paint you in that lovely gown."

"Thank you, Miguel. Perhaps before the summer is over we can arrange a sitting," she said, and withdrew her hand just as Chris strode up to the table.

As much as she liked Miguel, at this moment she could have cheerfully wrung his neck. She hastily introduced the two men and winced a little at Miguel's flowery apologies, now in hesitant English, for having interrupted a rendezvous on the *zócalo*. Amid Chris's cool insistence that another time could be arranged, Miguel, with cavalier gallantry, bade them goodbye and cheerfully wandered away. Watching the exchange of surface civilities, Holly had found Chris's aloofness hard to bear and didn't know why. It was as if a raw place had been touched.

"My landlord," she explained as Chris pulled out a chair and sat down.

"You're sure? Sounds like someone out of a Cervantes novel."

"Don't underestimate him. He's an avid student of history, a classical guitarist and an excellent painter. I find a little old-fashioned courtliness quite refreshing."

"So Felicity has developed a tart tongue in the interim. I must say it suits you better than I would have imagined."

The use of her old name threw her so that for a moment she couldn't speak. The way he said it, lingering over the vowels as he had when they'd first met, brought a lump to her throat. She gestured toward her coffee. "Would you care to order?"

He motioned to a waiter, and the interruption gave her time to recoup her poise. "So let's have it," he said, after his coffee arrived and her cup had been replenished. "I confess you left me curious."

Silently she pulled out Lee's carving and handed it to him. "This should tell you more plainly than any words I can use. I watched your son work on this yesterday morning. He tossed it into the wastebasket when you admonished him."

Frowning, Chris took the head and stared at it for a few minutes. Surprise, followed by chagrin and then pain crossed his face.

Finally he set it down. "Well, I guess that spells out pretty plainly the state of our relationship, and the boy isn't my son. My brother and sister-in-law adopted him two years ago, but were killed in an auto accident recently. He was made my ward at the time. Lee, as you probably noticed, is from a mixed marriage. He was orphaned as a toddler and was placed in one home after another until my brother took him in. He's insecure as hell. I guess that's part of the problem. I've tried every way I can to get along with him, but so far it's been disastrous."

At Chris's words, Holly felt relief wash over her and refused to examine the reason. "Look at the carving again, Chris. Naturally you're offended at Lee's view of you, but can you see anything else?"

"The boy knows how to whittle. That much is obvious."

She leaned forward demanding his attention. "More than that, he bursts with talent. Haven't you noticed?"

"I confess I haven't. Been too busy with my work I guess. And I've only had him for little over a month."

"Too busy? And is that the reason you want to ship him off? 'Out of sight, out of mind?'" She sat tautly, clenched hands poised on the marble table, knowing she'd made him furious.

A muscle tensed in his cheek. "My God, what an opinion you have of me! I was glad to make him my ward. I looked forward to being a father to him." He hunched his shoulders in a helpless motion. "But I can't find any way to reach him. If things don't improve by the end of the summer, I intend to find another home for him."

"Listen, Chris. All of Lee's life, everything he's loved has been snatched away. Maybe he's afraid of getting too close to you. He's certain that eventually you, too, will be taken from him."

Chris shook his head. "Believe me, you haven't lived with this kid. He couldn't care less about me. He needs the kind of discipline I haven't been able to give him."

"Chris, for heaven's sake, why are you insisting that a boy like Lee spend his summer in a military school? Think about it!"

"And you believe I haven't?"

"No! You're turning your back on his real needs. I'm positive his attitude will change if you pay attention to those. Here is someone with abundant talent," Holly said passionately. "Get him a good teacher, let him study. There are wonderful instructors here!"

"Dammit, Holly, how much time have you spent with Lee? Five minutes? Even a psychiatrist wouldn't rely on your snap judgment. Live with him a week and you'll see what I mean."

She leaned forward, unconsciously seeking his hand, then quickly releasing it. "Trust me, Chris!" she pleaded.

He looked at her oddly, and his mouth twisted as if in pain. "*Trust* you?"

She felt as if he'd slapped her. "Are *you* questioning *my* integrity? If so, don't you think you have your pronouns confused?"

He waved a hand. "Forget it," he said sharply. "I didn't mean to stir up something that's over and done with."

She took a deep breath. She desperately wanted to pursue this new thrust. If trust were the issue, he was treading on thin ice. With difficulty, she shifted the focus back to the subject at hand. Nothing should sidetrack them at this point. "Then you'll find a teacher for Lee? Forget about the military school?"

He fiddled for a moment with his cup. "I'm afraid you can't change my mind, Holly, but perhaps I can change yours. Since you're so dead set on your convictions, maybe you ought to talk with Colonel Hidalgo. He's interviewed Lee at some length and is familiar with his background. He's certain the school will solve the problems."

"I'll be happy to talk to the colonel. Where can I reach him?"

"Tomorrow evening, if you wish. I'm having a few friends over for a poolside patio supper. Colonel Hidalgo will be present. I was hoping he and Lee could get better acquainted. If anyone can make you see the light, he can.''

She looked at him warily. "Is that an invitation?"

"It is."

"And if he doesn't convince me?"

"Oh, I lay my bets on him. But if you come up with some overwhelming new argument, I'll listen to it."

"How kind of you," she said, not bothering to hide her sarcasm. "Well, I assure you I'll hold you to that promise."

He rose. "Tomorrow evening around seven. Bring a bathing suit." He scribbled an address on the back of a card and handed it to her. "See you then," he said abruptly, and left, striding with quick steps across the *zócalo*.

CHAPTER THREE

CHRIS HIKED ACROSS the *zócalo*, fists jammed in his pockets. His head pounded. The air seemed to have subtly taken on the heaviness that precedes a storm. He got into his Jeep parked on a side street and headed up Garcia Vigil to the hillside where his rented home was located.

Chris had realized long ago that Holly would always be in some area of his consciousness. It was a condition he'd come to accept. He'd sometimes wondered if the feeling would last forever. When he'd run into a professor from her college last May and had learned that Holly planned to spend the summer in Oaxaca, he had decided at once to go there. Maybe she'd mellowed after all these years. Maybe there would be a chance for them again. Besides, he'd always wanted to film Oaxaca's little satellite villages.

But now that he'd seen her, he almost wished he hadn't come. Over the years, he'd learned to handle the pain. Now he'd stirred it all up again. She was more desirable than ever, more beautiful, and she'd exorcised him completely. Her actions left no doubt about that. It would take careful strategy to get close to her again.

He hoped he'd shown appropriate surprise and restraint when they'd met at La Tienda Artesanías. It hadn't been easy to find out where she worked. He had wanted their meeting to appear accidental, so he'd first

visited numerous shops with no results. Finally he got
Ramona, his housekeeper, to call Doña Elena's studio to
get the information.

Holly hadn't been at the shop the first time he'd visited, but he'd played the interested customer anyway. The
manager had enthusiastically shown him around, eventually pointing out the pottery made by the talented
young woman who worked there part-time. He'd purchased one of Holly's fruit bowls, meanwhile managing
to find out what hours the "talented young woman"
worked.

Restraint was the key word now, and he couldn't let
himself forget it. He knew full well that she would erect
impossible barriers if he moved too quickly, especially if
she found out he'd followed her down here. Maybe it had
been a mistake to invite her to the party at his house.
Well, he'd remain the disinterested but courteous former
husband for the time being. But it wouldn't be easy to
look at her lovely, long-lashed blue-green eyes, their color
as ever-changing as the ocean; to watch the movement of
her endearingly feminine, slender body; to be close and
not be able to touch her.

He'd told himself that, if he could only see her once
more, he would be able to banish his fantasies once and
for all. Reality had a way of putting one's feet back on
the ground, after all. He'd probably made her larger than
life during the years they were apart. Yes, seeing her
again would bring perspective.

At the time of their divorce there'd always been that
question about her role in the disappearance of his ten
years of accumulated research. In his heart he knew
Holly hadn't destroyed it, but the evidence had sharply
denied that. Perhaps now he'd be able to hear the an-

swer from her own lips. He'd always trusted her in spite of his ridiculous outburst at the *zócalo*.

There'd been a dozen or more computer disks and tapes filled with priceless information and interviews, much of it impossible to replace, all waiting in readiness for him to start the book he'd wanted to tackle ever since he'd begun in the film business. The hours he'd spent, and all sent to the dump in a Salvation Army truck!

He'd been incredulous when he'd talked to the landlady. His wife had been very specific about which things the truck was to pick up and which were to be left for him, the woman had said. Holly had even left a note for the driver so there would be no mistake. Chris had been astounded. Someone had goofed. Holly had never been careless, much less vindictive, but when he'd tried to get in touch with her, she'd refused his calls and hadn't answered his letters. The disaster had caused all kinds of fallout. His advance payment for the book had had to be returned and a proposed lecture series based on the material had had to be canceled.

During the years following the divorce, he'd come to understand why a girl like Holly couldn't accept his lapse of fidelity. He'd been stupid and weak, and he hated himself for it. Perhaps if she hadn't gone storming off to Reno, they could have worked things out. He might have convinced her that it was she he truly loved and not Marissa, who'd merely provided the warm fire and excellent Scotch after one late night's work.

The word *marriage* was not in Marissa's vocabulary, and she'd been determined that it wouldn't be in his. *Creativity can't reach its zenith with the distractions of family involvement* was item one in her creed. She was a manipulator. He knew that, and even prided himself on being able to work with her and still look on with amusement at her maneuvers. Except for that one time. Not only had Marissa succeeded in destroying his marriage, but she had broken up their relationship, too. Although Chris had run into her once or twice at conferences, he'd refused further collaboration.

The heavy bumper-to-bumper traffic thinned as he drove into the outskirts of the city. He looked forward to a dip in the pool the minute he got home. After a few laps, he might be able to put the whole frustrating day into better perspective.

He'd been lucky to trade houses for the summer with a Mexican professor who lectured at the University of Texas. The attractive home was set among jacarandas and overlooked the city. Magenta bougainvillea cascaded over the same kind of plain stucco walls that enclosed most Oaxacan dwellings. A housekeeper who was an excellent cook came with the house. Chris had never enjoyed such a luxury.

He took a deep breath as he left the Jeep and walked up the steps. He resolved not to get into a hassle with Lee tonight—no matter what. He'd looked forward to the companionship with the handsome, intelligent boy, a tangible link with his brother, when he'd accepted him as his ward. Chris had hoped to adopt him. But from the beginning there had been a thorn hedge between them.

"Cena en diez minutos," Ramona greeted him as she set the small table for supper adjacent to the pool. Chris had spoken no Spanish when he had arrived in Oaxaca, but he'd already picked up enough vocabulary so that, along with a few graphic gestures, he was able to communicate adequately with the ever-smiling housekeeper.

"Bueno," he replied, and turned to see Lee execute a perfect dive, entering the water with barely a splash. The

kid was an excellent swimmer. Chris's brother had seen to that.

"That was a great dive, son," Chris said as a scowling Lee climbed from the pool, picked up a towel and rubbed himself down.

"I'm not your son," he said crossly.

"Merely a term of respect, and as a matter of fact, I'd appreciate the same from you. So far you haven't called me anything. I sometimes feel I'm invisible. Uncle, Chris, Dad, I don't care, but I'd appreciate not remaining nameless."

"My real father died a long time ago, and my adopted dad is gone, too. You're nothing to me!" the boy said, and abruptly turned away, making a business of draping his towel over a chair.

"Oh, no?" Chris said evenly, controlling his temper with effort. "Look, kid, I'm all you've got right now. What's with you? Most boys would give their eyeteeth to spend their summer in a classy place like this."

The boy faced him, eyes flashing with resentment. "And you can't wait to get rid of me, right?"

They glared at each other for several moments, mentally circling, each waiting to see what tack the other would take. "Listen, Lee," Chris said after a long pause. "Since you've come to stay with me, you've made it quite plain you hate it. Life, at least for me, is more than an armed camp. Obviously you don't like it here, so I'm providing you with the best alternative I can find."

Moisture filmed the boy's eyes. "Some alternative! Who needs it? I'm doing okay by myself."

"Oh, you think so? No person is totally self-contained. People need each other, even you and I. Get dressed. Dinner in five minutes," Chris said tersely.

Lee sniffed the succulent stew, a specialty of Ramona's, and gave an exaggerated sigh. "Why can't we ever have burgers and fries?"

Chris watched him go inside the house with his chin set stubbornly and felt a helplessness that had become all too common. Living with this boy demoralized him, made him feel inadequate. Worst of all, if their relationship were any indication, it was apparent that Christopher Brooke would be a complete washout as a father.

A few minutes later Ramona served the meal, her cheerful chatter failing to lighten the mood of the two silent males at the table. Chris observed Lee's remote countenance and caught a lightning glimpse now and then of the vulnerability the boy strove to hide. *What's the matter with us?* he wondered. *Why can't we communicate?* He'd always believed he could figure out solutions to any problems, but he could find damned few right now. He didn't even know the right questions.

His throat tightened at the despondent droop of Lee's shoulders. In the soft glow of the lamplight, Chris recognized the promise of manly planes in the childish curve of his cheek and felt a sudden and terrible loneliness. *This boy may be the only son I ever have, and I can't reach him.*

He'd planned to tell Lee about the party tomorrow evening and enlist his help in acting as lifeguard around the pool. Instead, he went to his room and tried to lose himself in a lengthy, dryly written history of the Zapotec Indians.

HOLLY SLUMPED INTO a chair on the cool veranda of Casa Avalon. Today the air felt soft and sweet, but she knew that June was a capricious month capable of producing warmth one minute and showers the next. The amaryllis edging the patio rose like flames. Faint sounds of Miguel playing a Spanish habanera on his guitar came from somewhere in the Casa. She inhaled the fragrance of freshly baked *pastelerías* wafting from the kitchen, but the pleasant ambience was dulled by the fresh memory of the past hour with Chris on the *zócalo*.

It had shredded her. She hadn't expected Chris to be so unyielding. Had the years turned him cold and unfeeling? And what was that business about trust? How dare he? No doubt he'd manufactured some imaginary hurt to compensate for his own indiscretion. It rankled like a persistent itch.

Somehow she had to find a way to reach Colonel Hidalgo without attending Chris's dinner party. Just being with Chris for the past hour had shaken her up so completely that she wanted no more of it. Today was Friday. Monday morning Chris planned to enroll Lee in the academy. She had to act fast. Not only had Chris's invitation been less than cordial, it was downright condescending. He'd been so certain that Colonel Hidalgo's arguments would demolish her. She determined that if she had to resort to a sit-in in the colonel's office in order to get his ear, she would do so.

She went to the outside phone on the patio and dialed the number of the academy. A secretary informed her in chilling tones that the colonel couldn't see her then nor on any weekend. Holly got the feeling that the woman enjoyed rebuking her.

Maybe she ought to forget the whole thing. Chris's attitude left no doubt that he considered her an interfering busybody. He was probably right, but the image of Lee's bleak young face as he had chucked his carving into the wastebasket would not go away. Well, one could arrive a little late at a party and go home early. One could also become so involved conversing with the colonel that one could avoid the host. As for the colonel, she'd have to put out feelers to figure out how to approach him. She hoped he wasn't the sort who monitored his favors like a miser doling out centavos.

THE NEXT EVENING she chose a sea-green casual cotton dress shot through with sapphire and was tempted to wear the pearls Chris had given her one Christmas. The strand would be perfect with the dress, and she'd long since disassociated them from painful memories. But Chris might interpret the action differently. She didn't want to risk anything that might interfere with her purpose.

After a shower and a discreet but effective makeup application, she whirled around in front of the mirror, gauging her reflection. She would do. She had no qualms about using a few innocent wiles to try to capture the colonel's attention.

She'd brought home a wood-carving set for Lee, planning to give it to him the next time he came into the shop. Impulsively she put it into the native basket she carried as a handbag, and with reluctance, added her bathing suit, hoping she could avoid going into the pool. If Chris remembered her phobia, he wouldn't insist.

For years she'd fought an excessive fear that had plagued her since childhood. At a lake one day with several playmates, she'd waded offshore to an anchored raft where they'd pretended they were pirates walking the plank. Once, after jumping into the water, she'd come up under the raft and a strap had caught on a protruding bolt. She'd almost drowned before someone had rescued her.

The green darkness, the frantic gasps for oxygen, the agony of knowing she was drowning still brought nightmares. Since that time, the very thought of going into water beyond her depth panicked her. Rather than call attention to her problem, she would sometimes paddle around in the shallow end of a pool to be sociable. People didn't seem to notice. Nevertheless, her fears persisted.

A taxi delivered her to the address Chris had given her, and the massive door in the stucco wall opened promptly at her ring. A maid ushered her through the house and onto the patio overlooking the pool. Torches burned inside colored paper cones, and the air was redolent with some sweet-smelling flower. City lights spread a sparkling mantle below as far as she could see. In the background a trio of musicians played a medley of Mexican tunes on guitar, muted trumpet and violin.

Heavens! She hadn't expected this! Chris never was one for the trappings of lavish entertainment. Coffee and cookies in their modest apartment were all he'd ever wanted. As for houses, how well she knew his lack of interest! A thatched hut would have sufficed to hang his hat once upon a time. What had changed him?

Several swimmers splashed energetically in a game of water polo, and other guests sampled hors d'oeuvres around a buffet. She finally spotted Chris. At the sight of him her heart gave a painful leap, sending a tautness through her. She took in the eager way he spoke, head bent forward, flames from the flickering torches dancing on the strong planes of his face. Memory became a tangible thing. How many times had she watched him like that as he expounded on some favorite topic? Suddenly he saw her. He flashed a smile and raised his hand in a gesture of welcome. Then, as he walked toward her, the smile changed subtly, remaining but lacking warmth.

They stood looking at each other a long time without speaking. "Hello, Felicity...Holly," he corrected quickly. "I didn't recognize you at first. You're looking stunning tonight. I can't get over how you've changed."

"That's a rather poverty-stricken compliment."

His eyes narrowed. "I don't mean your looks exactly. You were always beautiful. It's as if I'm speaking to someone I've never met."

"Perhaps you haven't," she said lightly.

"And is the new Holly as prickly as her name?"

"Absolutely," she said, and caught her breath. He wore a hand-loomed cotton shirt she'd made for him a few months before their divorce. So he'd kept it all these years! What impulse had led him to wear it tonight? She'd dyed the fabric an electric blue to complement his sun-bronzed skin. It seemed new, as if he'd never worn it.

"You're looking well. The years have been good to you. I like your shirt...it's very becoming."

He shrugged. "It's comfortable. I've had it a long time, but I keep forgetting to wear it. Can't remember where I picked it up, though. Maybe Guatemala."

"Probably. It looks like that kind of fabric." She experimented with a smile, but knew it didn't come off.

He took her arm and led her over to the other guests, and his touch suddenly brought back memories she wanted to forget. Recollections rose to claw and torment her. Would there never be an end to that feeling? Holly wondered. Chris made introductions, then excused himself, walking over to talk with the maid, who said she had a telephone message for him.

Several couples were in the group, along with a man who said he owned a travel agency. "Paul Dalton," the fellow said heartily, repeating his name as if to accent it in her memory.

Everyone was already in bathing suits, the girls standing unself-consciously, almost nude except for a few wispy nods to propriety. Her suit would instantly set her apart with its modesty, Holly thought, and hoped she wouldn't have to wear it. Paul pointed out the dressing room.

"Later," she said, and joined a spirited argument regarding the merits of the more than fifty varieties of Oaxacan chili peppers. She told of her own experience the first time she had made *salsa*, inadvertently reversing the proportion of tomatoes to hot peppers and almost frying her guests. Everyone laughed heartily.

Once she caught Chris studying her, his face a closed book, but he abruptly turned away when she met his glance. She felt annoyed and wondered why. Did his attitude challenge something in her that she didn't want aroused?

Paul, the travel agent, effusively assured her that he'd bring his very next busload of tourists to visit the shop where she worked, but she gave him only half an ear as she watched Lee sitting on the edge of the pool, disconsolately swinging his feet in the water. Chris called something to him, and he got up and headed out to a storeroom, returning almost at once with a couple of folding chairs. As he stepped back onto the patio, he collided with the maid, sending a tray of food flying.

"Sorry," Lee cried, and scrambled to clean up the mess, casting anxious looks at Chris, who strode over to survey the disaster.

Please, Chris, don't say anything, Holly thought, and took in the boy's agonized expression. She joined them, knowing she ought not to interfere, but unable to stop herself. "Don't worry, Lee. It was an accident."

Chris grabbed a broom and swept the deck clean, mumbling under his breath as he put the broom away. "By the way, I received a call from Colonel Hidalgo a few minutes ago. He missed his plane from Mexico City, so he won't be here tonight after all. I'm sorry."

"In that case maybe you'd better call a taxi for me. I'll make an appointment with him later."

He shrugged. "As long as you're here, take a swim. The dressing room is at the end of the patio. And don't forget to sample the buffet. Ramona is an excellent cook." He left her in order to welcome an attractive brunette who'd just arrived.

At an umbrella table Lee sat alone, his head buried in his arms. He looked up as she joined him. "So you're ganging up on me, too," he muttered.

"Why, what do you mean?"

"You know, sending me to that school. I heard you and him talking about that Hidalgo guy."

"Listen, I'm on your side. In fact, I came here tonight to convince Colonel Hidalgo and Chris not to enroll you."

He gave her a searching look, all attention now. "How come?"

She opened her basket and pulled out his carving. "Because of this."

He snatched it from her. "Where did you get that? It's mine!"

"But you threw it away in my shop, remember?"

"It's no good. I don't want anyone to see it, especially him." He nodded sullenly toward Chris.

"Why?"

"I was trying to get back at him, I guess. He really bugs me."

She felt a rush of warmth at his honesty. "Do you have any others?"

Lee ducked his head. "No, I threw 'em all away. He thinks I'm wasting my time."

Without warning, Holly felt stung by an old ache. She recalled her father's criticism when she'd been about Lee's age. *Why are you spending all that time messing around with silly frills like clay pots and weaving? You're still back in the dark ages, for Pete's sake. Why don't you study something that will do you some good, like accounting or math?* So she had put away her tools and the creations he'd derided until she had got to college and away from her parents. *That must not happen to Lee,* she thought to herself.

"You have a talent," she said, "but you'll have to do something about it, just like the artist who carved the horse you admire in my shop."

"Yeah, I get it. Go to that military academy."

"Maybe you'll have to go. I'm not sure I ought to meddle in Chris's decisions, but that doesn't mean that I can't pick you up on weekends. We can visit a master carver, find out about woods and maybe enroll you for lessons."

He got up and left without a word. Had she gone too far? Too fast? But he returned immediately. "I didn't throw them *all* away, he said shyly, thrusting a carving into her lap. "You can have this one if you want." It was a rooster, its neck arched in a pose of pure self-adulation. The work was considerably finer than the rough-hewn head.

"Thank you, Lee. It's beautiful. Look, I have something for you, too." She pulled out the wood-carving tools.

"For me? Awesome!" His eyes shone as he took them from the case. Reverently he tested the sharpness of each blade, and she saw the depth of feeling he had for his talent.

If only she could use it to create friendship between Chris and the boy! He set the knives carefully on a table and gave a sudden spread-eagle leap of pure joy. "All right!" he cried, and dived into the pool. In sheer exuberance he undulated through the water like a playful porpoise.

Once, before a flip turn, he shot up in the water and gave her a salute. She waved back and looked for Chris. Nothing more could be done for Lee tonight. She'd say her goodbyes and leave. Chris was still talking to the dark-haired girl with whom he now sat at the edge of the pool. The girl was dangling her toes reticently in the water, and even at this distance she looked as if she'd feel more at home in a painter's smock than a bikini. Like herself, Holly thought with a start. Maybe she should just slip away. There was no earthly reason to stay, and Chris wouldn't even miss her.

Paul Dalton came running up and pulled her to her feet. "Hurry! Change into your suit. We need another player!" Someone had stretched a net across the pool, and a game of volleyball had started. The players were standing, and Holly deduced that the pool had to be shallow. There should be no problem, she told herself. Still, she felt uncomfortable about accepting Chris's hospitality when it seemed so reluctantly given. Several others set up a chant for her to join them.

Unwillingly she went to the small dressing room at the end of the patio, tucked her thick wavy hair under a cap and put on her suit, a simple white knit maillot, elegantly cut to fit her like a second skin. She'd bought it, telling herself that owning a good-looking suit could be an impetus to learning to swim. She'd never got past the wading stage of her childhood; after the accident in the lake, she'd avoided swimming completely. Holly felt she'd conquered the past in all ways but this one. It was time she got over this, too.

She hesitated at the edge of the deck. The noisy game had already churned the pool into white water. *Jump in, you fool, before anyone sees your panic,* she told herself. She saw that Chris now watched her with a sardonic expression, his eyes sweeping slowly over her body as if to reidentify every curve that he'd once known so intimately. She looked down at the green water sloshing in stormlike waves from the activity and felt her heart pound violently. *I can't do it. Yes, I can. This isn't a deep pool. Jump in, damn it! No, I'm going to put on my clothes and go home.*

Paul left the game and swam toward her. "Man, oh, man, what you do to that suit!" he cried, and climbed out of the water. He let out a slow wolf whistle. "Smart lady. Covered up more than any woman here and you still manage to look the sexiest!"

She didn't even have time to answer before he took her hand and jumped back into the pool, dragging her with him. "I'll race you to the net," he cried, and took off.

She thrashed wildly, unable to gain a foothold, and felt herself sinking, sinking as if the pool were bottomless. She knew there must be a deep end after all. A roaring filled her ears, and she was that child again, caught under the raft, struggling vainly.

With enormous effort she somehow shot up and heard her crazed voice screaming with hysteria. Why didn't someone hear her? A terrible weight now made her limbs almost powerless, and the thrashing of her arms only seemed to keep her under. Surely her lungs would explode any minute.

Floundering, she churned the water into a froth and managed a few gulps of air. "Help!" she cried, her voice ragged with terror, and she glimpsed a sea of faces staring at her as if she were some flapping insect impaled on a pin.

Suddenly her body was caught in a fierce grip, and she felt hard arms on hers. "Calm down, you little wildcat," Chris said. "The pool is shallow. Stand still and you'll touch bottom."

CHAPTER FOUR

CHRIS'S WORDS WHIPPED her as effectively as if he'd used a leather strap. She planted her feet on the hard bottom of the pool where they would have been all the time had she not panicked. Energy drained, she hid her head against his shoulder. Humiliation all but suffocated her. How could she face Chris, much less all his guests?

"I'm sorry, I'm sorry," she said, gasping. "As you see, I still haven't won my private battle, but I never planned to publish the fact so thoroughly."

"Never mind," he said. His arms shifted suddenly, and the bruising grip turned into an embrace that was firm but unexpectedly gentle. With a quick movement, he lifted her and carried her up the ladder of the pool. Grabbing a towel from a stack on a table, he rubbed her dry, then settled her on a chaise longue. He turned to the people who stood dripping and silent around them. "She's okay, folks. Go on with your game. Holly doesn't swim and, for a moment, she just got a little panicky."

The group dispersed with a unison sigh of relief. Soon shouts and splashing sounds told her the game had resumed. Paul Dalton hurried over with a brandy. "I'm not sure which one of you needs this the most."

"Give it to Chris," Holly said. "I need something more potent, like a good ten-minute lecture on how to screw my head on straight."

Paul laughed heartily, handed the drink to Chris and went back to the bar to get one for himself.

Chris smoothed her hair back from her face, and his hand lingered on her cheek. "You know, I'd forgotten all about that phobia of yours or I would have told you the pool was a shallow one."

The familiar touch brought sudden tears, and she quickly closed her lids against them, but she couldn't shut away the concern she'd glimpsed in his eyes. She felt her breath quicken and was chagrined at the reaction, then rationalized that she might be excused, considering the shock she'd suffered.

His fingers remained on her cheek a moment longer, and she held her breath wanting the feeling to continue and at the same time willing it to cease. As if the unspoken will were communicated, he suddenly yanked his hand away as though it had been burned. She caught her breath at his now fiercely frowning expression.

What was it with him, one minute solicitous and the next a stranger? He had never been a man of moods, and nothing had ever thrown him. But now he was a different Chris, someone she didn't know at all. "I'm okay now. I'd better go," she said, and started to sit up, but her limbs refused to support her, and she fell back against the chaise longue, shivering.

"Rest awhile, then I'll call a taxi for you," he said, tossing a light serape over her. Then he went over to join several of his friends.

She felt as if he'd thrown a blanket of ice on her instead of the warm serape. How changed he was. What had happened to his never-failing wit? It had been one of his most endearing traits. In the old days he would have stayed and teased her out of her fright. Had the act of divorce wrung all the humor from him?

The evening had been a complete disaster. Not only had she disgraced herself, but Colonel Hidalgo hadn't arrived. Nothing had been accomplished for Lee. She curled up under the serape and wondered which aspect of Chris's behavior was harder to deal with—his detachment or his concern.

She stopped shivering at last. Sounds of laughter and music grew faint, and vaguely surprised, she began to feel drowsy. A few minutes later she fell asleep.

STARS STUDDED THE VELVET SKY above her, and for a bewildering moment she wondered what she was doing lying outdoors in this strange place. As far as she could tell in the surrounding darkness, she was entirely alone. Chris's patio! Good heavens!

A shadowed form moved in a chair next to the chaise longue. "Feeling better?" Chris asked quietly.

"Why didn't you wake me?" Holly cried, sitting up and pushing at her tousled hair.

"You deserved a little rest after that nasty experience."

She looked around the darkened patio. "Where is everyone?"

"In bed, I imagine. It's after two."

She gasped. "I can't believe it! Honestly, this isn't my night!"

"Oh, I don't know. You seem to have made quite an impression, especially on Paul Dalton, and even more on Lee. They hovered around like a couple of honey bees and drove me up the wall with advice on how to take care of you."

"How dull for you," she said wryly.

"How about some coffee, or better, some food? I'll bet you haven't eaten a thing." Before she could answer, he went to the buffet and heaped two plates with leftovers and settled down to join her.

She bit into a pastry filled with a hot chili mixture and swallowed slowly, glancing at a tub of geraniums nearby. Then she concentrated on the restless shadows caused by a flickering torch. The silence lengthened and became awkward. What did one say at two in the morning to an ex-husband from whom one had parted in rage and bitterness?

"Excellent chili. Brings back memories, doesn't it?" Chris said cheerfully.

He was referring to the first time she had prepared it—for a Sunday evening get-together for some of his colleagues. It had turned out so hot, the guests had had to wash it down with inordinate quantities of beer.

She shrugged. "I never was much of a cook."

"You were an excellent cook. It was a successful party, if you recall. Anyway, I like spicy food."

"No, I was the one who liked the hot stuff."

They both laughed, and she started to eat again. "So do you prepare it for yourself now?"

His smile faded. "Not anymore. My biggest efforts go into opening cans of spaghetti."

"Well, you always were fond of spaghetti. Remember Tony's?"

"You bet. Dark as a dungeon and ankle-deep in sawdust, but the best damn Italian food in San Francisco." He licked his lips at the recollection.

"Actually, I preferred Pierre's."

He looked startled. "Why didn't you ever say so?"

She shrugged. "'Let's go to Tony's tonight,' you'd say, so we went."

He squinted, giving her his full range of attention. Although she had at first considered it flattering, now it made her feel vulnerable.

"I'm just beginning to realize how you held everything inside you," he said.

She met his eyes unflinchingly. "Lucky we got everything back in focus."

"I wonder," he said as though to himself only.

"So how was Texas?" she asked, hoping he'd launch into a lengthy description so she'd have a little time to control the ache that flared every time she looked at him.

"Nothing earth-shattering. I did several documentaries, and one on Alaska's endangered species won an award. Besides that, I earned my pilot's license, and someday I want a plane of my own. I've arranged to rent one here and hope to explore the area, especially the archaeological sites. Did you know they date from before Christ, the oldest on the North American continent?"

Exploring. That was his forte, wasn't it? "I've only visited Mitla so far. Don't miss it. The ornamental facades are fabulous, and so is its history."

"You were squired there no doubt by Miguel, your gallant historian." He narrowed his eyes critically as if to evaluate her words, her features and actions, before calculating the sum total. "You're more beautiful than ever, Holly, but you've changed. I'm not certain what it is. Perhaps it's that you're more open."

And much too feisty, she thought, not caring for the conversational direction. "Well, I'm no longer a schoolgirl, if that's what you mean. What about you? Married?"

"No. Oh, I met a lot of charming Southern belles, but I always had the feeling they saw Christopher Brooke through the haze of their own fantasies, something I couldn't live up to.''

What happened to Marissa? Holly wondered but didn't ask. Already they'd begun to sound like a bad play performed by an inexpert cast.

As if he divined her thought, he said, ''And Marissa and I were never a couple, but I could never convince you of that.''

No, he couldn't.

''In fact,'' he said, ''I haven't seen her for several years. I've run into her once or twice at conferences, but we've never worked together again. And you?'' he asked, looking at her ringless left hand. ''Is this thing serious with your Señor Avalon?''

She hesitated. It was none of his business. ''I met Miguel only recently. He's been very kind to me.''

Chris lifted an eyebrow. ''Handsome devil. Talks quite a line. One of Oaxaca's elite, I hear.''

''You hear rather quickly.''

''Yeah, I keep my ears open. Miguel Avalon, the wealthy dilettante who owns the splendid Casa Avalon.'' He spoke as if he were quoting someone, and his tone was faintly cynical.

She didn't wince. ''Yes, I love living there. It's a fabulous place. It's been in Miguel's family for over a century.''

''Tradition and the kind of home where you can put down roots, right? That was always the bottom line for you, wasn't it? You haven't changed in that respect.'' She was taken aback by his caustic tone.

Something squeezed her insides. ''About Lee...'' she said, changing topics abruptly. ''I owe you an apology for coming on so strong. I have no right to challenge your authority, but I do want you to realize that he has unusual talent.''

He grimaced. ''That carving of his made me painfully aware of that.''

''This town probably has more artists per square foot than any city in the world,'' she continued eagerly. ''What a chance for him to study! If you still feel that Lee should attend military school, would you allow him to take lessons on weekends?''

He twisted a towel, then shook it out. ''That might be something to consider.''

She leaned forward and placed a hand on his arm to underline her plea. ''I'll wager a lot of your problems with the boy will disappear if you're supportive of his carving. Who knows? You may have a famous sculptor in the making!''

He looked at her hand as he seemed to evaluate her enthusiasm. ''You're quite an advocate,'' he said finally.

''Oh, Chris, you're such a creative person yourself. I can't understand your not being sympathetic. I'll swear you must have a blind spot!'' She realized she still clung to his arm and quickly released it.

His eyes swept over her, lingered on the curve of her breast and her small waist so clearly defined by the white suit, then dropped to her toes now curling under his surveillance. ''Blind spot? A lot more than one, my girl,'' he said, his tone filled with irony. ''All right, you've convinced me. We'll give it a try. No military school at least for a few weeks. You find him a teacher immediately.''

''Thanks, Chris,'' she said quietly. ''I promise, you won't be sorry.'' She started toward the dressing room at the far end of the patio.

"Hold on!" he called. "Before you get dressed, don't you think you should get into the pool again?"

She stopped in her tracks and stared. "Surely you don't want to risk a repeat performance?"

He walked over and took her hand. "Come on, I'll go in with you. Prove to yourself you can do it."

She looked at the quiet pool. *Nothing can happen. I can't possibly drown.* With some reticence, she followed him down the ladder and clung to it for a while.

"Come on," he said quickly, reaching up and lifting her into the water. Then he set her down and led her toward the center of the pool.

The water was warm and welcoming, almost sensuous as it undulated around them. Above, the royal blue sky sparkled with more stars than she'd known it could hold. The lights around the patio were turned off, but a late-rising moon softly lit the area. A distant clock chimed the half hour. The air felt soft and carried the scent of honeysuckle; it was a blessing after the exhausting evening.

"I'll teach you to float," Chris said. "It's good insurance against panic. Lean back in the water and try to relax. Imagine yourself resting on a feather bed. Don't worry, I won't let you sink."

Holly stiffened at first, but as she felt his muscular arm support her back, her tension diminished. A sensation of buoyancy took over. "What a marvelous feeling," she said, and wondered how much of the pleasure depended on Chris's nearness. Somewhere in her mind a warning bell sounded, but it was too distant to heed.

"Now I'm going to remove my arm, but only for a second or two," Chris said. "Try not to tighten up. Remember, I'm right here. You can depend on me."

Depend on him. How would it have been if that had always proved true?

"There, you see how easy it is!" he cried jubilantly as she floated free for almost a minute. They tried again, lengthening the time span.

She laughed aloud. "I'm really doing it!"

"Of course!" he cried, as happy as she. Her eyes met his sparkling ones, and for a few seconds they locked in a kind of silent celebration.

Suddenly he pulled her into his arms and held her close as the water grew calm and sheltering. He bent and kissed her, then slipped the strap off her shoulder and kissed the soft division between her breasts and the fullness of each one.

As fire swept through her, he took her lips, probing them open in sweet exploration. Her hand slipped up to cradle the back of his head, to caress his thick hair. She remembered it all: the good feel of his arms around her, the clean scent of his warm breath, the curl of his lashes as he looked down at her, and most of all, the feeling of rightness, that she'd come home. They stood swaying, half floating, in an exquisite embrace almost impossible to tolerate. The moment reached unabashedly toward joy.

Mentally she wrenched herself away, but she didn't have the willpower to turn reason into action. What was it with her, anyway? Some traitorous urging of the blood? She didn't want to recall how solid and neatly formed he was. She hated to admit how comforting it felt to rest in his arms again. Nor did she wish to compare the sweetness of his kiss with those of other men.

Panic rose, both at his ardor and her growing awareness of the body locked against hers. Almost forgotten sensations rose to engulf her, and she returned his kisses, unable to keep her own lips from pleading for more. Her fingers glided across his shoulders and locked around his neck as if to hold him even closer.

Waves lapped around them, caressing and voluptuous, weakening her capacity to reason, dispersing it in the ever-widening arcs that disappeared at the edge of the pool.

They became weightless as his hands moved over her in tandem with the caressing water, tantalizing, exciting her with the caring intimacies that had once been so precious to her. He cupped her hips, and she felt new tension as his aroused body held unmistakable significance.

The sudden wail of a distant siren rent the air, and the warning forced her to identify her own sublimated one. She pulled away from him, reached for the ladder, climbed it quickly and slumped down at the pool's edge. My God! What had got into her? Resentment, anger, shame all fused into a spear of anguish that shot through her and left her empty. Why had Chris come to split open her past, which she'd wrapped up and stuffed away in some dark corner?

"Okay. You've proven your point," she said, trying desperately to keep the tremor from her voice. "Your charm and persuasion are still intact. But this is it. No repeat performance. Finale. The end. Just consider this regrettable little interlude a bit of sentiment for old times' sake." She listened to herself go on and on, endlessly justifying, then apologizing for her behavior.

"Hey, may I say something?" Chris asked finally, breaking into her tirade. "I mean, if you've finished evaluating our actions, motives, words and other assorted nonessentials? It happened. Maybe it was supposed to. Maybe we even proved something."

"Oh, sure, we proved something all right, spurred along by all this moonlight and starshine. You always were one to make the most of your environment!'' She couldn't conceal her bitterness.

His jaw tightened. ''You never gave a damn about my work, did you?''

''Nor you mine! That was another strike against us, among many.''

''At least I wasn't malicious!'' He flung the accusation at her.

She stared, incredulous. ''Malicious! What are you talking about?''

''Forget I said that. I didn't mean it.''

''I don't think so. Out with it!''

''I said forget it!'' he shouted.

Fury shot through her. She wanted to shake him, pound on his chest. With effort she controlled her temper. ''I suppose you've cooked up some imaginary injury in order to salve your own guilt.''

''My God, woman! You call destroying ten years of accumulated research an imagined injury?''

She leaned against the table for support, looking at him in disbelief. ''Chris, what in heaven's name are you saying? Didn't you find all your materials, the disks, the tapes?''

He gave her a measuring look. ''Not a blasted thing! The landlady said you were very specific, left a note telling the Salvation Army driver exactly what to remove.''

''Yes, I did. I told them to take only the things that were boxed. I stacked your research stuff on the table. Oh, Chris, I knew how long and hard you'd worked, the hours you'd spent.''

''I was out of my mind. I couldn't believe you'd do such a thing, but I checked with the driver, and he still had the note in your handwriting.''

She felt sick. She tried to speak, but a sob came out instead. Her eyes glazed with tears, and she laid a hand on his arm. "Chris, you must believe me. Never would I destroy your work. I don't know what happened. Maybe the landlady or some of the tenants thoughtlessly moved things around.

She met his cool gray eyes, willing him to believe her. How could he imagine her capable of such wanton destruction? He looked down at her for a long time, his expression gradually softening. "Thank you," he said quietly, laying a hand against her cheek. "Deep down I never believed it."

His gentle caress brought tears to her eyes, and she abruptly pulled away. "I'd better get dressed. Would you mind calling a taxi?" she said more sharply than she'd intended.

"It's pretty late. I'll run you home."

She hurried to the dressing room, and a few minutes later, came out to see Chris tearing out of the house, his expression grim. "The Jeep is gone," he cried, "and Lee isn't in his room!"

CHAPTER FIVE

"WHAT CAN WE DO?" Holly asked when Chris got off the phone with the police. Her eyes were full of concern.

Frustration chained him as effectively as handcuffs. He gave a hopeless gesture. "Sit and wait. If the border is his destination, the police will pick him up in an hour or two. The Pan-American Highway is the only main route. The Jeep will be easy to spot."

He paced the deck. Holly sat quite still, her hands clasped in her lap, the picture of self-containment. He tried to draw the attitude inside himself to still his agitation. How many times had he seen her in that pose during their marriage? It had been part of what he adored about her, the poise that allowed her to handle any situation. Well, almost any situation. She had an Achilles' heel after all—her phobia about drowning. Other forces moved behind that serene facade, too, forces she'd hidden deep inside, ones that he'd been oblivious to. How could he and Holly have moved on such different planes?

"I still can't believe Lee took off like that," Holly said. "We had a talk earlier in the evening, and he seemed excited about the prospect of studying with a wood sculptor. I saw nothing to indicate he planned to run away."

"Well, I'm not surprised. The kid hates me." The words tasted acrid on his tongue.

"He doesn't hate you," she said, as if annoyed with him. "I've watched the way he reacts to you, and I'm certain he puts you on a high pedestal."

"Nonsense. He hardly even talks to me."

"Because he thinks you want a superboy, someone he can't possibly be, someone who isn't worthy of that high place, so he just crawls into his shell. Somehow you've got to convince him that you like him for himself. Oh, it's probably all mixed in with his growing up and achieving independence. He's not unique in that respect." She hesitated as if she weren't certain she ought to proceed. "For starters, why don't you try getting to know him?"

"Know him! I've known the boy since my brother adopted him six years ago!"

"I don't think so. From what I've seen, you two have little more than a nodding acquaintance. I mean find out who he really is, what turns him on and what turns him off, what books he reads, who his friends are, that sort of thing."

Chris realized he couldn't answer one of her questions. It jolted him. He hadn't thought of himself as being so self-centered. "Since when did you get to be such an expert on adolescents?"

"I'm not, but I taught a high school summer session one year and bumped heads with the breed, a rare and wonderful lot if you can understand them."

"And you're saying that I haven't done that with Lee?"

"I don't think so." Her answer was not unexpected, but it still wounded.

"I see. Well, if anyone is qualified to report on my outstanding sensitivity, you're number one," he said bitterly.

She ignored the comment. "I wonder when he left. I saw him talking to Ramona, and then he went into the house. I thought he intended to try out some wood-carving knives I gave him."

"You bought him tools?"

"Just a few. Why? You don't object, do you?"

He shrugged in a gesture of futility. "If I'd used my head, I'd have seen to that ages ago. That's what you were talking about. Awareness. Right?"

"Yes, Chris." Even though she spoke softly, the underlying conviction was unmistakable. Did she speak for herself as well as for Lee? When she looked up at him like that, her dark-fringed eyes meeting his without flinching, her chin firm and unyielding and yet so damn feminine, something intensely masculine churned within him. Holly had evolved rather than changed, opened and flourished like a lovely blossom, making her an even more exciting woman than before, even more beautiful.

"Listen, Chris, I don't want to interfere or sound preachy, but if you want to try another angle in dealing with Lee, I can tell you what works for me."

"Go ahead. It's apparent I'm at the bottom of the class with my tactics." He'd eagerly taken on the challenge of fathering this boy. He'd wanted it to work, maybe to prove something to himself. He'd believed that no matter how deeply involved he was with his career, he'd never shortchange his humanity. But Holly had left him, so he'd failed. And now he'd failed with Lee.

He saw that she watched him with eyes that had softened. She started to touch his arm in an old, familiar gesture, then quickly put her hand in her lap again. He felt desolate at the rejection.

"Just remember. Curb the fireworks and try to cool your inclination to pass out judgments on what happened. Instead, describe your feelings and his, too, if you like. What you need most right now is a decent climate where you two can talk to each other.''

"Well, one thing's certain. I'd better clamp down hard in the future.''

Holly shook her head. "No, Chris, not unless you want more of the same.''

He slammed a fist down on the table, making their cups teeter and rattle. "So what the devil do you suggest?''

"Lee is trying to learn who he is. If you restrict him too severely, you'll lose him.'' Holly reached over into a tub of succulents and filled both hands with sand. She squeezed one hand hard, and sand escaped between her fingers. She kept the other open, and the sand remained.

"I see,'' he said, and fought his desire to take those slim fingers and interlock them with his. They sat in silence for a while as if mutually willing the phone to ring and announce that Lee had been found, unhurt and safe. A little later she asked him to call a taxi for her, and he sent her home with the promise he'd call her the minute he had any news.

He remained at the patio table for a long time, feeling oddly unsettled. He kept picturing her as she had sat across from him. It had sent exultation beating like drums all the way through him. Her conversation hammered away in his mind, forcing him to look inside himself. What he saw troubled him. Had he been such an insensitive clod when they were married? So it seemed. And now he was behaving the same way with Lee. There had to be some way to keep one's antennae pointed in the right direction.

Now that he'd manipulated himself into Holly's life again, he had to play a whole different ball game. He was certainly going to back off a little and arrange the kind of quality time it took to get to know the persons they'd become. She was no longer a schoolgirl to be swept off her feet. He hadn't realized the depth of the turmoil she'd harbored during their marriage.

Overall, her actions indicated she'd written him out of her life. But what about the incident in the pool when they'd clung so intimately to each other? It had to have been a fleeting reaction to the brief understanding he'd shown toward her phobia, something he should have shown during their marriage, he thought miserably. But the way she responded to his kisses indicated that the chemistry was undeniable. Maybe there was a spark he could nourish after all.

He hoped this Avalon fellow wasn't a serious consideration. He hadn't fully sized the guy up yet, but somehow he didn't come off as genuine. He seemed to be playing a part, as if he were some lord of the manor straight out of a past century. Was it an act? If so, Holly would surely see through it, and fast.

Stop your wishful thinking. Señor Miguel Avalon is no wimp. He offers the kind of gracious life any woman would cherish. He holds a position of respect and power in the community. He comes from distinguished lineage with roots firmly established in the area. If what Chris had heard was true, Miguel's home was classic Spanish colonial, full of tradition and quality. Stability and things that stood the test of time, that was what counted with Holly and that was what Miguel Avalon represented. Christopher Brooke didn't qualify in either area. Well, he'd fight hard to win her back, and he'd damn well do it without all that hand-kissing business.

The police called an hour later and said they'd located the Jeep at the turnoff to Teotitlán, a small village a few miles south of town. South? The border was north. And Lee was nowhere to be found. What was he up to? Had he gone to the coast to get a job on a fishing boat? Had he abandoned the Jeep and hitched a ride? Did all parents go through such harrowing experiences?

An hour later a bedraggled and tired Lee walked in. Chris took in this boy-almost-man who had so thoroughly upset his night. Worry, anger and frustration exploded. "Where the hell have you been?" he shouted.

Lee sat down, kicked off his shoes and socks and stared at the blister on his heel. "What's it to you?" he muttered.

Chris walked over and glared down at him. "You disappear with my Jeep and ask a stupid question like that?" Fury blistered the words. Lee's dark eyes looked haunted and miserable, but Chris wondered if he'd imagined it when the boy's expression turned sullen.

No fireworks, Holly had said. But already he'd become a verbal pyromaniac. He silently cursed his temper and took in the boy's bowed head, his posture now slumped in utter dejection. "You look beat," he said quietly.

"I sure am. I took Ramona home. Just after I started back I ran out of gas, and I didn't have any money to phone you."

Dammit, what got into you to take the Jeep in the first place? he started to say, but this time a warning light flashed. *Describe feelings*, Holly had said. He managed a fair if studied calm. "I've been out of my mind. I didn't know what happened to you." Did that qualify? he wondered.

Lee hung his head. "Sorry. I didn't know what to do except get home as fast as I could. I walked all the way. It seemed like a million miles."

"You and I always let each other know where we are, so I got pretty teed off when you left without telling me."

Lee's head snapped up in surprise. "But I left you a note."

"Where?"

"I propped it on the chest by your bed."

Chris hadn't found it, but he'd only gone to his room briefly to change out of his bathing suit. "That still doesn't explain why you took the Jeep without asking. You've never done that."

Lee toyed with a fork he'd found on the table, then shrugged. "Yeah, I admit it. I was afraid if I asked, you wouldn't let me. You were busy with all your friends, so I just split."

"You must have felt mighty stupid when you ran out of gas and had no money."

"You'd better believe it. I'll never do that again."

"Can I count on it?"

"I promise."

Chris laid a hand on his shoulder. "You promise? That's good enough for me. Shall we turn in? It's late."

Lee nodded. His eyes blinked rapidly as he hurried off to bed.

ORDINARILY HOLLY WAS a morning person, but as she walked to work, she knew it would be a long day. She'd stayed awake until Chris had called last night with the explanation of what had happened to Lee. After that, the events of the entire evening had nagged her, allowing only fitful sleep. It didn't take long for Juana's sharp eyes to notice her lethargy.

"So you're not yourself this morning. Too much romance or too little?" she teased, and shook a finger at her, then lowered her voice as if she were a conspirator. "I have an herb potion for such a condition." She rolled her eyes and fluttered her hands. "¡Bueno! ¡Maravilloso! I'll prepare it for you. Tell Juana the problem."

"It's Lee. He disappeared for a while last night, and we were worried sick."

Juana nodded. "Ah, yes, teenagers! My cousin José in Guadalajara can turn those little savages into guacamole. We'll consult him."

As far as Holly could tell, Juana had a least one in-law in every town of any size in Mexico, and a lot of villages, too. More than that, each relative was a specialist in almost anything, from how to pickle quail eggs to the secret of why there were few gray-haired Oaxacan Indians. According to Cousin Rosarita in Topolobampo, no hereditary or dietary bonus kept their hair jet black. The truth of the matter was that both men and women were as reluctant to age as any other race, and many simply dyed their hair.

Holly said she'd be happy to hear Cousin José's advice, but this time the problem had already been settled. And rather well for a change, she thought, if she had correctly read between the lines when Chris had called with a brief explanation this morning.

But that was all he had discussed. The conversation had been a bare-bones outline, but she had gleaned enough to realize there'd been no angry confrontation. For a while last night, as they were steeped in mutual concern for Lee, they could have been two loving parents concerned for their son. It had been an oddly satisfying time, but this morning Chris had turned into a stranger again.

What sleep she'd managed during the night was plagued, not only by concern for the missing boy, but by the memory of her own behavior. If only she could bury forever the recollection of her paranoia when Paul Dalton had dragged her into the pool. She hoped she would never run into any of the guests again. She'd never been so embarrassed in her entire life, nor had she ever lost her cool to that extent. Well, she'd learn to swim this summer even if she had to neglect her pottery.

And as for the way she had allowed herself to respond to Chris's embrace, her face burned at the thought of it. Did old emotions always lie in wait to trap one? The worst part was that he was quite aware of her response. He was probably amused that he could still charm an ex-wife to the point of seduction. What must he think? Well, she'd won his agreement to arrange a teacher for Lee. She'd do that, then bow out of any further business with Christopher Brooke.

For the next few days she worried about her lapse, unable to put it out of her mind. She went over and over the scene in her head. If only she'd said this, done that, would it all have turned out differently? And throughout, visions of Chris flashed before her—his broad shoulders, how it felt when he held her—and something wept soundlessly within.

She had taken Lee's rooster carving to show to Elena at her lesson yesterday. Elena had examined it thoroughly, taking it to the window and turning it slowly. "Who is this boy? I tell you, he is a prodigy."

"I'm glad you think so, Doña Elena. I agree."

"So! We must find him a good teacher at once. I know just the person. He has refused any more students, but I'll call him. He'll take this one!" She wrote a name in clear round letters. Señor Jorge Hamilton.

Holly read the name. "Hamilton?"

Elena smiled. "His grandfather was Scotch. You'll find such names here—a result of colonial times—but he couldn't be more Mexican. He's a demanding one. Can this boy take discipline?"

"I believe so," Holly said, and prayed she was right.

"Then I'll make the call and let you know." Holly's own lessons were going well, and Elena was particularly enthusiastic about her birds. Elena's accolades were balm to her gloomy spirits. She'd already learned they were not passed out lightly.

As soon as Elena gave her the go-ahead, she'd relay the information to Chris. Maybe she would write him an impersonal note giving Señor Hamilton's name and address. It was time to cut off further meetings with Chris. A relationship between them was futile. They'd found out the hard way how wrong they were for each other. Why go through all that misery again? A remnant of physical attraction was no excuse. If only they hadn't run into each other again.

She worked the rest of the afternoon in Elena's studio completing some fruit bowls. They sold at La Tienda as fast as she could make them. As always, Elena prodded her to invest her work with her distinctive style. "Add the touch that shows it's yours," she often said.

As Holly pounded a fresh lump of clay, it occurred to her that the evolution of a pot could be likened to the human life cycle from birth through the struggle to achieve a unique identity. The potter took clay from the earth, prepared it, chastened and wedged it. It grew on the wheel, gaining form and shape. Rough edges were smoothed, slip applied. Individuality emerged through decoration and design. There was trial by fire, followed by glazes and color. Back into the kiln, tempered by heat, at last it arrived at maturity.

Around the edge of one of the bowls, she painted a ring of stylized girls' profiles, their noses up in the air, ignoring the handsome fellow sketched in the center. Elena's eyes twinkled. "The barometer of your love life, *hija mía?*"

LATER IN THE WEEK Lee came into the shop. He'd dropped in so frequently of late that Juana had begun to give him odd jobs. He obviously enjoyed helping, and pitched in to wait on customers whenever there was a crowd.

Today he seemed restless. Several times he started over to where Holly was dusting a shelf of terra-cotta candlesticks, and then he wandered off to carry out some empty cartons. A little later she joined him. "How are things going?"

He frowned. "I blew it already."

"What do you mean?"

"I still can't believe it, but things have been a lot better since the night I took the Jeep."

"So what happened?"

"Yesterday he had to leave early, so he asked me to take his latest batch of film to the post office and airmail it to the place in the States that processes it for him. I started to work with the new knives you gave me and forgot all about it." He spread his hands in a hopeless gesture.

"Well, is that such a big deal?" Holly asked.

"Yes, it is. He wanted the film back as soon as possible. This is the weekend, and now it won't go out until Monday. Man! Did he blow his top!"

"I see," Holly said, and did. So the truce was too good to last. Chris was a perfectionist about his work and appreciated the quality in others. Maybe that's why he got along so well with Marissa. Holly was certain that the woman had never made a mistake in her entire life. "Did you apologize?' she asked.

"Barely. He took off to check out an animal market for future filming, then he had to go to the airport to pick up someone who's coming to see him on business." Lee fumbled with a figurine and almost dropped it, then set it on the shelf. "Listen, I figured maybe I could get him a little present. Maybe it would patch up things a little."

"Good idea. Give him one of your carvings."

He looked appalled. "No way. They aren't nearly good enough. He's not interested in my stuff."

"You're wrong, Lee. 'A gift from the hand is a gift from the heart,'" she quoted.

He shook his head. "Not for him," he said doggedly. "Will you help me choose something?"

Holly understood Lee's lack of confidence in his art. She'd behaved in much the same way. One had to be a veritable Leonardo da Vinci before showing one's creations to Chris, she'd thought. How wrong she'd been not to share that part of her with him.

She made several suggestions from the merchandise in the shop, but Lee seemed to want something more personal. They finally settled on a handwoven belt from Santo Tomás. None was left in Chris's size, and there would be no delivery until Monday. Later they walked to the old market several blocks on the other side of the zócalo where the belts were also sold. They selected one in shades of beige and brown, eagles in flight interspersed with Indian motifs. The weaving had the look of fine petit point and was sewn onto a strip of leather. Eagles in flight. The design was particularly fitting.

They walked companionably back to the *zócalo* and sat down to rest on one of the white wrought-iron benches in the shade. It was the siesta hour, and few people were in the square. Tonight the place would be crowded with listeners for the brass band or the marimba group that alternated performances. Lee pulled out the belt from the package and inspected it again. "Do you really think he'll like this?"

"Of course he will, and why can't you call Chris by name? You always refer to him as 'he.'"

"I don't feel comfortable calling him Chris."

"I'm sure he'd prefer it over all those dispassionate hims and hes. You call me by my first name."

"That's different. You're kinda like a big sister. I don't know who he is yet—who he is to me, I mean. When I find out, I'll call him something."

"In the meantime, keep in mind that those pronouns are putting up a mighty big barrier between you two."

He looked at his watch. "I'd better hike over to the corner. He said he'd pick me up by the hotel on his way home from the airport."

Holly rose quickly. "I have to go to my pottery class. I'll be in touch soon." No way did she want to be around when Chris arrived. He'd think she wanted him to take her home or some other such nonsense. She merged into a throng of pedestrians and crossed the street just as Chris's Jeep swung to the curb where Lee waited.

Lee hopped into the back seat. A woman sat in front beside Chris. The shade of her hair and the distinctive upturned chin left no doubt about her identity. So, Chris didn't see her anymore! Without a doubt, the stunning auburn-haired woman in the wide sun hat and the Yves-Saint Laurent dark glasses was Marissa Levesque, the woman who'd devastated their marriage.

CHAPTER SIX

So CHRIS AND MARISSA were still an item after all. Well, it was no concern of Holly's. They could carry on forever as far as she was concerned. She walked quickly to Elena's studio, a walled conglomeration of primitive-looking buildings and kilns surrounding a dirt courtyard right in the heart of the city. For an hour she worked on an eagle poised for flight, and in the end, mangled it and threw it into a bucket.

Doña Elena gave her a knowing look. "Go home and drum out your devil and come back when you're ready," she said in her soft Spanish.

How perceptive the kindly teacher was, Holly thought, putting her tools away and then cleaning the working area. As she started toward the door, Elena put a hand on her shoulder.

"Momentito," she said, and handed her a slip of paper with an address on it. "I have arranged for the lessons with Señor Hamilton, the wood sculptor. It wasn't easy to convince him to accept another pupil. I don't want to eat my words, so caution the boy to be prompt and work diligently."

"Muchas gracias, maestra!" Holly thanked her warmly and hoped the lessons would prove to be the answer both Chris and Lee so desperately needed.

For no reason at all, she felt depressed and was glad she had a date with Miguel in the evening. They were going out to dinner and afterward to the Museo Regional to see the treasures from Monte Albán's famous Tomb Seven. Miguel was determined to educate her concerning the background of Oaxaca, wanting her to love it as much as he did. She was grateful for his interest. It couldn't have come at a better time.

Twenty minutes later she turned off the hot dusty street and rang the bell at the great door of Casa Avalon. As always the beauty inside came as a welcome balm. Lush greenery and blooming flowers met the eye after one passed through the little entry office sternly guarded by the manager. The only sounds this late afternoon came from the fountain that sprayed in the courtyard and from Pepe, the caged parrot, who squawked occasionally. With relief she slumped into a chair on the patio, picked up a magazine from the table and absently thumbed through it.

Drum out your devil, Elena had said, but it wasn't easy. It was as if some perverse force inside her was filling her mind with images of Christopher, whose steady gray eyes never crinkled with laughter anymore, with the problems concerning Lee, with the question mark of Marissa, and in spite of all efforts to banish the thought, the recollection of his arms about her when they'd been in the pool.

She willed herself to focus on her surroundings. Casa Avalon had been built a century ago in Spanish colonial style with a *U*-shaped tiled patio around a grassy courtyard that bloomed with an unstructured array of poinsettias, geraniums and amaryllis. A grape arbor shaded a pleasant walkway across the open end of the complex, and beyond that there was a vegetable garden, its produce helping to provide the Casa's delectable meals.

The place had a dozen bedrooms that were nearly always filled. Each room opened out onto the covered patio where comfortable chairs invited restful contemplation or chatting with other guests. Even now a group gathered on the far side to sip cool drinks, sometimes mescal, while they awaited the cook's clanging bell for the evening meal at seven. The early hour was a concession to the mainly American tourists. Most Mexican households served *cena*, a light supper, much later.

She looked at her watch and reluctantly headed for her room. Her spacious thick-walled suite was furnished sparingly with sturdy antiques, hand-loomed spreads and area rugs. A carafe of purified water rested on a table, with a bouquet of daisies beside it, and a full bookcase offered a potpourri of reading material.

She'd learned from one of the other residents that only recently had Casa Avalon been opened as a guest hotel. Inflation was riotous in Mexico now; the peso had devalued drastically. Fortunes had shrunk, and although Miguel still lived well, even he had found it judicious to open his house to paying guests, all of whom he screened carefully.

She showered and put on the turquoise gown Miguel admired, the one he wanted her to wear for his painting. She would have to make time for that soon. He'd reminded her frequently.

A little later a maid knocked on her door, saying Miguel was waiting in the foyer. As she walked around the patio, she pictured young women of early days passing along this same gracious walk to accompany their swains in carriages, no doubt properly accompanied by chaperones.

Miguel's dark eyes shone as he reached for her hand, giving it a whisper of a kiss. "How beautiful you are tonight, dear Holly. I am honored to have your company."

"Gracias," she answered, trying to imagine Christopher speaking those same words and failing completely.

Miguel drove a spotless, shining Rolls-Royce, probably at least twenty years old, but it looked and seemed to perform like new. Someone had told her it was the only such car in Oaxaca, and everyone knew it belonged to Señor Avalon.

It took only minutes to drive up the hillside and through the tree-lined approach to Hotel Victoria, one of the most charming in the city. From the attendant who parked the car to the maître d', all behaved as if they were welcoming royalty. Miguel accepted the attention graciously, apparently quite accustomed to it. It occurred to Holly that he might even have been hurt and bewildered if such were lacking.

Holly had to admit that it was pleasant to bask in the solicitous climate, and she couldn't help feeling amused at envious looks cast her way by women at surrounding tables. No wonder. Miguel's aristocratic manner would command regard anywhere.

A plate of *gorditas*, tortilla dough wrapped around various stuffings and deep-fried, was served with their margaritas. Chilled gazpacho followed, then an entrée of red snapper smothered in the most delicious mole she'd ever tasted. Miguel kept up a continual patter, explaining the ingredients of the various foods, and he seemed inordinately pleased at her enthusiasm for the dishes chosen for her enjoyment.

His expressive dark eyes seemed to compliment every word she spoke, and at times she grew uneasy with such enveloping attention. There was also more than a hint of invitation there. For an innocent flirtation? Or for something more? Was he waiting for some response to the hand that often rested fleetingly on hers? Or was his behavior merely a result of his cultural heritage, more decorative than meaningful?

The candlelight, the soft music of a classical guitarist and a handsome, attentive escort provided the most romantic ambience she'd ever experienced. Why, then, didn't she feel at least a nudge of chemistry?

To her dismay a flush suffused her face, and it wasn't from the wine. She knew only too well the answer to her question. Ever since Christopher had unexpectedly checked back into her life, he'd insidiously projected himself into her thoughts on a nonstop basis. Memories accompanied her every waking hour. Well, it had to be stopped. Where was the sensible, mature Holly who knew what she wanted out of life? A fling with an ex-husband had no part in it.

She summoned a brilliant smile for Miguel and held her glass up for refilling. Immediately she found herself comparing Miguel's flowery, somewhat formal conversation with Chris's lively, straightforward speech. Miguel turned to wave at some acquaintance at a nearby table. Holly studied his patrician profile, so different from Chris's imperfect one, which was a little too strong actually. His sun-bleached hair was often tousled, a condition she had once regarded as eminently endearing. As for Miguel's thick black mane, not once had she seen a hair out of place.

Miguel launched into a description of a painting by a young Mexican artist, which he planned to show her later. "Not at all what you'd expect from Mexico. Unless you knew, my dear, I swear you'd peg him as a fugitive from the French Impressionists.'' Holly made herself listen, hoping her eyes wouldn't glaze. Having at last secured her undivided attention, Miguel's rhetoric flowed silvery and expansive as he discussed the painting. He repeatedly filled her glass as if the wine were some magic elixir that had helped win her acknowledgment.

The rest of the evening passed in a continuous blur. On the way to the museum they stopped at a gallery to see the painting—a dark-haired beauty sitting in a garden with a basket of daisies in her lap—that Miguel had raved about. The work showed talent and was unabashedly romantic. Did the painting reflect Miguel's ideal of femininity?

They walked around the block to the Museo Regional where the Tomb Seven artifacts were housed. Around A.D. 500, Mixtec Indians had placed the articles in the tomb: jewelry, incense urns, vessels and art objects of gold, alabaster, jade, pearl, onyx and rock crystal.

Miguel pointed to a display of gold necklaces. ''*Cara mía*, I shall see that you have a gold necklace designed like one of these. You have only to choose. I know a superior jeweler who is talented at such work.''

''Beautiful,'' she murmured, knowing she would refuse such an expensive gift. Later she struggled to recall even one fact that Miguel had reported, but failed. She hoped her vague comments went unnoticed as they drove back to the Casa.

Miguel escorted her to her room and raised her hand to his lips. ''*Buenas noches,*'' he murmured, and the lingering kiss seemed to promise that future good-nights would hold greater ardor. She sincerely hoped he hadn't been offended by her distracted manner and promised herself that from now on she'd give this attractive man the attention he deserved.

She crept into bed and knew at once that sleep would be a long time coming. Drawing the sheet over her head, she tried to recall the colors in the painting of the lady with the daisies, hoping the concentration would invoke sleep. Instead, the muted colors wavered and grew bold. The elegant woman became an erotic nude in another portrait she'd almost forgotten. The ache she felt now filled her entire body. Suddenly she wanted very much to recall every detail of the time she had seen that awful portrait.

She and Chris had been driving home from a weekend trip to Lake Tahoe in the early months of their marriage. It was midnight when the timing chain suddenly broke on Christopher's ancient M.G. A friendly highway patrolman pushed them off the freeway into a little one-horse town whose one garage had been closed for hours. They locked the car and walked across the street to a seedy motel.

A sleepy clerk rented them a room. Chris unlocked the door and burst out laughing. Huge red cabbage roses bloomed on stained wallpaper, and a frayed pumpkin-colored rug didn't quite cover the cement floor. Over the bed hung a dreadful portrait of a voluptuous nude woman painted on black velvet in garish colors. Chris whooped, lifted Holly in his arms and whirled her around dizzily.

"Darling, I always wanted to take my bride to the Waldorf. Lucky we found this place."

She gave a rapturous sigh. "What class!"

"Early rummage sale period," he chortled. They howled with laughter at each new discovery in the room: the long beaded fringe on a faded lampshade, embroidered pillows blessing "home sweet home" and "mother," and cheap vases with plastic flowers adorning dresser top and tables.

Holly plopped down on the bed and promptly sagged into the center. "A true honeymoon bed," she cried, convulsing into giggles. Christopher sat down on the other side and rolled against her. She kissed him lightly, jumped up and headed for the shower.

"Hurry!" she cried a few minutes later. "This water is tepid going on freezing!" He hurried to join her. When they were covered with suds, they embraced, and for a little while, with the clean scent of soap all around them, they basked in the stinging spray, rocking rhythmically as if to music, reveling in the sensuous feel of their soapy, wet bodies against each other. In no time at all the water turned cold, and Christopher turned it off. He kissed her shoulder, then vigorously dried her in the unexpectedly generous towel.

A little shyly, she rubbed him dry. Even though they'd been married almost two months, she still felt a catch in her throat when she saw his firm, lithe body. She knew he would scoff if she told him he could have modeled for one of those ancient Greek statues. And what of herself? She could never equal the female Greek counterpart. In fact, she wondered if Chris ever felt regret that he didn't have a more curvaceous armful when he held her slim, small-breasted body.

He swept her up and dumped her unceremoniously on the terrible bed. She grabbed a pillow and hurled it at him. He ducked, caught it and threw it back, then fell into bed beside her. They rolled over and over, arms and legs entwined, pinching and nipping like playful cubs. Then, as if with one mind, they stopped clowning. Chris cupped her face in his hands, and his eyes softened. His kiss was gentle at first, as she knew it would be, but soon it became more urgent.

He'd made love to her often during the past weeks, but he still touched off sensations that were new and fresh, telling her continuously with his lips, his hands, his eyes and voice how deeply he cared for her.

The intimate words of love didn't come to her as easily as they did to him, but she ran her fingers through his fair hair, felt for the laugh lines already etched at the corners of his eyes, then lingeringly explored his body, relishing not only the texture of his skin, but thrilling to his eager reactions.

Passion rose in overwhelming waves, and their consummation brought tears of elation. She lay still for a long time afterward, her head on his chest as she listened to his heartbeat return to normal. Christopher never fell asleep immediately. He'd hold her close and continue to murmur words of love like a tender lullaby until slumber came. "Darling, I never cease to marvel at the tiger under all that decorum," he finally whispered.

She snuggled closer. "So you arranged this detour entirely for your evil purposes?"

"You'd better believe it," he replied.

But his good-night kiss had held no such flippancy. It had acknowledged their commitment to share special joys as well as the inevitable anxieties, and her throat had ached with happiness.

Now she tried to banish the memories of that wild and joyful night, and she wept for the broken promises, the worthless commitments.

Something had prevented her from enjoying this evening with Miguel, all right—an indestructible core of feeling for Christopher. Well, she must be strong. She would refuse to let it run through her life like a quivering thread. She would not allow it to keep her from finding love again. First thing tomorrow she would give Chris the information about Lee's teacher, and that would be the end of it.

However, the next morning Chris called first. After he identified himself, she crisply enunciated the teacher's name, address and lesson time, then conveyed Elena's warning to be prompt and conscientious.

"I think you'll be pleased. Señor Hamilton is said to be a strong disciplinarian requiring total commitment. That's what you wanted, wasn't it? Perhaps that will make up for Lee's not attending military school. Goodbye, Chris. I hope you have a pleasant summer."

"Hey, hold on," he said. "I haven't had my turn."

"I can't think of another thing we have to say to each other."

"Believe me, there is. I need to talk to you. How about tomorrow at two? I'll call for you at the shop when you finish work."

"What's to say?"

"Something that concerns both of us."

"You and I are finished, Chris. We're not related anymore. We're strangers now. Best to keep it that way."

She heard his voice tighten. "I realize that, but—"

"By the way, Chris," she interrupted. "Wasn't that Marissa I saw you with yesterday when you picked up Lee at the *zócalo*?"

The silence at the other end seemed endless. "Yes, it was," he said finally.

CHAPTER SEVEN

CHRIS STOOD at the kitchen counter, helped himself to a bowl of hot oatmeal with raisins from the Crockpot and put brown sugar and milk on it. He set it on a tray, added a sweet roll from the batch Ramona had purchased at the *pastelería* yesterday and took his breakfast outside on the patio. Damn. Of all the times to receive a contract to do a book revision. It would throw a wrench into his time-table. Today he'd planned to film the colorful animal market at Ocotlán, where the farmers came to buy, barter or auction their stock. Instead, he would have to spend hours with Marissa Levesque, of all people.

They'd coauthored the book eight years ago, and the publishers wanted them to update it for a new edition. It was an in-depth manual on how to make a documentary film and had become something of a classic on the subject. Film schools had begun to use it as their bible, and the publishers, with foreign markets assured, planned to translate it into twenty languages.

No way could he turn down the handsome advance. The unexpected assignment would save him from going into debt, a lever he suspected the canny Marissa had depended on to con him into accepting the offer. He already had a lot more money than he'd counted on tied up in the Oaxaca documentary.

He'd been firm in letting Marissa know he could spare only a week for the revisions. They'd have to work night and day to finish in that time, but it could be done. He hoped that she wouldn't complicate the work with any notions of extracurricular activities. He'd been brutally clear in getting the message across yesterday. Her pride, if nothing else, should keep her in line.

She'd called two days ago with the publisher's offer and, in typical operating procedure, had announced she'd already booked a flight to Oaxaca.

"How did you know where to get in touch with me?" he'd asked after she'd made explanations.

"Darling, need you ask? I merely called the university."

"Well, I wondered. It's been a while, hasn't it?"

"Too long, Christopher. We were quite a team. A shame you didn't recognize it. Think of the beautiful music we could have made."

Music? Oh, sure, Chris had thought. Professionally they were dynamite together, but when it came to his personal life the word for her was *poison*. Marissa didn't need him. Not really. She had a nose for smelling out upward mobility and not only latched on to it, but soon manipulated, outwitted and maneuvered until she held the reins. Not that she wasn't good. She was one of the best screenwriters in the business.

MARISSA'S PLANE was an hour late, but when she got off, her step was vigorous and she looked as fresh and vibrant as ever. *She could have had a career as a model*, he thought as she walked toward him. She wore a stunning red suit, no doubt from some designer's salon, which looked surprisingly dashing with her auburn hair. *She must be forty-seven now*, Chris reflected. He recalled she was about ten years older than he, but she could have passed for someone a lot younger. She probably devoted as much time to keeping that flawless skin and trim figure as she did to her writing.

She kissed him firmly on the lips and took his arm. "Darling, how wonderful to see you after all these years. What a glorious tan! This Oaxacan sun must agree with you."

"I hope you brought an umbrella. We get frequent thunder showers during the summer." They continued to bat a few comments back and forth about the weather as he lifted her luggage from the carousel and carried it out to his Jeep. She wrinkled her nose as she climbed into the dusty vehicle.

"Is this the accepted mode of transportation in these parts?"

"It happens to cooperate very well with the dirty roads in the villages and mountains," he said dryly.

He'd reserved her a room in a hotel overlooking the city a few blocks from where he lived. His suspicion that she had planned to stay with him was soon confirmed.

"I thought you lived in a house. I mean, I gathered from my conversation with someone at the university that you'd traded places with a professor," she said as he drove up to the hotel.

"That's true, but I thought you'd prefer more privacy. I'm staying with a teenage boy for the summer. I didn't think our pad would be comfortable for you."

She laughed, and it jarred him. That hearty chortle coming from such a chic woman always came as a surprise. She laid a hand on his arm. "You ought to know a bachelor's pad never offended me, Chris. Cancel the hotel room. You must have a couch somewhere. I'll sleep on that. You know very well we'll need every minute of that ridiculous little time slot you've allotted us."

"It'll work best this way," he said firmly. Then he got out of the Jeep and set out her luggage for the bellboy who came running. Her face looked stormy, but he knew she wouldn't stoop to begging.

"I see. So where are we going to work? The hotel lobby?"

"A friend is letting me use a vacant office in his building. It has a couple of desks and typewriters. It's only three blocks from your hotel, a brisk little walk on tree-lined streets. I recall how you always insisted on your morning constitutional, or I'll pick you up if you prefer."

"So the Brooke household is off-limits?"

He grinned. "Would you settle for a swim in our postage-stamp-sized pool when we've completed our revisions?"

"I'll look forward to it," she said, her tone waspish.

He hoped he'd set the ground rules, but he knew he'd have to be vigilant. Managing Marissa was like trying to put form into quicksilver and, unless she'd changed, she undoubtedly had other projects in mind aside from updating their book. Well, she could forget them!

Angrily he crumbled the rest of his sweet roll into bits. The woman had unerring timing. What must Holly think? He'd tried to tell her about the unexpected offer to do the book revision when he'd called her yesterday, but nothing he'd said had come out right.

"You owe me no explanations, Chris," she'd said, but her words had been pure frost. Damn! Their newfound relationship was precarious at best. Now, with Marissa's arrival, they were back to square one. Well, he'd try to clear up the matter the minute he could persuade Holly to listen. His mouth twisted. Considering her actions lately, that would take some high-powered tactics.

HOLLY TOOK A TAXI to work so that she could bring along her latest batch of pottery. Doña Elena had pointed out early on in their lessons that Holly's forte was whimsy, and she'd urged her to cultivate it. This morning Holly brought several candelabra, one balanced on a mischievous-looking two-headed goat, and another decorative pair from which tiny birds and fanciful flowers dangled. There were also several flower-festooned trees of life, each holding five candles. She'd adapted the forms from some of the more sedate ceremonial candelabra she'd studied in Elena's studio.

No sooner had she arrived and set her pottery on the display shelf, when a busload of people burst into the shop. Such mass arrivals were rare. Oaxaca wasn't as well known to tourists as the coastal cities. Most foreigners went there because it was unique, not only because of its ancient archaeological ruins, but because of its culture, mainly Indian, which had not only survived for centuries, but still flourished in the high valley surrounded by mountains. In fact, no bus had ever made the shop a stopping place before. Holly soon found the reason—Paul Dalton.

She'd hoped never to see him again. For a moment the humiliation of her behavior in Chris's pool reached up to strangle her, then subsided as the man gleefully hailed her. His beaming, open face showed no recollection of the incident. He was a squarish, thickset man with sandy hair and a kind of genial ugliness that was rescued by his cheery grin. He was dressed in rumpled slacks and a nondescript pullover shirt; his body obviously resented anything but the most informal attire.

He hugged her as if she were a long-lost relative. "Holly, my love, didn't I tell you I'd come? And," he added sotto voce, "I've brought along my chickens, ripe for the plucking." He gestured toward the tourists now avidly zeroing in on the merchandise.

"Thank you, I think," Holly muttered to herself as she viewed the suddenly crowded, noisy shop. Then she introduced him to Juana. The manager's eyes sparkled as if she'd just been handed a dozen roses and a five-pound box of candy.

"Ah, *señor*, you have come to the right place. We carry work from the finest artisans in Oaxaca." She took his arm and proceeded to bombard him with a rhapsodic account of the merits of her stock.

"I can see that you appreciate fine work," Juana said, and stood back to survey the man. "You're just like my cousin Chole. I saw it at once: the broad forehead, the discerning eyes. I am right, no?" Her gestures dramatically underlined her assertions.

"You are right, yes," Paul said, not displeased with the flattery. "And I see that you also carry the works of Oaxaca's famous Doña Elena." He lifted one of Holly's candelabra to inspect it more closely.

Holly quickly joined them. "The work is mine, Paul. I study with Elena, so her influence is undoubtedly apparent."

Paul examined the work closely. "I'll be damned," he said under his breath. "I know her work well, but you could have fooled me. You're terrific. Did you know that? Listen, would you let me take one of these pieces to the States? I have connections with several galleries, and I'm certain they'll want your ceramics."

The shop sold only on consignment, so recalling one of her pieces was no problem. "Well, if you wish, but it doesn't matter that much to me. I'm just here for the summer, you know."

"But this will establish you as a first-rate ceramicist in the U.S. It's a real opportunity! You see that, don't you?" he asked eagerly. He counted out the price of the piece and handed the money to Juana in the event that Holly changed her mind.

She laughed, throwing up her hands. "I see you're a man who gets what he wants." Paul had pizzazz. It went out in waves and enveloped anyone who was near him.

"Hey, I can promise you at least triple the profits you make here. You can use them to invest in the lottery. Who knows, you might make a million."

"Aren't you getting ahead of yourself?"

"Never. I believe in lucky breaks. There are always plenty around. All you have to do is snag 'em." He grinned, but his tone was deadly serious.

A plain, middle-aged woman from his tour group timidly touched his arm and asked his opinion of a rebozo, a fine wool shawl, the kind no Oaxacan lady would find herself without. Paul draped it around her in a way that framed her face, then tossed one end over her shoulder, achieving a natty effect. "There, love, have a look," he said, leading her to a mirror. "You'll knock 'em dead in Sioux City." The woman blushed and stared at her reflection for a moment, then selected several more of the shawls for purchase. Meanwhile, Paul circulated through the shop, dispensing advice, outrageous flattery or jests, all expertly tailored to the individual tourist. It was clear they adored him.

As they made ready to leave, Holly saw Juana discreetly hand Paul an envelope. She guessed it held the customary tip for bringing in the busload of customers. He promptly returned it. "For you, *amiga*. Invest it in a lottery ticket," he said, and left with the others.

Holly smiled, knowing there was no way Juana would part with her pesos in that frivolous pursuit. The woman lived in a tiny apartment above a bakery, scrimping to save enough money to buy a small place of her own.

The petite manager rarely spoke of her past. From various remarks, Holly gathered that around seven or eight years ago, Juana, defying her parents' wishes, had left her affluent family home in Spain to marry a well-to-do Mexican businessman. Apparently the man had made bad investments. When he had died a few years later, he'd left her with nothing. Too proud to go home to her estranged parents, she'd made a life for herself in her new country.

Juana's exuberant nature allowed no complaints. Without a single member of her own family in Mexico, she embraced a huge number of in-laws and cousins whom she often called upon for advice and comfort. Her one passionate goal in life was to own her own home. No one considered her thrifty ways tightfisted, because they knew why she hoarded each centavo and peso. Everyone around her, from customers to artisans, was caught up in her enthusiasm. They could picture the walled brick cottage with space for flowers and a few vegetables. There would be a courtyard with a fountain and a birdbath. Someday they would help her move the few good pieces of furniture she had accumulated. *When Juana buys her cottage* had become a dream they all shared.

Holly often wondered why the attractive, effervescent woman hadn't remarried. In spite of her earthy attitudes, she had an air of class about her. Perhaps she frightened off the local gentry or, more likely, she didn't have the opportunity to meet them.

When the shop closed for siesta at two, Holly walked the mile back to Casa Avalon for *comida*, the large meal of the day. She'd found it difficult to adjust to the big several-course meal when her usual habit was a salad or yogurt. No wonder everyone needed a siesta.

After *comida* she unpacked and hung up the gown she planned to wear that evening. Miguel was taking her to the Monte Albán Hotel for dinner and to see the regional dancers who performed there on Saturday nights. She had splurged on a new dress by Mima, one of Mexico's talented young designers. It was made of crinkled white gauze, and the tiered skirt was bordered in turquoise ribbon decorated with occasional, tiny bunches of handmade flowers. The wide, scooped neckline barely tipped the shoulders and had the same trim. It fit her like a dream, and the moment she'd tried it on at the boutique she'd felt it had been made for her.

Would Christopher have approved of the dress? she wondered as she performed a few pirouettes around the room, the skirt floating gracefully about her. She'd worn mainly her own muted homespuns when they were married. Obviously he preferred women with brighter plumage if Marissa's outfits were any indication. She recalled the high-fashion scarlet suit.

A light knock on the door proved to be a maid who handed her a gardenia wrapped in tissue. Holly breathed in the exotic scent of the velvety white flower and opened the note that accompanied it. "*Señorita hermosa*, beautiful lady," it read. "I shall await you at eight in the library. Time will crawl until we meet. Your servant, Miguel." Dear man. He'd been born a hundred years too late. She wondered if he were considered an eccentric in this ancient city as he surely would be in the States and hoped no woman had ever been cruel enough to scoff at him.

She pinned the flower in her hair and knew it added a becoming touch. Miguel would approve the romantic look. There was no way she could become the idealized version of femininity that he sought, but at least for this evening she could enter into the spirit of the make-believe world in which he lived.

She had become used to Miguel's flowery compliments, but tonight, as he drove her the few blocks to the hotel, superlatives flowed unchecked. Her dress was a dream. She looked like an angel, no, a bride! She was a queen! It was a relief to arrive at the hotel and end the deluge of compliments which had become embarrassing.

Hotel Monte Albán was a colonial building on the *zócalo*. Its facade, tiled floors and antique furniture had seen better days but, like an aging countess, class and dignity remained intact. They walked to an inner courtyard that had been turned into a restaurant, now glass-domed in order to protect the patrons from Oaxaca's sudden showers. In the center, surrounded by tables and potted palms, was a dance floor, and musicians performed vintage tunes on accordion, trumpet and drum.

A raucous laugh caught her attention, and Holly felt as though someone had doused her with ice water. Marissa? And if it were, Chris would probably be with her. She glanced quickly around the room, but she didn't see them. No doubt she suffered from an overactive imagination. Still, the thought that they might be present flawed the evening. She wasn't interested in parrying civilized niceties with the woman who had destroyed her marriage.

Miguel ordered their dinner, and when the instrumental trio began a waltz, his dark eyes sparkled. "My favorite," he said, and invited her to dance. He rose, took her hand and led her to the edge of the dance floor, where they awaited an appropriate beat to meld into the music. She loved to dance, but if Chris and Marissa were there she'd rather not advertise her presence.

At once, she realized that Miguel was a superlative dancer. In her lovely, white gown, she no longer feared comparison with a woman in a tailored scarlet suit. Suddenly she hoped Chris and Marissa *were* somewhere in the room, *wanted* them to see her in the arms of the handsomest man there. Adrenaline flowed.

Forgetting all else, she lost herself in the movement and melody. She floated among the other dancers, whirling smoothly through the intricate steps Miguel improvised as if they'd danced together always. Suddenly she realized the spotlight that had played randomly among the dancers now followed only her and Miguel while the others stopped and edged away to watch. Colored lights bathed them in rainbow colors. It was unreal. It was magic.

Her eyes locked with Miguel's in acknowledgment of the joyous experience, and his arms tightened. For a vagabond moment, Miguel's dark eyes seemed to turn to gray, and the face that was close to hers had a shock of sun-bleached hair. Her eyes stung. Chris rarely danced. He'd always insisted he had two left feet.

As the music drew to its ending cadence, Miguel led her through a stunning series of turns concluding in a graceful pose. The room burst into applause. They bowed in acknowledgment. He kissed her hand, and they made their way back toward their table.

"Señor Avalon," a male voice called, and they paused to greet Miguel's friends, Judge Juárez and his wife. Another couple was seated with them, and the judge made introductions. Holly clung tightly to Miguel's hand. *Well, you got your wish, old girl,* she thought as she stared straight into Christopher's astonished smoke-gray eyes. The men rose, and the judge made introductions.

"Señor Brooke, an eminent filmmaker who is making a documentary here, and his colleague, Señorita Levesque, from Texas."

"Ah, yes, I believe we've met," Miguel said as the men shook hands. "Señorita Levesque, I never cease to marvel at the lovely ladies your state produces. And may I present my dear friend, Señorita Jones." He gave the *J* the Spanish pronunciation, so that her name came out sounding like Hone-ess.

"How do you do," Holly murmured to the judge and his wife, and nodded briefly toward Chris. "I know Señor Brooke."

"Hello, Holly," Chris said stiffly. Marissa tossed a sharp look at Chris, then back at Holly, swiftly appraising her. There was no sign of recognition. *Why, Marissa doesn't remember me!* Amusement welled up and filled her with elation. Had she changed so much? But of course they'd met only briefly years ago.

"What beautiful dancers!" Marissa said, directing the words to Miguel. "I simply adore a waltz."

"You must try one with Chris, then," Holly said sweetly. "He has a way with it." Chris glared at her. There followed a few minutes more of polite conversation and then they returned to their table.

Miguel seemed subdued as the waiter served their soup. "What kind is it?" Holly asked, tasting the delicious mixture.

"*Sopa de ajo,* garlic soup. Eat enough of it and it will keep away stomach ailments, mosquitoes and unwanted guests," he said, and again lapsed into silence. She studiously refrained from glancing across the room at Señor Juárez's table. Miguel had no reason to suspect any undercurrent in that direction. What was the problem? Didn't he feel well?

He warmed up a little as dinner progressed and eventually regained his usual enthusiasm when he described the regional dancers they would see a little later. They'd barely consumed their flan when Chris and Marissa appeared at their table.

"Señor Avalon, we have a time-honored custom in the States of occasionally trading partners for a dance," Chris said with uncustomary formality. Already the musicians had started a rhumba.

Holly's eyes widened. Chris couldn't even waltz, much less rhumba. But maybe he could. It was arrogant of her to assume he hadn't learned during the intervening years.

"But of course. Charming custom," Miguel said, rising with alacrity and taking Marissa's arm.

"I'd simply adore it," Marissa said, her Southern accent becoming thick as honey.

They moved at once onto the dance floor, but Chris made no move to join them. "My goodness, what are we waiting for?" Holly asked when it appeared that he'd planted himself there for the duration.

"You know damn well," he growled, then put a firm hand under her elbow and guided her into the adjacent, dimly lit salon where the bar was located.

"Why go in here?"

"For starters, I like girls named Holly who wear flowers in their hair," he said, his mouth twitching in the old teasing manner she remembered so well. The small pain under her heart became a stab. He'd shown little sense of humor since she'd arrived in Mexico, and she'd counted it a grievous loss.

"Bum answer. Try again. I know you, you're afraid to dance. So whose idea was it to trade partners?"

"Not mine!" he said emphatically.

"Your flattery overwhelms me."

"Oh, I can't hold a candle to what's his name."

"No you can't, and his name is Miguel Domingo Anastasio de Avalon."

He rolled his eyes. "How old is the guy, anyway?"

"I have no idea. Does it matter?"

"Old enough to be your father, I'll wager, but then you always did go for antiquity."

"You bet. Quality and lasting value—the name of the game."

"Care for a drink?"

"No, thanks. We should go back soon. I've already had enough alcohol, and anyway, I'm having too good a time to risk dulling the evening."

"That's obvious. You provided quite a spectacle."

"Glad you enjoyed it."

"Okay, I'm so jealous I'm out of my mind, and on top of that I'm a lousy dancer." He leaned forward, forcing her to meet his eyes. "I'd give anything to be able to hold you in my arms and lead you in a dance like that. I had no idea you were so good. Why is it that you bloom spectacularly in anything you undertake with everyone except me?" he asked, his tone almost angry.

She swallowed hard. "Good question. Think about it." Strains of the rhumba indicated it was drawing to a close. "We'd better get back."

He reached over and ran his fingers lightly across her cheek. "Holly by candlelight," he said softly, then clasped her hand in his, his eyes intense. "Sit out another with me, please. I have something I need to say to you."

For a moment she allowed the warmth of his fingers to travel through her body, filling her with an excitement she had no wish to define.

"You're getting repetitious, Chris. Come on." She pulled her hand away and walked toward the restaurant. He followed, but at the ornate entryway he drew her behind a pillar, gathered her close and kissed her. Not just an ordinary kiss, but one with a fundamental, individual message, urgently and forcefully administered. Her heartbeat quickened, and it frightened her to admit that she'd longed for his touch ever since they'd come in here together.

As always when near him, she sensed her complete vulnerability and perceived that her body was separated from his by only thin layers of clothing. Were such emotions valid, or did they perform like trained animals in accord to finely honed sets of stimuli? The latter was correct, Holly decided, and as the music ended she pulled away and headed back to the table.

"For heaven's sake, Chris," she called over her shoulder, "What are you trying to do?"

"I'm trying to tell you something as quickly and succinctly as possible. You're not very generous with your time."

"Forget it. I hate rehashes."

A fanfare by the trumpet indicated the intermission that was to precede the folk dance exhibition. Miguel and Marissa ambled back to the table at a leisurely pace. She clung to his arm, looking up at him in rapt attention, the very picture of an adoring female. What had happened to that independent, take-charge woman? Why ask? Holly thought dryly. Obviously the canny redhead had known from the age of puberty how to zero in on any man who caught her fancy.

Chris apparently didn't notice. He had his eye on Miguel. "Listen," he muttered into her ear. "I don't like to knock my competition, but you'd better realize that guy is on the ten-most-wanted list and besides that he's a top Communist spy and a paid undercover agitator."

She burst out laughing, and he gave a rueful grin. He shrugged. "You can't blame me for trying."

"Darling," Marissa cried breathlessly to Chris, her smile flashing as brilliantly as her diamond earrings. "I had no idea Oaxaca was such an exciting place. Señor Avalon has been filling me in. I'm tempted to stay on for a few weeks." She looked up at him, as coy as any sixteen-year-old. "Why didn't you tell me Mexican men were so charming?"

Miguel bowed and kissed her hand. Marissa seemed touched, and her reaction was no put-on. *Why, she really is enjoying Miguel's brand of chivalry*, Holly decided. Who would have thought it? Perhaps, after all, there was a secret place in every woman's heart that occasionally reveled in Miguel's brand of gallantry.

Marissa turned to Holly and extended her hand. "Nice to have met you too, Miss Hone-ess." In an aside she said, "My dear, you're quite beautiful. I'm happy to see that Chris's taste in women has improved. You can't believe the type that used to run after him. He was so readily taken in, you know. One plain Jane, barefoot and in homespun, if you can imagine, even captured him for almost two years!"

"Really? What happened?" Holly asked, almost strangling.

"Oh, he finally came to his senses. That's one thing about Christopher Brooke. You have to be patient. It may take him a while, but when all is said and done, he usually comes up a winner!"

CHAPTER EIGHT

MAYBE SHE NEEDED VITAMINS, Holly thought as she walked to work on a sparkling July morning, wondering if she would be able to serve up the usual cheerful amenities to the customers today. She inhaled the fresh air, recently cleansed by the brief but torrential shower an hour earlier, and nodded at an Indian woman carrying a basket of huge red radishes to market. The woman's shy, sweet smile didn't cheer her; neither did the sight of the magenta bougainvillea spilling like a tidal wave over a neighbor's wall. There was positively no reason why she should have slept so poorly last night. Nor should she be feeling so depressed this morning, she thought. Any normal person, given her present situation, would feel on top of the world.

Her pottery lessons with Doña Elena were going well, and the teacher was as thrilled as she that Paul Dalton thought enough of her work to find a U.S. market. Even local critics had begun to take notice, if the squib in the local paper had any significance. It was only a couple of sentences among a review of other artists, but it was encouraging. *Works by newcomer Holly Jones show outstanding originality and skill. Her ceramics can be found at Las Artesanías.*

True, the way that Chris kept popping up in her life had become disturbing, but she could handle that. Anyway, there would be scant likelihood of running into him again. He'd mentioned several times that he had a tough filming schedule ahead.

He was an enigma. What was this business of coming on so strong during the dance Saturday night? Was that his style now? Well, he could cross her off his list. Trust had been the issue in their breakup, and she saw nothing to indicate he'd changed. Obviously there was still something going on between Chris and Marissa, despite his assertions to the contrary. Marissa. She'd brought all those memories back in her Gucci handbag, opened it and allowed them to gnaw at Holly's cringing consciousness.

Chris hadn't trusted *her* either. If he could have believed for even a minute that she would destroy ten years of his research, he'd believe anything. Well, no relationship could survive without trust, and there'd been precious little of that.

Still, if she were honest, she had to admit there existed some current between them, or remnants of it. With discomfort she recalled the moment of weakness she'd felt when he'd brushed cherishing fingers against her cheek, and the fierce exultation she'd felt when he'd kissed her. She thrust the memories away. There'd be no problem dealing with them. She was a big girl now, and perfectly aware that chemistry was always on the alert to sabotage reason.

"*¡Buenos días!* A day for angels!" Juana sang out as if she had a personal share in its arrival. "And how did you enjoy the folk dancers? *¿Fantástico, no?*"

"I've never seen such colorful costumes, and I hadn't expected to have so much fun." They discussed the flirting routine where dancers snatched kisses behind fans while performing the intricate footwork. In the dance of the drunkards, slapstick comedy was skillfully choreographed to interweave both humor and grace.

But in spite of the color and excitement of the dancers, for her the highlight of the evening had been the moment Marissa had finally recognized her. Holly would prize it for a long time.

It had amused her to no end that there hadn't been a glimmer of recognition during the introductions. Of course Marissa hadn't known her maiden name, so she'd had no clue. After the program was over, they'd all stood chatting together for a few minutes before parting, then Marissa had turned to Holly. "I can't get over the feeling there is something familiar about you. Are you certain we've never met? Perhaps at Chris's sometime?"

"Yes, we have, but you knew me by my married name."

"You must forgive me. I have a terrible memory for names. What was it again?"

"Brooke. Remember? The barefoot girl in homespun? Actually, I always wore sandals."

"My God!" Her mouth had dropped open, and color had rushed to her face. No doubt that had been the first time in her life she'd ever been tongue-tied. Amazement and embarrassment had vied in her expression. She'd painted herself into a corner with the remarks she'd made earlier, and Holly had waited with interest to see what she'd do next.

"Damn Chris! Why didn't he tell me?" she'd said angrily.

"Why should he have? Our marriage was over and done with a long time ago. We ran into each other quite by accident down here."

Marissa had stared intently, apparently still trying to find that shy, young girl in the self-assured woman before her. "Why didn't I see it? My dear, I hardly know what to say."

"It was all said and done a long time ago, and you probably don't care for redundancy any more than I do. Goodbye, Marissa. Oaxaca is a great town. Enjoy." Marissa had looked as if she were still groping for words. Well, such new experiences would be good for her.

Holly unpacked a batch of rugs from Teotitlán, a little village outside Oaxaca where almost every house had a loom. One weaver specialized in copying designs from Picasso and Escher, an extremely intricate process. She chose one whose all-over pattern cleverly interwove sea gulls and fish and hung it on the display rack. A few customers browsed in the shop now, and she looked up at the sound of a familiar voice.

It was Miguel, and contrary to his usual aplomb, he looked anxious and harried. "My dear Holly, I need your expertise. I promised a dear friend I would select something *típico* of the area for her to take as a hostess gift when she visits a Canadian friend. I was to deliver it this morning, but it completely escaped my mind. What do you suggest?" He passed his hand across his forehead, closing his eyes for a moment.

Holly showed him some lovely table mats by the Santo Tomás weavers.

"*Perfecto.* I knew you would come to my rescue," he said, relief apparent on his drawn face.

All concern, Juana joined them. "Señor Avalon, your head aches?"

"*Sí, señora.* It seems filled with serpents today. I can hardly think."

"The pain is located in this area, no?" She touched her temples lightly. Juana looked particularly attractive this morning, her thick black hair piled on top of her head.

Curly wisps escaped to frame her face, and gold earrings swung vigorously. He nodded with the look of a man about to face death.

"Aha, just as I thought. Tension, the bane of our busy times." She hunched her shoulders in a hopeless gesture. "You have a few minutes, yes? I'll fix that head of yours. I need only time to brew you a cup of my special herb tea." She looked around as if someone might be eavesdropping. "Cousin Florentina in Barcelona shared the secret."

He glanced up sharply. "*Señora*, you are Spanish?"

"*Sí*, it is my birthplace," she said as she went to put the teakettle on the gas plate in her little office. Then she fluttered around him, seating him in a chair in an alcove behind the rug display. She massaged his shoulders and talked continually in her soft, persuasive voice. "Close the eyes, let the head fall forward, feel the pain dripping down, down and out of the finger tips."

"*¡Maravilloso!*" Miguel murmured with a sigh. Juana continued her ministrations, and a little later she handed him a cup of her mysterious brew.

"Sip slowly, slowly," she admonished.

Holly smiled. The shoe was on the other foot, and how Miguel reveled in it! Nothing defeated or baffled Juana. She met life with glowing eyes and the determination to beguile it into handing over the best it had to offer. If Miguel didn't recover immediately, Juana would bait, snare and outsmart his headache until it did her bidding!

"*Señora*, you are an angel. How can I thank you?" Miguel said, declaring himself completely recovered after he had finished a second cup of the tea.

Holly had to wait on a customer then, and Miguel left after he and Juana had outdone each other with enough hyperbole to fill a book.

A few minutes later Lee burst in, his expression ecstatic. "Guess what, Holly? I sold one of my carvings! Someone actually wanted to buy it! She did!" He beckoned to a startled-looking Marissa, who'd followed him into the store.

"Lee and I have been shopping, and he recommended Las Artesanías," she explained, obviously surprised to find Holly there.

Awkwardness was minimized as Holly introduced her to Juana, and Marissa quickly made a business of unwrapping Lee's carving to show them. It was an amusing life-size roadrunner whose body and long legs were thrust forward in a supreme effort to reach some unknown destination.

"I adore it," Marissa said, and handed it to Lee. "Look, you've forgotten to sign it. Some day, when you're famous, I can brag that I have a piece from your early period."

Lee proudly affixed his signature underneath the pedestal. Holly watched the woman with suspicion, but Marissa hadn't been patronizing. She'd meant every word she'd said. For a moment Marissa's urbane facade faded to show a look of such wistfulness that Holly caught her breath. Was it regret for the children she would never have?

"You've improved a lot, Lee," Holly said. "That's an excellent piece. Did you show it to Chris?"

"He's too busy to look at any of my stuff!"

"Too busy is right," Marissa agreed vehemently. "I'm here in this marvelous city for only a few days, and he vanishes."

"Oh, he left earlier to go to some little village to film a wedding," Lee said.

"Why didn't he tell me? I could have ridden out with him."

"No, you mustn't! That village is different. They don't like tourists shooting pictures. He made special arrangements. Only he can be there," Lee said emphatically.

"Nonsense. Chris always invited me to come along when he was shooting. He probably didn't want to wake me this morning. I'll call a taxi. It isn't far, is it?"

"About thirty miles," Holly said.

Lee looked worried. "Hey, I don't think that's a good idea."

Holly agreed. "Lee is right. It's best to respect the wishes of the villagers. Ugly Americans, you know."

Lee took in the frowning Marissa. "I'll take you around Oaxaca, Miss Levesque. There's lots to see, honest. The new market at the edge of town is a blast, and Santo Domingo Church is only a few blocks away. Its interior is something else, gold all over the place—the finest in Mexico, my teacher said. When we get tired, we could have an ice cream on the *zócalo*."

"You're a prize, Lee. What do you say we have the ice cream first, then we'll talk about our day." They said their goodbyes, and Holly looked after them. Marissa's taut expression indicated wheels were spinning. Holly suspected she had more on her mind than sight-seeing.

CHRIS PARKED HIS JEEP on a dirt street at the edge of the tiny Zapotec village, wedging it between two ox carts. Even though it was the only motor vehicle around, it no longer attracted the attention it had when he'd first arrived over a month ago. The villagers knew it belonged to him now, and they trusted him.

One didn't earn a Zapotec's confidence overnight. Archaeological evidence had proved that Oaxaca was the site of one of the earliest fully developed civilizations in the world, and the Zapotecs had been influential since 1500 B.C. They were fiercely protective of their heritage.

Slowly but surely he'd won their trust, first making friends with the male schoolteacher and a lot of the children. The teacher spoke adequate English and had offered to act as interpreter, since most of the villagers spoke only the Indian dialect and very little Spanish.

Then he'd mingled with the men over a beer or mescal, had shown them his camera, had explained how it worked and had invited them to shoot some footage. They'd laughed nervously and had dared one another to try it. One by one they'd gingerly held the whirring black box and had looked through the lens. Soon others had clamored for the experience.

Many of the villagers held to the belief that cameras snatched away one's soul, and they hid their faces when they saw him. It hadn't been easy to break down that superstition, but with the help of the teacher he'd succeeded with most of them. Today he would probably be the first cameraman ever to put a Zapotec wedding on film from start to finish.

There had been one strong proviso. No outsider must be present. That posed no problem. Tourists steered clear of the little village. It had no distinguishing features, such as interesting buildings, archaeological sites, or even a sizable market day. Gardening and some weaving formed the main livelihoods, but most of their products were marketed in the city.

At the outset he'd promised Lee he could come along for the day, and Lee had seemed pleased and interested. They hadn't spent much time with each other, and Chris

suspected that's what they needed most. Fathers and sons
did things together—chucked balls in the park and went
fishing and on Boy Scout outings. At least that's what
movies and TV programs led one to believe. He wouldn't
know. He didn't remember his own father, a pilot who
hadn't returned from Korea. Well, he'd make time, as
soon as today's filming sequence was over. He harbored
the wistful hope that such a course might make a difference.

But after he'd promised the village's five town council
members, two justices and every one of both the bride's
and groom's families that they could destroy all his film
if he showed up with a single outsider, he'd had to tell Lee
that the expedition was off. When Chris had explained
the reason, Lee had been a good sport, but it was apparent he was disappointed.

Marissa would have jumped at the chance to come
along today, too, but he'd purposely not mentioned it.
The presence of an American woman would have really
ruined the filming. He knew it was only natural for her
to want to do a little sight-seeing while she was here, but
damn it, he wished she'd go home. Their manuscript was
completed, and she was proving to be an albatross. Marissa was manipulative, so he'd kept up his guard. He'd
allowed her to ruin his marriage seven years ago, and he
wasn't about to permit her to come between him and
Holly again, even though their present relationship was
tenuous. God, what a fool he'd been!

Throughout the entire confrontation at the dance festival the other night, he'd masked his glee at the way
Holly had deftly remained in the driver's seat. Mentally
he'd waved a pennant and shouted cheers.

She'd looked incredibly lovely that evening. Her fair
skin was still flawless, and her delicate facial bones

promised the kind of beauty that time would not alter. He was so envious of that oily Miguel he could have killed him. But, as usual, he'd blown it. For a few minutes he fantasized about what it might be like to kidnap Holly and whisk her away to some heavenly hideout, in the manner that today's groom had acquired his bride-to-be. Capricious thought. Mayte, the bride, had been a willing victim, aiding and abetting the kidnappers; he could see Holly fighting like a tiger.

Mayte's parents had wanted her to wait another two years for marriage. She was fifteen, the only daughter in a family of seven younger brothers, and her help was needed to do the heavy amount of washing, cooking and cleaning. Chris had learned that marriage in the Zapotec tradition was ordinarily thought of as an economic arrangement between families, negotiated through an intermediary with love holding no part in it. But youth was beginning to rebel, and occasionally the custom of *robo*, which permitted couples to choose their mates, was becoming more common.

Even *robo* had its prescribed ritual. Mayte and Curro, the groom, had been meeting secretly for over six months when they'd decided to marry, knowing full well that Mayte's parents would object. So plans had been made secretly, and Curro, with a couple of his close friends, had literally stolen the girl from her home, with her consent of course, and had taken her to the house of his godfather. They'd remained hidden for one night, which promptly put a blight on the reputation of the girl's family.

Formal negotiations had followed at once, with one of Curro's relatives acting in his behalf. That was the point at which custom decreed that gifts, such as chocolate or wine—perhaps even a goat or turkey—had to be presented to Mayte's family. Chris had been amused at the way the two young people had followed the ritual, even to the turkey, so that consent to the marriage had been finally granted.

Chris had spent days getting the shots he wanted of the village and the members of the two families. Now he lugged his cordless lights into the church and set them in an alcove with a fine view of the altar but invisible to the congregation. The sanctuary had been built during the time of the *conquistadores* in the 1500s. Crumbling bricks, peeling plaster and rickety benches identified its age, but a wealth of flowers and flickering candles transformed it into a place of dignity and beauty.

After he set up his gear, he took his camera and climbed a little hill adjacent to the church and stood among the trees, adjusting his telescopic lens to zero in on the arriving guests. Men wore straw hats, white pants, cotton shirts and sandals. Women, many barefoot, were in long dresses with richly embroidered tunics, their regional costume reserved for such special occasions.

They walked slowly and gracefully as if to the measured rhythm of a processional, with a dignity that paid homage to the solemnity of the coming ceremony. The women's faces were unusually grave. Perhaps they were thinking about the youthful bride, about how she would escape the drudgery of waiting on seven brothers and a demanding father, only to become the veritable slave of her domineering mother-in-law. Young couples invariably lived with the groom's parents until the birth of their first child.

The men seemed more relaxed. No doubt they anticipated the mescal that would flow later. It was considered quite acceptable, even expected, that the men would become roaring drunk.

Back inside the church he set up a cordless lamp as the wedding party assembled at the altar, then used a fast f/ 1.2 lens to zoom in on individual faces. The tiny bride, looking childlike and vulnerable, kept her frightened eyes on her husband-to-be, pleading for reassurance. In contrast, the groom displayed a jaunty macho facade as was expected of him. But although the church was cool, perspiration beaded his brow.

When Chris had got the footage he wanted, he slipped out of the church in order to set up his gear at the home of the groom's godfather, where the reception was to be held. It would be about forty minutes by the time the long prayers were said and the guests were reassembled for the reception. A flicker of scarlet caught his attention as a woman ran out of the church and down the steps to join him. My God! Surely it wasn't Marissa!

She flashed him a brilliant smile. "Darling, such an amusing little wedding!"

Fury erupted as intense as any volcano, and he suspected his color was as fiery. Without a word, he grabbed her arm and roughly hustled her behind a tree. "What are you doing here?" he asked between clenched teeth. "I gave these people my word that no outsiders would come. Don't you realize you are jeopardizing my entire documentary?"

She pulled away and rubbed the place where his fingers had bitten into her flesh. "Don't be ridiculous. Grease their palms with a little silver and you can do as you damn well please."

He felt like strangling her. "These people are my friends," he said coldly. "Damn it! Get out of here before you insult them in person."

"Come off it, Chris. Honestly, can you blame me for wanting to see what there was about a primitive dusty

Indian village that would keep you from leaping at the chance to film the wedding of the year in Europe?''

"I have my own priorities. How did you find me, anyway?''

"Well, Lee—''

"Lee!'' He groaned. Couldn't the kid have kept his mouth shut?

"Don't worry, Chris. I'll pretend I don't know you. I'll act like a nosy tourist who got off at the wrong bus stop.''

"Well, get moving, and maybe I'll be lucky. The wedding will be over any minute.''

He hurried her down the hill toward the plaza, looking over his shoulder repeatedly to see if people were coming out of the church yet. At the plaza he pointed to a bench on the far side. "The bus stop is over there. I trust you know the schedule.''

"And ride with all those goats and chickens? No, thanks. Lee will pick me up soon. Actually, I rented a car.''

"Lee *brought* you! How could he do this to me?''

"Cool it, Chris. I insisted. Don't be angry with him.''

"Well, where is he?'' There wasn't a car in sight.

She took out a tissue nonchalantly and wiped some invisible dust from her face. "You *are* a fussbudget. He'll be along soon. I told him he could take the car for an hour while I was here. You used to be very partial to my presence. What happened?''

"You were writing the script then. It was a whole different ball game.''

"And who's writing it for you now? Your former wife? Why didn't you tell me she was here? I didn't recognize her at first. It got rather sticky.''

His jaw tightened. "Holly has nothing to do with the documentary. We've been divorced a long time. We're practically strangers. Anyway, you never did understand about our relationship.''

Her eyes flashed angrily. ''I understand that you're squandering your talent in this godforsaken place. Don't tell me you're using this little expedition as an excuse to dally with your former wife? Is that the kind of challenge that turns you on nowadays? My God, what a waste!''

He clenched his fists. ''Leave Holly out of this.''

''God forbid that you're considering marrying her again. For heaven's sake, use your head! Marital encumbrances only sap the creative juices. Haven't you figured that out? Stay single, Chris, and you'll reach the stars.''

''I've been single for seven years, and I haven't yet managed to get off this planet,'' he said dryly.

''That's because you need *me*. You know how we take off when we work together, and I'm not talking marriage. I've seen all too often what happens to creative people who think they have to marry. The condition cuts you up into little pieces and scatters you by the wayside.''

''In about five minutes you're the one who will be responsible for cutting me into little pieces if I don't get back to my filming.''

Marissa continued to rave. She'd found her private soapbox and she wasn't about to relinquish it. ''I tell you, Chris, great talent has an obligation to itself. It has the right to be selfish!'' It took several minutes before she finally ran out of things to say. Cheeks flushed, eyes shining, she waited for his agreement.

''Hogwash,'' he said, and frowning furiously, he steered her into a small dark café and ordered her a beer.

He pulled out a chair for her. She reluctantly sat down, but he remained standing.

"You know very well I prefer gin and tonic."

"Not on the menu," he said gruffly. "Sip it slowly. You may have a long wait. Lee isn't known for his punctuality, especially when he gets a chance to drive."

She pushed the beer away, almost overturning it. "Okay, Chris. Indulge your fantasies. Take a vacation from reality. But, believe me, not too far in the future you're going to sing a different tune." As he started for the door, she cried, "Hold on!" Reluctantly he turned. Her upswept auburn hair enhanced the fever in her face, and her eyes were on him like hooks.

Suddenly they changed and softened, and a teasing smile lit up her face. "Darling, you know what I'm like. I'm devastated when I don't get my own way. Humor me a bit. Really, I only want what's right for you."

"A matter of opinion," he snapped impatiently.

"Wait and see," she said sweetly with the confidence that had intimidated legions. "I'm going home tomorrow, but before the summer is over I'll return. After you hear what I have to tell you, you'll not just ask, you'll *beg* to work with me again."

CHAPTER NINE

THE NEXT MORNING Chris and Lee ate breakfast in silence on the patio. Raindrops from a recent shower glistened like amethysts on the jacaranda petals. A wild canary hopped down from a tree and grabbed some hapless insect, then flew back up and bragged to its companions in an impressive series of turns and trills.

Chris had come in late the night before after the wedding festivities, elated that, in spite of the near catastrophe Marissa had imposed, the filming had gone on without a hitch. He could hardly wait to preview the segment. He'd worked hard to convey the dignity of the people in that poor village, to show how they managed to combine their Zapotec heritage with their 16th-century Spanish roots and their efforts to strive toward social betterment in present-day Mexico. In his bones he felt Curro's wedding day would be a highlight of the film.

Lee had darted apprehensive looks at him ever since they'd sat down. Finally he cleared his throat. "Sir, I'd like to explain about yesterday. Miss Levesque said you were really angry."

So it was *sir* now. He wasn't certain if the word was a hint that the fence was going to be lowered a little between them, but at least it was an improvement over the anonymity of pronouns. "*Angry* is a pretty mild word for the way I felt. You knew the situation, so why didn't you explain it to her?"

"I did! I tried to keep her from going, honest!"

"Strange. You drove her there."

"Well, she said that you used to work together on documentaries and that she knew the ropes. All she wanted to do was to look over the village. She promised she wouldn't offend anyone, and, man, was she convincing. I was driving that car almost before I knew what hit me."

"She's quite able to drive, you know."

"Well, she said she was worried about the narrow dirt roads, and besides, she wanted me along for protection."

Chris lifted an eyebrow. "I can see your problem." Yes, he could.

Lee's dark eyes brightened. "You're not going to chew me out?"

"Maybe I overreacted but, as you know, those scenes I filmed yesterday are a crucial part of the documentary."

"So, if Miss Levesque had stirred anything up, it might have been a different story?"

"Exactly. In the future, you'd better stick harder to your principles, particularly around persuasive ladies," he added, and suspected he could use the advice himself.

"I sure will!" Lee said heartily. "And, sir, I have a special favor to ask."

"Oh?" Chris said suspiciously. "My mood is mellow, but I do have limits. Let's have it."

"Well, I promised to give Holly swimming lessons, and I wondered if it would be okay to use this pool—when you're not around, that is. I don't think she likes you much."

"You're some kind of analyst?"

"No, sir, I just kinda got that impression. She sort of closes up when you're around and doesn't smile or anything."

"You're a keen observer," Chris said, and wondered if the time had come to reveal the facts of his marriage. He toyed with a spoon, then cleared his throat. "Perhaps the lady has some unhappy recollections. You see, Lee, Holly and I used to be married, but we've been divorced for a good many years."

Lee's eyes widened in amazement. "What happened? She's a real neat lady."

"Agreed. In fact, I had hoped to clear up some of our misunderstandings while we were in Oaxaca this summer, but so far I haven't made much headway."

"Wow! That's really incredible! Did she know you were going to be down here?"

His mouth twisted. "If she'd known, she'd never have come."

Lee seemed to think about that statement for a long time. "I'm really sorry."

"That goes for both of us, and about the pool, go ahead. What makes you believe she'll accept your offer?"

"I haven't asked her yet, but I'll come on strong, like Miss Levesque."

"I don't think that's the best tactic to use with Holly. As for using the pool, you can tell her that I'll be on location every day for the next month."

"Great. I have to go to my wood-carving lesson now, but when it's over I'll stop by her shop and tell her." He went over to the little shed where he kept his bicycle and wheeled it across the patio. "And, sir," he said as he paused by the table, "if there's anything I can do to help clear up your misunderstandings, just call on me."

"Stick to your wood carving, son." *Son*. The forbidden word came out quite unconsciously, and for once Lee didn't flicker an eyelash. He hopped on his bike and pedaled off, whistling.

When Lee proposed the arrangement to Holly later, she adamantly refused, but after thinking about it for several days she began to realize it was a good opportunity. She wanted, needed, to learn how to swim. It was ridiculous for a woman her age to be so afraid of water, so the sessions were set up for Tuesday and Thursday afternoons when she didn't attend Doña Elena's classes. Lee proved to be a good teacher; demanding, yet sensitive to her fears and endearingly businesslike.

"You're doing great, Holly!" he said after a few sessions.

She gave him a salute. "Thanks, teach. I owe it all to you." She loved the way he glowed with pride at her use of the affectionate nickname.

"But," he said sternly, "you could use more practice."

"Another *but* to complicate my life! You're a hard taskmaster."

"Any chance you could come tomorrow?"

"As it happens, I can. Doña Elena has to go to Mexico City for the weekend, so my class is dismissed tomorrow." She still felt a remnant of panic every time she went into the pool, and she was determined to get rid of it. Practice would do it. She knew she should take advantage of every free afternoon while Chris was away.

"¡Perfecto! I have a soccer practice, but I'll give you my key. Don't forget to keep your eyes open when your face is under the water."

"Yes, sir, teach. You're sure it's okay to come?"

He gave her a knowing wink. "For sure. *He's* got a heavy date with a camera."

The next afternoon she arrived promptly at two and unlocked the massive outer door, which, as in so many homes in Mexico, formed a part of the outer wall. All morning she'd looked forward to the workout. The temperature soared today, and the shop had been unusually busy with demanding customers and a lot of mail orders to fill between times.

How inviting the pool looked. The tiled deck glistened, and the water was clear and sparkling and smelled faintly of chlorine. Lee was conscientious about his job of keeping it immaculate. She hoped Chris was aware of that.

She changed in the small dressing room and cautiously lowered herself into the water. She hadn't yet the courage nor the skill to dive in. After practicing the exercises until she was breathless, she floated for a while on her back, then fell forward, arms out in front of her, in the relaxing dead man's float. These were the only techniques she could handle with total assurance. After twenty more minutes of Lee's workout, she again lay back and rested in the water.

The scent of honeysuckle wafted above her, and she gazed with delight at the delicate traceries the mimosa made against the sky. She lay deliciously suspended as the sounds of lapping water played a somnolent lullaby. The tranquillity was heavenly; an oasis of perfection in her hectic day. She'd come a long way in conquering her fears since that awful night when she had fallen apart at the party. Her thoughts turned to the caring way Chris had helped her to face her terror after her humiliating display. Now she reveled in the remembered feel of his strong, supporting arms, visualized the concern in his face and could hear his quiet voice encouraging her. Strange how the recollection made the day seem so full of color.

"Well, what do you know. My pool has sprouted a pretty little angelfish. I've always wanted one." Chris's voice seemed to come from somewhere nearby.

She smiled. How clear it sounded in her daydream. Languidly she called up the visual image from the sound, then opened her eyes, promptly sank and came up sputtering. Chris's muscular form cast a shadow over her. The sight of him sped up her heartbeat and stole her breath away.

"Pretty clumsy for an angelfish," he said with a broad grin.

She planted her feet firmly on the bottom of the pool and ducked so that only her head showed above water. "What are you doing here? Lee said you were on location."

"Yes, I know, but this is Friday," he said with an aggrieved air. "Lee informed me you came on Tuesdays and Thursdays."

"We made an extra date for practice. Didn't he tell you?"

"I'm afraid he failed to mention it. Of course he didn't know I planned to come home earlier today. Or did he? The rascal."

"What does that mean?"

"I suspect it comes under the heading of Junior Matchmaking Department."

"You're talking nonsense."

"I'm often accused of that."

She got out of the pool quickly so that he wouldn't think she wanted him to help her.

"Don't mind me. Go ahead with your workout. I can use a little female company, even if she is cantankerous," Chris said as he settled himself in a nearby chair.

"I've finished, thank you," Holly said crisply, and continued to the dressing room, where she changed in five minutes. If this was to be the pattern, there'd be no more workouts. Maybe no more swimming.

With as much dignity as she could summon, she crossed the patio toward the gate. It wasn't easy to maintain her poise when it was through Chris's generosity that she used the pool.

Holding two margaritas, Chris blocked her passage. "Guaranteed to cool edgy tempers," he said with an engaging grin.

She looked at the inviting frosty drinks, decided to refuse, then took one. She'd stay, but only until the drink was finished. At this point it was easier than battling him. She hoped the drink would douse the rogue fantasies that were turning her into a distraught and confused creature and change her back into a clear-thinking human being.

They sat down at an umbrella table and sipped the fragrant margaritas. "Thanks for staying," he said. "And I didn't know you would be here today—honest— but I'm glad. I've been trying for weeks to arrange some quality time with you."

She lifted an eyebrow. "I've noticed how busy you've been."

"Not fair. Marissa and I were up against a deadline. Anyway, she went home."

"Well, what's with this quality time bit? You know everything about me."

"No, I don't know everything about you, but I want to." His expression turned serious, and he leaned forward and folded his arms firmly on the table. "May I speak plainly?"

"Of course. I never liked beating around the bush."

"It's been seven years, right?"

"That's plain."

"And we've both agreed that we're practically strangers now."

"Quite clear."

"We're only here for the summer. That's not very much time, so I have a suggestion."

"Now things are getting cloudy."

"The point is, if we continue to let our past intrude on the present, we'll never have much of a future. I suggest that we start fresh, as if we'd just met."

"Just how do you propose to do that?"

"Easy. I say, 'Hi, Holly. Good to meet you.' You say, 'Hello, Chris, I'm glad to meet you, too.' Then I say, 'I happen to know this great little Italian restaurant,' and we go on from there. Boy meets girl, an unbeatable formula."

She smiled in spite of herself. This was the Chris she'd loved. "We'd have to come down with amnesia concerning our earlier relationship."

"You've got it! That way we could stop playing all these witless games and really get to know each other."

"I imagine you're talking about ducking behind pillars and a coy clinch or two in the shadows."

"That, too, if the occasion calls for it."

"I see. Well, then I'm a little puzzled as to your definition of *quality time*."

He seemed prepared for the statement, even eager to explain it. "I'd like to introduce you to a wonderful Zapotec family who live in a tiny hut with dirt floors. They've become very special to me. I want us to see the fabulous architecture of ancient Mitla together, to hear what you have to say from an artist's viewpoint. I'd like to tell you about my documentary—what I'm trying to show and how I do it. I want you to tell me all about how you make pottery—what you do with clay and glazes to create all that beauty." He watched her intently as if gauging her reaction.

That would be novel, all right. He'd barely noticed that she was an artist during their marriage. Not only had he not encouraged her talent, he had seemed unable to reach that secret creative part of her and share in her delight in it. But, she thought with a start, if she were honest, she'd have to admit that she'd never taken more than a surface interest in his filmmaking. "I'm not given to illusions," she replied finally. "We'd be fools to think we could discard our past. We would interpret every action, every word in terms of what we already knew about each other."

"What's wrong with giving it a try? If it doesn't work, nothing lost."

"Pardon the old cliché—I can't think of anything better at the moment—but that would be about as useful as beating a dead horse."

He winced. "I never thought you were one to avoid risks, to take a chance on a little adventure."

"See what I mean? You're already calling up past judgments."

He sighed. "Since we're dealing in clichés today, I'd say you were a hard nut to crack."

"Good insight. Thanks for the margarita. It was very refreshing, and now I'm going to take myself off to the bus stop. Just a couple of blocks down the hill, right?"

"Let me drive you home."

"That's thoughtful of you, but I've had a busy week. I'll just climb into the back seat of the bus and vegetate."

"Oh? Have you ridden on our local buses yet?"

"No, but I've noticed they travel at a leisurely pace." She rose and took their glasses into the kitchen. He followed.

"Okay then, wait a minute, I have something I've been meaning to give you."

She washed and dried the glasses and put them away, then leaned against the counter, idly wondering what he had for her. After a few minutes, when he didn't return, she walked to peer into the room where he'd disappeared. It was a den, very masculine with its heavy, comfortable chairs, a cluttered desk and film gear piled on every surface.

He had his back to her, and he seemed to be going through items in a large cardboard box. He ran a hand through his wheat-colored hair in apparent exasperation. The action brought an ache deep inside her. He was always losing things, and that gesture usually accompanied his irritation. She didn't know why it brought tears to her eyes now, but it did. She wished he weren't so good-looking. Even more, she wished that she didn't have such a keen memory. Suddenly she didn't want him to find her there, to see the emotions her face might reveal.

Quietly she started to back out of the room, then stopped short as she took in a glass display cabinet. It held four of her own creations, one on each shelf: a candelabrum, an ornamental bowl, a figurine and the blue quail, all made in Elena's class. Each piece had been for sale in La Tienda Artesanías. She'd been in the shop when he had bought the quail, but not the others. Chris was no collector, and he'd never been interested in pottery.

She returned to the kitchen and sat down on a window seat looking blindly out at the patio.

He hadn't meant her to see the case or he would have invited her in, so what did it mean? Perhaps he wasn't aware the pottery was hers—except for the quail. He probably hadn't looked at the signature. Still, her style was distinctive, and there'd been four things—all hers!

"Here we are," he said, and handed her a small jewelry box. "It had slipped between some folders, and I had a devil of a time finding it. You know how untidy I am." Yes, she knew. For months after the divorce she'd looked around her immaculate, empty apartment and had wept because there were no books cluttering the table, no jacket cast carelessly across a chair, no jogging shoes set half under the bed.

"I spotted it at Casa Victor's recently and couldn't resist," he said as she pulled off a cord. "It suits the new you, your new name, all that."

She opened the box and caught her breath. It held a slender gold bracelet. Holly leaves etched the surface, and tiny rubies formed the berries.

"It's exquisite, Chris, but I can't accept it."

He took the bracelet and slipped it onto her wrist. "Indulge me. The jeweler will be highly offended if I return it. Let's just say that it's a token of friendship. Ours. No strings attached."

Holly started to take it off but caught his expression, a picture of boyish anxiety. He'd chosen it especially for her. No strings attached, he'd said.

"It's beautiful, Chris. You always did have exquisite taste. Thank you."

Impulsively she reached up and kissed his cheek. He looked stunned. She gave a little wave and hurried out of the house and through the heavy door to the street. Damn, why had she kissed him? Her face still felt hot at her gaffe. The gesture had come so naturally she hadn't had time to stop it. Old habits. Would they always sneak up on her like that? She pondered her actions as she impatiently awaited the bus.

After fifteen minutes, she considered hailing a cab, but not one had passed by. She considered walking. It was at least five miles, but the walk might help clear her mind.

A squeal of tires interrupted her thoughts as a vehicle pulled up to the curb. "Local bus to Casa Avalon and points east and west," a male voice sang out. "Back seat guaranteed excellent for vegetating."

"I don't believe this!" Holly said, looking up at Chris's grinning countenance.

"Believe it, *señorita*. I just remembered that buses from this stop go in the opposite direction."

"You're making that up."

He got out of the Jeep and caught the attention of the small group of people waiting at the bus stop. *¿A la derecha, no?"* he asked, pointing east.

"¡Sí!" they chorused, nodding vigorously.

Chris opened the door. "Get in. I'm blocking traffic."

Noting every eye upon her, and muttering with embarrassment, she climbed into the Jeep. The crowd burst into enthusiastic applause. *"¡Olé!"* they cried in one voice. Chris waved jauntily, and they took off.

"You're bizarre!"

"Thanks, but you needn't resort to flattery, and the bus really does go in that direction."

"But I'll bet it circles around the city and eventually passes near my street."

"Without a doubt," he said airily. "But you'd have to transfer so many times you wouldn't have time to vegetate. So put your head back and close your eyes, and I'll drive carefully so as not to disturb you. Don't think you have to make conversation. I always did get a thrill out of watching you sleep, the way those long curly lashes sweep that petal-soft cheek, the way..."

"That's enough, Chris! And where are you going, by the way? Don't tell me this bus also takes the circular route?"

"Actually, we're taking a little detour. I left one of my tripods where I was filming yesterday, and I want to get it."

"Figures. I swear you need someone to follow you around to pick up after you."

"I know. I had that luxury once, but something happened. Anyway, there's a place I want to show you. It's special."

"Absolutely not. What's with you anyway? Do I have to hit you over the head?"

He sighed. "You are a challenge. Since you seem in need of a little R and R, I thought I'd try out an honorable old Zapotec custom."

"I can hardly wait to hear it."

He looked at her scowling face. "Well, when there are strenuous objections to a couple getting together, the young man kidnaps the young woman and takes her to a friendly retreat. It has a way of nullifying problems."

"Oh, sure, Miguel told me all about that. Anyway, it's a marriage custom. You really twist things around. Besides, the young woman always *wants* to be kidnapped."

"Don't fuss over trivialities."

"How long will this little jaunt take, if you don't mind my asking?"

"It's not far. Ten kilometers."

With an exaggerated sigh, she curled up in the seat with her arms clasped over her face, knowing she would never sleep. Something inside kept telling her to relax and enjoy the outing; it was a good opportunity to see the area. On the other hand, she was still furious over the way he had manipulated her. *No strings attached to the bracelet?* She wondered.

Surprisingly he respected her wish for silence. Once, he started to whistle, then looked over at her and stopped. Occasionally she moved her arms slightly in order to steal a quick glance. What thoughts went on behind that impassive expression? She'd often wondered the same thing when they'd been married. Apparently two years hadn't been enough to learn about each other. How many years would it have taken? There were probably parts of each other they would never have been able to understand, even if they'd been married a century.

In the beginning they'd been so in love, constantly needing to touch, to be near, to speak tender words, to allow the burning passions within them to set fire to their bodies. But they'd been lovers then, and everyone knew lovers weren't real people.

They were out of the city now, and she felt the car slow to a crawl in order to take the bumpy road as gently as possible. The brilliant sun warmed her body, and the breeze that played freely in the open Jeep caressed her. Through her fingers her eyes dwelled on Chris's strong profile and the outline of his wide shoulders. His strength of mind and body had largely been what had drawn her to him.

She felt a sensuous stirring and willed her senses to reject it. But the yearning persisted, grew and enveloped her, shutting out everything else. She wanted him to hold her close, to make love as of old with his hands, his lips, his voice, with his entire body. The torment seemed endless. Dear God, what was wrong with her?

"WAKE UP, SLEEPING BEAUTY. Nap time is over," Chris said, and leaned over as if to kiss her, then quickly drew back.

Holly felt a fleeting rejection as she sat up and stretched her cramped muscles. "I haven't been asleep," she said primly, keeping her eyes down. Eyes could reveal emotions far more than words could.

He chuckled. "Oh, no? How long do you think we've been sitting here? We reached this place almost an hour ago."

"An hour!" she cried, and looked at her watch. "I'm sorry. How boring for you!"

He grinned. "Don't worry. I had to pick up my tripod anyway. Then I came back to check up on you. Incidentally, you seemed to be having some mighty interesting dreams."

She felt her cheeks burn. Oh, no! Had she said or done anything to indicate the turn her thoughts had taken? "You must remember that I sometimes talk in my sleep," she said, hoping desperately she hadn't.

"Yes, you do!" His eyes gleamed wickedly. "It'll come in mighty handy when I get around to blackmailing you."

"You could have been a gentleman and left me a little privacy."

"Yes, I could have, but it would have been difficult, and I didn't want to disturb you."

"Meaning?"

"That the way you clung to me was somewhat restrictive but, I hastily add, mighty satisfying."

"You're lying," she said, and wished she could believe it. "Where are we?"

"Cuilapan, an ancient monastery. Come on, I can't wait to show it to you."

The edifice was located in the middle of a barren, dusty field. No sign of habitation was visible in the immediate area, but the dramatic quality of the building instantly minimized the bleak setting. Chris rattled on about its history, mentioning that it had been built in 1555 by Dominican friars but had been abandoned shortly before completion because of financial disagreements. The Zapotecs had eventually taken it over as a center for their own exotic blend of ancient and modern religion.

They stood and looked at the twin towers at the entrance, reminiscent of a medieval fortress, then walked through magnificent pillars and lofty arches surrounding a chapel whose roof had been blown off a century ago by a hurricane. Arched shadows splashed the area, making stark patterns of dark and light across the brick floor. Holly stood transfixed. "I had no idea such beauty could be found in this lonely spot. How sad that no one can enjoy it."

"It looks deserted all right, but there are small farms all around, and on certain religious occasions as many as ten thousand Indians gather here for services."

They paused at the entrance. One uniformed attendant, whose prime duty appeared to be to collect a fee from the occasional tourist, guarded the place. They walked up to his desk, and he roused himself long enough to accept their pesos, then nodded off again.

Inside the sanctuary it was cool and dark. Brick walls appeared to be several feet thick. They examined shadowed naves, lovely frescoes and trod up dark, winding stone stairs to the second floor to see the tiny rooms that had been intended for the religious men who had never occupied them. Holly pictured a crude bed with a nightstand and a candle beside it. The place had a haunting quality, as if it hungered for life.

There appeared to be a huge lighted painting at the end of the dark hallway, but as they drew closer it turned out to be a window with such an extraordinary view that Holly looked out in wonder. The opening had been framed in wood, and the panorama, with its warm, muted tones, could have been a masterwork by Pissarro. They sat down on the broad base of the window. Tiny farmhouses dotted the landscape, trees formed green oases and a silver ribbon of a river sparkled in the distance. Above, the sky was a cloudless blue. Just below, an Indian woman rested under a jacaranda with her little flop-eared burro. No glass panes covered the window. The view would never blur.

"A great place to get things in perspective," Chris said. "I've come here several times. Better than a dozen visits to a therapist."

"I love it. It's a setting for a poem, or some romantic novel!" she cried. "You've filmed all this?"

"Only as a background for my family."

"Your family?" she asked with a start.

"The family whose members are the subjects of my documentary," he said. "I've become very close to them. You see..." He hesitated as if suddenly reticent about discussing his work with her.

"Yes?" she encouraged.

"Well, most documentaries use what is called a generalized method, which shows a condition or situation that affects a certain group of people. But it always seemed to me that the audience doesn't get truly involved using that process. For example, a film that shows hordes of starving people in Africa doesn't touch us nearly as deeply as one that introduces us to a few members of one of those starving families, showing us how each life is altered.

"I'm committed to that viewpoint," he continued with surprising intensity. "I wanted to show life as it is today in a Zapotec village, so I made friends with one of its families. I filmed their joys and sorrows: the sadness at the death of a newborn infant, the wedding of their oldest son and the mores and taboos connected with their traditions. I've shown how they till the soil, what food they eat and how they prepare it. The father of this family is a weaver of consummate skill, yet he performs his miracles on an unbelievably crude loom, using centuries-old techniques."

His mouth twisted bitterly. "It's probably all for nothing. I don't have a written contract, and only this week I learned that Rapitch and Corrigan, a big film company from L.A., has just moved into Oaxaca to do a documentary. They'll probably be able to submit theirs before I'm able to finish. I'm practically a one-man operation. They have a whole crew as well as a lab at their disposal." He slapped his fist on his knee. "I want that TV contract so much I can taste it, but it will probably go down the drain like my hopes for filming those remote villages in the Andes."

Holly knew about that dream, all right. He'd worked every angle he knew in order to get a grant to film there. At times she'd wondered if it meant more to him than she did.

Although she'd known little about his work, she knew he was tops in his field. After all, film schools all over the country as well as abroad clamored for him to lecture. No one could be more deeply committed to his own creative ideas, techniques and philosophies. No one would show more integrity in his craft.

"You'll win! I know it," she cried, and knew that she wanted that for him as passionately as he did.

He looked at her in surprise. "You say that as if you really mean it."

She laid her hand against his cheek for an instant. "But of course, Chris. I mean it with all my heart."

"Your heart, Holly?" he asked softly.

She swayed toward him, as if to a magnet, as the question hung in the silence. Suddenly they were in each other's arms, and he covered her face with kisses. She felt a wild sweep of pleasure as their lips finally met. Holly knew that both of them were fulfilling a thirst too long unquenched. Remotely she felt all her well-ordered intentions teeter and slip.

It was if another woman had taken over her body, a woman of wanton passion. Her arms crept around his neck, and she pressed herself against him, loving the hard feel of him, the clean smell of his freshly shaven cheek, the caring way he touched her.

Her fingers outlined the familiar planes of his face and traced the fine shape of his head. She then clasped her hands tightly behind his neck again. Oblivious to all else but the sensations swirling within her, she pulled his head down again for a kiss that left them both breathless.

She arched her body, making her sensitive breasts more available to his caresses. His touch teased and tantalized until sensations rippled out to every nerve ending. She seemed possessed by a passion that bordered on explosion.

They rocked together for a while, savoring their closeness, and she was suspended in star-studded space a million miles away.

"My darling, I'd almost given up hope that you'd love me again. And you do, don't you?" Chris said exultantly, holding her away from him and searching her dazed eyes for assurance.

A quivering sensation filled her. My God, what was he asking? She stiffened and hid her face in her hands. "I must be out of my head!" she cried.

He looked as if she'd slapped him. "Explain that remark, please."

She straightened, and held back tears. "You were always an expert lover, Chris. I guess I got carried away." Oh, God, why had they opened themselves up to all this pain and unhappiness again? Why was it so difficult to get rid of a love that was of no use to either of them?

He got up and paced down the dark hall as if to purge himself of fury, then returned, glaring at her like some menacing wild animal. "Are you blaming this little episode on me? I admit I wanted it more than I can say, but I didn't initiate it. I'd promised myself not to touch you again until I got the right signs and, lady, you passed out plenty." He leaned forward and shook a finger in her face. His gray eyes grew cold and glistened like steel. "You know something? You're a tease and a fraud. I would have never believed it of you if I hadn't experienced this. Dammit, you send out all kinds of signals, then berate me for accepting them."

She cringed as if his words seared her. He was right. Her face flamed with humiliation, and shame filled her until she could hardly speak. "I apologize," she said huskily. "Blame it on the ambience or whatever."

"I don't believe that. Emotions don't lie. I'm sure yours were real."

"Emotions make pretty shaky foundation for real love. They distort one's perception. Something more stable is needed—like trust."

The word slashed him as surely as if it had been a knife, and he turned away for a moment, clenching his fists. "What about forgiveness?" he asked in a low voice, then turned around again, his face a study in pain.

She shook her head sadly. "We've been over this before. There is no future for us, Chris. Face it. We're completely wrong for each other. I want a home where I can put down roots. You're basically a nomad. I cherish solitude. You aren't happy unless you have wall-to-wall people. You go for every new gadget that comes out. I cherish lovely old things. I want—"

"Surface considerations," he interrupted with an impatient gesture. "They don't count when real love is present."

"I want children," she continued, as if she hadn't heard him, "and I'm convinced you aren't interested, at least if your relationship with Lee is any indication."

He looked stricken, his face so bleak that she wanted to rush over and apologize, to comfort him. She'd gone too far, accused unfairly. What had made her lash out with so much bitterness? Was she still punishing him for his one lapse of fidelity?

Despair almost overwhelmed her. Logic flung a clear message, but her heart would have none of it. There must be a hundred other reasons not to renew their relationship. She'd gone over them for days, for years. They were muddled and indistinct now, but as soon as she struggled out from under all this confusion she'd remember.

"I've thought about us a lot over the years, and I can't forget how it was when we split up," she said. "I felt so alone, so abandoned. I don't think I could go through that a second time. Can you come up with a single reason why we should try again? I can't. We're basically the same two people. Aside from our physical attraction, which is still strong—at least for me it is—we have nothing going for us. We found out the hard way that chemistry isn't enough. I know now that I shared equally in our breakup. I'm not right for you, Chris. I'd hold you back, get in your way, and you'd hurt me, too. In the end, it would be our undoing, just like before. There's only one solution for you and me. I don't know how else to say it—I want us never to see each other again.''

He looked at her so long, she wondered if he'd gone into a trance. When he finally spoke, his voice shook with the effort to control his anger. ''Okay. I admit I've been pretty dense when it comes to understanding you, but I finally get the picture. I'll not bother you anymore. I promise. Finale. The end. Come on, I'll take you home.''

They rode in complete silence, not even a goodbye when he dropped her off at Casa Avalon. She felt as if she'd been sucked into a whirlpool and was drowning.

She'd managed to slip the gold bracelet into the pocket of a jacket that was thrown over the Jeep seat. Somehow the action, even more than their hurtful words, seemed to bring down the final curtain between them.

CHAPTER TEN

CHRIS LOOKED IN the rearview mirror as Holly got out of the Jeep and stood at the Casa Avalon door to ring the bell. She looked desolate. He recalled that wounded look, the way she caught her underlip between her teeth and widened her eyes as if to accommodate sudden tears. She looked so incredibly vulnerable that a spurt of tenderness shot through him, and for an instant he considered going after her.

Foolish thought. It would only prolong the agony. Holly was right. Christopher Brooke and Holly Jones were too different to make a marriage work, and apparently the changes had increased since their divorce.

It was the end between them. Somewhere in the back of his mind he'd clung to the dream that someday they'd find each other again, that time would have mellowed her and enabled her to forgive, and that they would be able to shed the bitterness of the past as easily as an old coat. But life didn't operate that way.

Thank God he had his work. He hoped the monumental amount of editing that still remained on his project would enable him to sublimate the very real pain he felt. Then he thought about the surprise he'd planned for her birthday, which was coming up next week.

Ever since he'd realized what a fine artist she'd become, he'd felt that she needed better exposure. Her works almost got lost among all the handicrafts in Juana's crowded little shop. They deserved to be featured in some uncluttered gallery so that their true beauty could be appreciated. Without her knowledge, he'd been collecting some of her best works for himself, harboring the notion that he'd have a part of her with him always, regardless of what happened. Holly's pieces told worlds about the woman he'd always adored, with their grace and beauty and touches of whimsy. They were never garish but were almost always understated.

Yesterday he'd taken samples of her work, the blue quail and one of her candelabra, specifically, to Hugo's Boutique, which was located in Hotel Victoria. The hotel catered mainly to affluent foreigners. It had the reputation for carrying only authentic quality goods. Not surprisingly, Hugo was excited about Holly's work and wanted to work out a deal at once.

Chris had planned to give her the good news on her birthday. At first he'd decided to ask Ramona to pack a special picnic. He wanted to take Holly out to the village that was featured in his documentary. He felt a special closeness to the place and its people, and he was anxious for her to share his feelings, to meet some of his friends there and to like and understand them as much as he did.

But then he'd thought the smarter thing would be to try to out-Miguel Miguel, with dinner on the terrace of Hotel Victoria and then later go to Rafel's Piano Bar. Knowing how she loved to dance, he'd even intended to attempt something basic. He had to remember to cancel the reservations as well as the white violets he'd ordered for her.

Now that they'd agreed not to see each other again, he would call Hugo and tell him to forget the deal. They'd both agreed to keep things clean and uncluttered.

No. He wanted this chance for her. She had no idea how good she was. Such opportunities didn't come often. He'd work it out without seeing her. But right now he was too drained to think. He just wanted to go home, have a stiff belt of tequila and hit the sack.

FOR THE PAST HOUR, Holly had sat unmoving in the uncomfortable high-backed chair in the Casa Avalon drawing room. She and Miguel had finally arranged a sitting for the long-planned portrait, but she could muster little enthusiasm.

Despair was the word that best described the way she felt. All morning she'd tried to hide it. At work, Juana had almost driven her to distraction, insisting that she consume her latest tonic. "Such doldrums! Pale as the alabaster Madonna in the cathedral, you are! Come, another spoonful of tonic."

"Don't tell me. Let me guess. A formula by Cousin Chole?" Holly asked, making a feeble jest.

"My own creation." Juana had beamed proudly, urging on still another bitter spoonful. Then she had put together a generous package of her magic elixirs and had handed them to Holly, insisting she go home and go to bed. Instead, she'd sat for the portrait.

Sometime between midnight and dawn last night she'd finally admitted the truth to herself. She'd wrestled with it ever since she'd come to Oaxaca, but no matter how she fought it one conclusion remained. She was still hopelessly in love with Chris. But the acknowledgment didn't change a thing; it only made life infinitely more difficult. The emotion had always seethed just below the surface, and she'd continually insisted it was merely a remnant of the old chemistry between them, something to be lightly dismissed.

The very thought of her actions at the monastery filled her with shame. She'd flailed around blindly to find something that would wound him. To accuse him of not being interested in Lee had been cruel. From recent remarks Lee had made, she could tell how hard Chris had been trying. Even worse was the way she'd thrown herself at him, then repulsed him. She despised women who did that. An apology was due to him, maybe a call or a note. But, no, she'd been the one to insist they sever all ties. It would be wrong to stir up the anguish all over again.

Miguel indicated that the session was over. "I'm afraid I've kept you too long," he said with concern. "Your pallor alarms me. You must get some of Juana's excellent herb teas."

"I'll do that," Holly said, not wanting to extend the conversation by telling him Juana had already given her a generous supply. "How are your headaches?"

"Much improved, thanks to that marvelous lady. She and I are *compatriotas.*"

"Yes, I know," Holly said, and knew the fact raised Juana even higher in Miguel's estimation. He, too, was of direct Spanish descent.

Years of intermarriage between the conquering Spaniards and the indigenous Indians had made most of Mexico's inhabitants mestizos. There was a kind of unspoken caste system, with those of pure Spanish blood considering themselves the elite of the population. Holly knew that Miguel felt this way without considering himself a snob.

"Ah, yes, we have much in common, especially our love for Spanish music," Miguel continued. "Last week we heard the symphony orchestra play works by Spanish composers. *¡Magnífico!*"

Magnífico indeed! Miguel and Juana were made for each other. Why hadn't she introduced them earlier? A budding romance? She hoped so.

Miguel cleaned a brush, and they made an appointment for the next sitting. "Thursday?" he questioned after she'd suggested it. "You're not going for your swim lesson?"

"Discontinued for the time being."

"Señor Brooke is your teacher?"

"No. Lee," she said a little too quickly.

Miguel raised an eyebrow. "My dear Holly, I sense a special link between you and Señor Brooke." He held up a hand as she started to interrupt. "I'm quite intuitive about such matters, and I'm rarely mistaken."

She laughed, and was shocked at how false it sounded. "Really, we're only acquaintances. We probably won't even see each other again."

"Ah, but that can change, and it should."

She shook her head, bit her lip and looked away, hoping she could hold back the tears.

"My dear, when I saw you both together at the regional dancing, I knew my own wishes were at an end. You see, ever since you arrived at my Casa, I hoped something meaningful would develop between us. Ah, but I never argue with fate." His words were heavy with pathos, and he tipped up his chin in a gesture of brave resolve.

The noble grandee will carry on despite adversity, she thought with affection in light of his never-ending sense of drama.

"I want your friendship, Miguel. I need it."

He held her hand between both of his for a moment, then kissed it. "Always, my angel," he said.

Holly went to her room and changed to another dress. The turquoise outfit had to be kept fresh for the portrait. She felt certain Miguel was no more in love with her than she was with him. He was merely enchanted with the state of *being* in love, and she was a convenient subject.

Paul Dalton had called the shop this morning and had asked her to meet him at 4:00 for coffee on the *zócalo*. "Wait until you hear the good news!" he'd said with his usual verve. Well, she could use some good news. She looked at her watch and saw that she'd have to hurry.

The *zócalo* was about a mile from the Casa. She hurried past the tiny shops whose sparse inventory negated any thought of great profit. There were the sidewalk vendors, too—mostly women who sat all day with their meager wares spread around them: a few packages of gum in faded wrappers, shoelaces, plastic earrings, individually wrapped needles and other trinkets worth only a few centavos. Everyone in Oaxaca had something to sell, it seemed. Bravo for them, Holly thought.

Closer to the center of town the buildings, though ravaged by time, were more classic in style, with arched doorways, ornamental grillwork, tiled floors and inner courtyards. Even in the newer buildings the latter feature was retained. Holly loved them. In a city where space was at a premium, the oases of flowers and greenery, with perhaps a fountain and a caged bird, were benisons to refresh the spirit.

But today she trod the familiar route unaware. Paul already sat at a sidewalk table and leaped up as she arrived. He held out a chair for her. "Holly, love, wait until you hear! Holly's Selecciónes! How does that grab you? It's already arranged. Two of Texas's largest galleries have contracted for your stuff."

"Back up, Paul. What are you talking about?" she asked, confused at the jumbled information.

"Your ceramics. They love 'em, can't wait to get an order, and they'll give you triple what you receive at La Tienda."

"But Paul, there's no way I can produce enough to fill orders for two large galleries. I barely make a respectable amount for our small local shop. I only work at Doña Elena's studio two afternoons a week."

"Don't worry your pretty little head about that. They'll take with grateful thanks whatever you can give them."

She looked dubious. "Sounds as if you're turning me into a factory. I don't know. That kind of pressure intimidates me."

"Listen, love, with the extra money you're going to make, you can afford to stop working at La Tienda Artesanías and work full-time at your pottery."

She didn't want to stop working at La Tienda. She'd come to enjoy meeting and working with the various artisans, hearing about their families, learning about their tools and techniques. Every item in the shop now held special meaning. And she'd come to love Juana, who was like an older sister. She would have been lost in Mexico without that wise and funny, very brave lady, and she didn't want to leave her until the end of the summer.

Paul ignored her expressions of reticence. He had enough enthusiasm for both of them. "Listen, I have one big favor to ask. The shops are pleading for those animal whistles. They'll pay well. I mean it."

Doña Elena had originated the figures, and there were copies all over the city. "I won't make those," she said. "I consider it forgery. I won't infringe on Doña Elena's territory."

"Forget it. She won't sue you. Everyone and his brother does it."

"Not I. Don't ask, because I won't do it."

He promised, but somehow it didn't sound like a well-intentioned pledge to Holly. He chattered on about their partnership, assuming it had already been consummated. "I want everything on a businesslike basis. That's the way I operate. In order to set up the deal, I had to jump the gun a little and give you a business name. Holly's Selecciónes." He handed her a copy of the contract and pointed out the name. "Isn't that a winner? Pure class! I'll collect the usual commission, but I'll earn it and get you every penny you deserve. All you have to do is ship the things to my Texas office. I'll do the rest. You won't be sorry." He reached over and gave her hand a brotherly squeeze.

She frowned. She would have preferred to name her own company. "And what is the commission?"

"Listen, love, I'll guarantee you three or four times your usual price, even if I don't get a dime. Is that fair enough?"

She was bewildered. Why should he choose her pottery over the work of so many others? Her things were good, maybe even unique, but so were those of a lot of other artists in this town.

She shook her head. "I hardly know what to say. It's all rather sudden."

"All you have to say is, 'Go for it!'"

She considered the proposition. If the profits were as fantastic as Paul said, she'd have no financial worries during her year's leave of absence from teaching. She'd planned to live on a very stringent budget. It might be fun to be a little extravagant for a change. "Well, okay, if you allow me to do my own thing and go at my own pace. No copying Elena."

"Meaning you won't make those whistling musicians?"

"Exactly."

He shrugged. "What a woman! I thought you'd jump at the chance. You artists are all alike. No head for business whatsoever."

He handed her a pen and the papers for her to sign, giving him exclusive rights to sell her pottery in the U.S. and establishing her business name as Holly's Selecciónes. They finished their coffee. "Come on, let's celebrate our new venture," Paul said. "I feel lucky today. I'll treat both of us to some lottery tickets."

"No, thanks. Don't waste your money on me. I'm not much of a gambler, and anyway, the chances of winning are too remote."

"Someone has to win. My chance is as good as the next guy's."

"Spoken like a true gambler."

"Besides, the Mexican lottery pays well. Sixty-five percent of the money goes back to the public as prizes." They walked over to one of the ticket sellers she'd noticed on the city streets, this one a tiny Indian woman sitting at the entrance of a grocery store, her strings of tickets hanging over a wire stand. Holly silently counted as Paul peeled off hundred-peso bills one after another. To her amazement, she estimated he'd purchased around five-hundred dollars' worth of tickets.

"Good heavens! Do you do this often? I could live for weeks on that much money."

"I told you I feel lucky. If I win, I'll buy a yacht and take you on a cruise."

"I'll not pack my bags yet."

He laughed, and they meandered around the square, pausing to window-shop, then had coffee in another of the sidewalk cafés. As they parted, he suddenly clapped a hand on his shirt pocket. "I almost forgot. I ran into a mutual friend of ours while I was waiting for you this afternoon—Chris Brooke."

"Oh?" she said with a start, and hoped the sudden anguish she felt didn't show.

"I mentioned I'd be seeing you in a few minutes, and he asked me to give you this letter." Paul pulled it out and handed it to her, then bent and gave her a light kiss on the cheek. "To the future of Holly's Selecciónes! May it be a long and rosy one."

She stuffed the letter in her bag and walked rapidly back to Casa Avalon. Her mouth grew dry. She'd felt tempted to sit down on one of the white wrought-iron benches in the *zócalo* and read it but, whatever Chris had to say, she wanted to be able to deal with it in privacy.

She walked quickly, then started to run, as if the message might disappear if she didn't read it as soon as possible. Pedestrians turned to stare as she brushed past. She saw one shake his head. *Crazy Americans. Always in a hurry!* his expression seemed to say. Breathless and hot, she at last reached the Casa and, cutting short the friendly gardener's attempt at conversation, she hurried to her room.

She sank into a chair and pulled out the envelope from her bag. It had her full address and a stamp on it. Chris had probably been on his way to the post office when he had run into Paul.

A small wisp of hope encircled her, a passionate longing that the words might open the door between them again. She'd insisted they had grown too far apart; but surely they'd become more mature, more tolerant in the

years they'd been apart. That meant something, didn't it?
With trembling fingers she opened the letter.

Dear Holly,
Enclosed is the card of a boutique with whom I've
arranged to feature your pottery. Your artistry deserves wider exposure, and I believe this place will do
it. As you may know, Hugo's is Oaxaca's top boutique.

I intended to give you this good news when we ce-
lebrated your birthday, but we've since both agreed
to end our relationship. I, too, now believe we are
taking the right course.

I sincerely hope Hugo's will prove a big break for
you.

Best wishes,
Chris.

The loneliness seemed incredible. It was as if it had
sunk into the thick walls of the building and would per-
meate the place forever. She'd dealt with Felicity's pain.
Now she had to learn to live with Holly's—a woman in
love without hope.

Tears glazed her eyes as she read the card. Hugo's!
Every artist in Oaxaca dreamed of being featured in that
exclusive shop. Never before had Chris evidenced such
interest in her work. What had changed him? And why
now, when it was too late? Regardless of the profits Paul
promised, she'd prefer to be featured at Hugo's a thousand times more. She read the letter again, searching for
a word, a phrase or some overtone that might serve to
open the door between them, but she found none. She
crumpled the letter, then threw herself onto the bed and
sobbed.

CHAPTER ELEVEN

HOLLY WOKE WITH A START as firecrackers exploded in a deluge of ear-splitting bangs. It had to be some kind of holiday, she thought, perhaps a saint's day. There were over a hundred during the year. Mexicans loved fireworks and used them at most celebrations. Had they known it was her birthday, they might even have shot off a round for her, she mused wryly.

There would be no birthday observance this year. She dressed quickly. She wouldn't mope. No, she wouldn't. Chris hadn't revealed his plans for her birthday. He'd insisted he wanted to surprise her. Would it have been a day to remember?

She breakfasted on fresh orange juice and a sweet roll, refusing the *huevos rancheros*, a hearty omelet smothered in cheese, tomatoes, peppers and a spicy sauce, which she ordinarily might have relished. Without appetite, she nibbled on the roll and tried to figure out how to handle the problem of Hugo's Boutique. What irony! Now that Chris had become supportive of her career, she had to refuse his help. She appreciated Paul Dalton's interest, but it was strictly business with him, and certainly self-serving. Chris had made the arrangements with only the good of her career in mind. Well, she'd have to straighten it out with Hugo the first thing this morning. As she walked back to her room, a maid said there was a telephone call for her.

Her heart began a rapid thumping. Chris? *Don't be ridiculous! Fantasy time is over.* Nevertheless, she was as conscious of him as if he were present in the room. She picked up the phone. *"¿Hola?"*

"Holly, this is Lee. How about coming over for a swim? It's safe, if you know what I mean. Honest."

"Thanks, Lee, but we'll have to discontinue the lessons for a while. I'm going to be pretty busy for the next few weeks."

"You two had another fight, didn't you?"

"You're a mind reader?"

"Don't have to be a mind reader when you see a guy go snorting off like a wild horse for no obvious reason."

"Are you and Chris having problems again?"

"Heck, no. Not this time anyway." His voice deepened and became very adult. "As a whole, I think he's improving."

"Oh, he is, is he? What about you?"

There was a pause. "I don't know, Holly. For sure I'll never be able to measure up to his expectations. But at least we've been talking to each other," he added, sounding pleased that he could mention at least one positive point. "Listen, what I really called about was this ticket. Someone gave it to me. It's for a symphony concert tonight, and I don't really go for that stuff, so I said to myself, I'll bet Holly would like it. It's your thing, right? I'll pedal over and leave it in the office for you. No problem."

He sounded so eager she hated to disappoint him. Actually, a concert might be just the tonic she needed, she thought. It had been ages since she had attended one. "Thanks, Lee. I know I'll enjoy it."

"Great!" he said, his voice cracking with enthusiasm. "You're going to go for sure? I wouldn't want to waste the ticket."

She smiled. "For sure."

A few minutes later she took a taxi to Hugo's. The place breathed class. A recorded Brahms string quartet sounded in the background, and each art object was displayed with studied regard for lighting and space. What a thrill it would have been to see her works featured here! Hugo, a charming gray-haired gentleman, was understanding concerning her problem.

"Let me know if matters change," he said. "Your work has great potential in my shop." She left with a distinct sense of loss.

The day stretched interminably. It was Sunday, and she didn't have to work either in the shop or at Doña Elena's, and again she wondered what she and Chris might have been doing. Why keep going over it? she berated herself. Even if they'd spent the day together, in the end it would have changed nothing. They'd both recognized the futility of their relationship. There was no way around their incompatibility. All that had happened was they had ended everything sooner. Why extend the agony? Right? Right.

Maybe she would get tickets for a charity event, a house tour she'd seen advertised. It would be interesting to see some of the fine homes of the city. There were five on the tour, from colonial to modern. She still yearned for a home of her own, a place to put down roots and raise a family with the man she loved. Stability. That was one of the foundations for a happy marriage, and that would never have come with Chris.

She decided to invite Juana to go along with her on the tour. Juana, too, yearned for a home of her own, perhaps even more passionately than she did.

"You come with me instead. I show you a real house tour, and we don't have to buy tickets either," Juana said when Holly called her. They agreed to meet in front of the Tomayo Museum near a bus stop right after *comida*. Holly was intrigued by Juana's plan and looked forward to her vivacious company. When they met, Holly was surprised to learn that touring houses that were for sale was Juana's favorite Sunday occupation.

"Every week I choose three houses listed in the newspaper, then I visit each one and have a splendid time. Better than TV!" She laughed merrily at herself.

Two of the places were old and in need of paint and repair, but the third was another matter. It was a small but beautifully kept cottage on the outskirts of the city, and it was owned by an artist who had moved to Guadalajara. It had everything Juana had ever said she wanted in a home: a lovely courtyard filled with flowers, bright airy rooms and even a space for a small vegetable garden.

Juana, eyes shining, stood in the immaculate kitchen and took a deep breath as if she could already smell the spicy mole being prepared in the kitchen. Then she sat down for a while by the fireplace, beaming as if a flock of children were seated at her feet. In a doorway opening on to the courtyard, she leaned her head against the frame and gazed at the purple passion flowers for so long that Holly wondered if the color had mesmerized her.

"Here's your chance, Juana. It looks as if you've found your dream home," Holly said.

For an instant Juana's usually animated face turned bleak, and she turned her back and bent to examine the floor tiles. A moment later she quickly brushed her hand across her eyes and stood up. "I must consult Cousin Carlos. Such a purchase is a big step for me." They left then, and oddly, Juana said no more about it.

AFTER *CENA*, the late evening meal, Holly dressed for the concert, wearing a classically simple midnight-blue silk gown that was flattering to her slender figure, emphasizing her small waist and high, firm breasts. She added the single strand of pearls Chris had given her so long ago and tried to do something with her hair. She'd washed it earlier, but it wouldn't behave. Noting the time, she hurriedly pinned it up into the simple knot that she'd favored during her marriage.

The taxi crawled, spending irritating minutes at every signal. She'd forgotten about the busy evening traffic. According to her watch, she was already ten minutes late. She hoped Mexicans were as relaxed about starting concerts on time as they were about other schedules. As she walked into the hall to find her seat, the lights dimmed and the cacophony of instruments being tuned faded. Breathless, she crossed in front of several people and slipped into her seat. She glanced at her program. Good. Beethoven's Ninth for the first half. She could use the strength of that music. A moment later the conductor lifted his baton.

A pleasant fragrance wafted by her, and she looked at the matronly woman on her left who drummed her ringed fingers in her lap in time with the beat. The man on her right sat a little forward, gripping his program, already immersed in the music. Light emanating from the stage outlined his rugged profile. She gasped.

Oh, no! What was Chris doing here? How could this have happened? Had this been the surprise he'd planned for her birthday? For a moment her spirits zoomed, then plunged just as quickly. Lee! Of course. The scamp. No wonder he'd been so eager for her to use the ticket. It must have taken some expert finagling to arrange this. He'd probably purchased the tickets, too. She couldn't help feeling affection for him and his earnest peacemaking efforts, regardless of how misguided.

The unexpected turn of the evening set her heart to hammering. How was she to get out of this? Chris would be furious. If he maintained his present concentration, perhaps she could slip out at intermission before he recognized her. She rested her elbow on the chair arm and spread her fingers against her cheek, hoping to camouflage her face. Thank goodness she'd styled her hair differently.

She tried to concentrate on the music, but it brought back painful memories. She'd heard her first live performance of Beethoven's Ninth with Chris at the university. She'd been so profoundly moved by the glorious *Ode to Joy* in the final movement that tears had run down her cheeks. Chris had squeezed her hand and had solemnly pulled out his handkerchief, his eyes warm and tender. Odd that one of the things that had clung to her memory through the years was the feel of his good, kind hands wiping away her tears. Moisture again flooded her eyes at the recollection. As she brushed it away, the program fell from her lap.

Chris started to retrieve it for her, but she managed to get it first, then felt irrationally disappointed that their hands hadn't touched. Maybe that was part of what had gone wrong with their marriage—reaching out and not touching. But that had been her fault even more than his, she realized now. One couldn't keep feelings bottled up; one had to show them, and she'd rarely done that. Talk was important, but there were other ways: touching, holding, listening, a certain look. Even a companionable silence spelled out a special kind of intimate dialogue. Why had these things been so difficult for her?

The strings soared in poignant melody, a perfect accompaniment to the lyrics that sobbed in her heart. What would happen if she reached for Chris's hand and said, "I know this is crazy. We have no future. We both know there are too many obstacles, but I love you"? Why was that so hard? What actually prevented her from doing it? Oh, she knew, all right. She was not strong enough to shove aside pride and propriety.

During the hushed pause between movements of the symphony, she kept her head turned toward the woman on her other side. Suddenly she heard Chris's quick intake of breath.

"Felicity! My God, is that you?" Chris whispered.

Felicity! He hadn't used her old name in ages. He stared at her as if she were an apparition. It had to be her hairstyle.

"Sorry, wrong person," she said curtly, and turned away.

She felt his avid surveillance. "Right. Not Felicity. It's Holly, isn't it?"

"Shh!" she warned as the persons in front of them stirred impatiently. There remained one more movement before intermission. They sat stiffly aware of each other in the dark. Was his face hostile? Did he also plan to escape the second the lights went up? She could almost feel the muscles tensing in his arm, only a fraction of an inch away from her. How close, yet how separate they were.

Now the music climaxed in the exalting *Ode to Joy*, and its emotion claimed her, thrilling, humbling, touching her very core. She knew that Beethoven had triumphed over the adversity of deafness to create this glorious symphony. What a tribute to his spirit!

She stole a glance at Chris, and his eyes were on her. He too was recalling that long-ago concert, no doubt. How she wanted him to reach over and squeeze her hand. Did he also wish they were touching?

The audience rose to its feet and exploded into bravos. Holly quickly slid across the row and headed up the aisle to the foyer. She'd gone only a few steps when she felt an iron grip on her arm. "Not so fast, Felicity, or Holly, or whoever it is you are now. I need a few answers."

He guided her firmly into the foyer and into an alcove partially hidden by a row of potted palms. None too gently, he pushed her back to the wall, then shot his arms straight out on either side of her, leaning them against the wall and effectively cutting off her escape. He glowered fiercely. "Okay, let's have it. Is this one of your on-again-off-again acts?"

"Surely you knew Lee arranged this."

"Lee!"

"He only wanted us to be friends. Is that so bad?"

"So the two of you hatched up this little pas de deux?"

"Lee gave me a ticket. I had no reason to suspect that he had also given one to you," she said wearily. "When I first saw you, I even thought this might have had something to do with your original surprise plan for my birthday."

"Many happy returns," he said dryly.

She ignored the sarcasm. "And speaking of birthdays, it was enormously kind of you to surprise me with your arrangement at Hugo's. I was truly touched."

"Did you contact him?"

"Today, as a matter of fact." She hesitated, hating to admit all the details, but he'd find out eventually. She gave an inward sigh, afraid anything she said would sound like a slap in the face. "It would have meant a real step forward in my career, and I appreciated your thoughtfulness," she said miserably.

"But?"

"But I'd already signed a contract with Paul Dalton as exclusive agent to market my things in the U.S."

"Paul, eh? You'll earn a lot more with him. I can't fault you for that."

"Money has nothing to do with it. It was a matter of timing. Believe me, I would have much preferred Hugo's."

"I imagine," he said coolly, obviously disbelieving. "Paul's a slick operator. Watch your step."

"Our relationship is strictly a business one."

"I imagine."

"You said that before. Why can't we talk like two civilized human beings? I can't stand all this tension. It's tearing me up inside."

"What do you think these past weeks have been doing to me, for God's sake?"

Holly looked up at him, trying to negate the choking sensation that seemed to be overwhelming her. She bit her lip and widened her eyes, praying tears wouldn't spill. At the familiar sight, his expression changed and for a few seconds became infinitely tender. He pulled a handkerchief from his pocket and brushed her cheeks and gently wiped her eyes. For a while they seemed enveloped in a cocoon of memories. It took all her control to keep from swaying toward him, from putting her head on his shoulder. Now, she thought. Now is the time for the right words, an understanding touch or gesture. *Please, God, let it happen. Let one of us break the barrier.*

Lights blinked the end of the intermission. Chris shook his head and dropped his arms. "Who are you? Who are you *really*? Holly? Felicity? Or someone else entirely? I'm not sure of anything anymore."

They merged into the foyer and were soon separated by the milling crowd. She hurried back into the hall and sat down in her place. Lights dimmed. The conductor walked in, lifted his baton and the music started. For the rest of the performance the adjacent seat remained vacant.

CHAPTER TWELVE

HOLLY HUNG THE HAND-PAINTED, tin Christmas ornaments over a T-shaped rack: saucy parrots, a gingerbread man, figures of men and women in colorful regional costume, angels, camels... The variety was endless. The ornaments were popular items in the store, reasonably priced and small enough so that the tourist could tuck any number in his luggage to take home with him.

She tried to focus on the original designs—no two were alike—but the rugged profile of the man who had sat next to her at the concert last night kept coming back to distract her. The memory of the evening's events touched a raw place and filled her with tension. Had Chris gone home after intermission, or had he found himself another seat? Probably the latter. He was a music lover and wouldn't want to miss out on last evening's treat.

Wistfully she recalled his brief moment of tenderness, cherishing the recollection and hugging it to herself. She could secretly claim comfort from it, couldn't she? No one would know. The heartening thing was that he still could show concern and warmth, no matter how briefly. She felt as if she were clinging to a fragile lifeline. It hurt a lot that he hadn't returned to sit by her. Chris had never lacked self-assurance. Couldn't he handle proximity to an ex-wife for an hour or two?

Lee rushed into the shop like a whirlwind, trading friendly insults with Juana and leaping over a couple of terra-cotta jars in a shortcut to reach her. What a difference from the withdrawn, sullen boy she'd first met. His self-confidence had burgeoned since he'd started studying with a teacher who appreciated and encouraged his talent. Creativity was one of life's most nourishing blessings, Holly thought, whether it took the form of stirring up a batch of of fluffy biscuits or designing a spaceship.

"Hi, how was the concert last night?" Lee asked, all breezy interest.

"Great music! I'm glad you thought of me. I really enjoyed it."

He watched her expression. "Uh, how was it otherwise?"

"Otherwise?"

"Oh, nothing. Just wondered if you saw anyone there you knew and stuff."

She managed to hide a smile. "Would you believe Chris had the seat right next to me? Quite a coincidence, right?"

"Sure was. How was he? I mean, he seems pretty preoccupied lately. Was he friendly and all that?"

"I don't think he was too thrilled at finding me next to him."

"No? I thought, I mean, I should think he'd have been pleased."

"Well, perhaps it's more complicated than you realize."

He shifted his weight uncomfortably. "I know. He told me you used to be married to each other."

"He did?"

"Yeah, and the way he talked I figured he was real anxious for you two to get back together."

"I'm sure you misunderstood. In fact we only recently agreed not to see each other again, so I hope we don't have any more accidental meetings. It gets pretty uncomfortable."

"Oh, Oaxaca's pretty big. It probably won't happen. Hey, what I really came in for was to tell you some great news. Listen to this. My teacher has been asked to provide an exhibition of the work of two of his best students at the El Presidente Hotel!"

"And you're one of them? Congratulations! What did I tell you!"

"Thanks, and they're going to have a special reception with refreshments and the works. You'll come?"

"I wouldn't miss it. Oh, Lee, I'm so proud of you."

He turned sober, and a shade of the old insecurity crossed his face. For a little while he studied some imaginary object on the floor, then stubbed a toe against it. "Do you think *he* will come?"

"Absolutely. He'll be the proudest one there besides me. Have you told him yet?"

"No chance. I just found out, and he took off early this morning. Maybe when he sees the exhibition my stock will go up a little."

"Whatever do you mean?"

"Well, he's so good at everything. I always feel like a kind of nonperson around him. I figure that he sort of puts up with me, and it makes me say and do weird things. It's a bad feeling to be a nonperson, Holly."

"True, but of all the people I know, you're the least likely candidate for that category."

"You're just saying that."

"Not at all. Do you have talent? A bundle! Are you kind and helpful? Ask your swim pupil. Are you good-looking? You bet! Are you the world's greatest peace promoter who buys expensive symphony tickets for two special people...?"

He grinned. "Who told you?"

"That proverbial bird. Listen, Lee, you don't have to be perfect to earn Chris's approval. If you want true respect, all you have to do is to be your very best self. Is that so hard?"

He sighed. "I don't think that's good enough for him."

"Give it a try. And in the meantime, you might think about *his* needs. Adults have those, too, you know. Chris is under a lot of pressure right now trying to complete his documentary. Did you know that a big film company moved in recently to do a similar one and may scoop him for the contract?"

"He said something about it, but I didn't pay much attention. Man, it will kill him if he doesn't get that contract. I'd better make myself scarce for a while."

"Is that your best solution?"

He stared at the ceiling as if it held an answer. "You don't think anything I could do would help?"

"You won't know unless you offer."

"Got it. So long. I'm due at the studio. I'm finishing some pieces for the exhibition. He gave her a jaunty salute that was so like Chris's that she felt a lump rise in her throat. How close Chris and Lee were to understanding each other, and yet how far!

Not five minutes later Paul Dalton called. The wires sizzled with his excitement. "Holly, love, pack your bag. I did it!"

"What on earth are you talking about?"

"Remember the lottery tickets I purchased recently? I won, sweetheart, and I won big! Get this. I'm throwing a fiesta to christen my new yacht, and I want you to do the honors."

"You bought a yacht?" she asked incredulously. "In heaven's name, how much did you win?"

"Hold on to your hat. In dollars, a cool million, love."

"I'm flabbergasted!"

"Wait until you see her—the sweetest little craft in the Pacific. She's anchored in a cove near Puerto Escondido. I've hired a plane to fly you and a few other good friends over for the celebration. Flight time is noon next Sunday. Can I count on you?"

"I'll be there."

"Great, and Holly, the Texas galleries love your ceramics. They want more as soon as possible. Wait until you see your profits. They're better than either of us expected. I'm calling from one of the galleries now. I'll fly back to Oaxaca tomorrow."

"With another tourist group?"

"Hell, no. I've turned the tourist business over to my partner. I'll run the export end. Less confining. I'm living it up for once in my life, and it's about time. See you Sunday. Bring your bikini."

He hung up, and she considered his good fortune. Would one of those tickets he had wanted to buy for her have been the winning number? Whatever she would have won, it wouldn't have mattered. Money couldn't buy what she wanted most in her life.

Nevertheless, her spirits lifted at the prospect of the celebration. Paul would surely invite Chris. The question was, would he come? *Don't think negatively.* In the close quarters of a small yacht, they couldn't avoid talking to each other. If the situation turned favorable, they might even become friends. Friendship would allow some communication, and that was better than nothing. She busied herself dusting a shelf of figurines. What a dreamer she was!

On Sunday she took a bus to the small airport, which was a few miles from town, arriving a little before noon. The place wasn't busy, and she found the chartered two-prop plane without difficulty. It was an ancient but dependable Grumman Goose, so Paul had told her when he'd called again yesterday.

She went aboard and looked around. Her spirits plunged. Chris was not among the passengers. There were four couples who all seemed to know one another, her lone self, and the pilot, a fiftyish man who seemed bored with the entire procedure. Possibly Chris had flown earlier with Paul, she thought, grasping at a straw. *Stop doing this to yourself! You know you'd be better off if you never saw him again.* Lord, she was as obsessed as any addict!

The flight over the Sierra Madre to the coast took less than an hour. The pilot set the plane down on the runway in Puerto Escondido, where a minibus waited to pick them up. Paul's million would disappear in a hurry if he kept this up, Holly reflected.

A few minutes later the bus, edging around a few donkey carts, unloaded them on the beach. Several sun-bronzed boys in rowboats waited there to ferry them out to the gleaming white yacht anchored a few hundred yards offshore. As they glided smoothly through the calm water, Holly drank in the beauty all around her. Gentle waves lapped the shore of the little cove. The beach sand glistened white, scalloping the deep turquoise of the ocean. Coconut palms stretched their slim trunks skyward among banana trees and mangoes. In prolific clusters, ferns and tropical flowers added to the South Seas aura.

The clean, graceful lines of the yacht sent a thrill through her. No sails were visible, which meant it was power-operated. That figured, Holly thought. Paul wouldn't want to fill his leisure time with work!

Paul, in natty white trousers, navy polo shirt and yachting cap, waved and shouted as they drew near. An accordionist played a nautical tune to pipe them aboard while the host extended a hand to help the ladies up the ladder. In the other hand he juggled a drink, which tilted precariously every time he hugged and welcomed a guest.

Paul was in his element—garrulous to the point of being a monologuist. He poured champagne and refilled glasses continually, not slighting his own. Later, at his signal, Holly dutifully broke the champagne on the prow of the yacht. She christened her *Buena Suerte*, which meant "good luck." Everyone clapped and shouted toasts, and uniformed caterers set out a bountiful spread.

She could have been invisible as far as the four couples were concerned. They were completely wrapped up in one another and had begun to dance on the limited deck space. She closed her eyes and imagined herself in Chris's arms, dancing among them. Her entire body warmed at the thought. She could feel the firmness of his jaw, imagine the clean scent of his thick hair, feel her breasts grow full against him.

The daydream ended rudely as the accordionist began a rock number, and the deck suddenly burst with energy. Now the four couples divided into eight separate entities; they didn't touch or even look at one another.

With a fine discipline, she managed not to ask Paul if Chris might be coming later. It would be embarrassing if he hadn't been invited. She looked around. If Paul considered her his date, he wasn't being very attentive. At the moment he was regaling one of the girls with a very funny story, judging by her giggling. Holly felt like a fifth wheel and wished she hadn't come.

The pilot eventually roused himself from a nap and asked her for a dance, then disappeared again, no doubt figuring he'd fulfilled his social obligation for the day. She curled up against a dinghy and watched the sunset, trying not to let her blue mood interfere with the spectacle of liquid gold melting into the ocean.

"Here now, we can't have this," Paul cried upon discovering her hideaway a few minutes later, pulling her to her feet. "You haven't danced with me yet, love."

His breath, heavy with alcohol, forced her to hide her head against his shoulder, and he held her so tightly she could barely breathe. Either he danced to a different beat or his reflexes were too dulled to perform. It was impossible to follow him, but he seemed unaware. "This is the life!" he said effusively, and stepped on her toes again.

"Your guests really love it." *Most of them anyway*.

"Money, that's what makes the world go round!"

"I thought it was love," she said, suppressing a groan at her injured toe and deciding she'd be a candidate for the Purple Heart before the dance ended. He stopped and shook a finger at her.

"No way, baby. Stay away from that stuff. No security, no interest, no borrowing power. Can't trust it." He gestured grandly, almost losing his footing. "Did love get me all this? No way! Here's what I put my faith in." He pulled out a crumpled lottery ticket and kissed it. She suggested a tour of the yacht, which he'd already given, but she hoped he wouldn't remember. Anything to keep from dancing again.

"Into the drink, everyone. Time for a swim!" Paul cried when they came back on deck again. He ambled inside to talk to the pilot. Everyone else started peeling at once. Holly headed for one of the small rooms below to change into her suit. With some apprehension, she wondered if four swim lessons were adequate preparation for a dip in the ocean. Well, she'd give it a try if it came to that. She could always float.

After putting on her bathing suit, she almost changed back into her clothes again. Although it was hot in the little stateroom, she felt as if she were freezing. Familiar fears snatched her breath away and spread to her limbs, piercing her like needles. She held her hands out before her and willed them to stop shaking, but there was no response, and she knew with certainty that she could no more climb down the ladder and ease herself into the dark depths than she could dive off the deck into it. She hugged herself in an effort to stop trembling. Oh, God, what to do? This tiny room! Claustrophobia zeroed in and wrapped her in a net, squeezing, tightening. She gasped for air. *Get out of here! Feign sudden nausea. Think of something!*

She climbed up on the deck and peered around to see if anyone remained there. All clear. Faint shouts and laughter indicated everyone was already swimming. Cautiously she edged around the deck and crouched down in the dinghy.

Eventually her heart stopped pounding, and she felt a cool rationality take charge. In disgust she climbed out of her hiding place. *Stupid woman! You're acting like a scared rabbit. Face up to the situation. All you have to do is tell people you don't know how to swim well enough to join them. What's wrong with that?*

The soft purring of a motor caught her ear. Looking across starboard she saw a launch pulling away from the yacht and heard hearty male voices ringing out in the cabin. Paul's, the pilot's, and yes, the third was definitely Chris's. Her pulse accelerated wildly. *Calm down. Except for the swimming problem, Chris thinks you're one cool lady.* She'd destroyed his other illusions concerning her; she had to allow him to hang on to this one.

How long before he'd come out onto the deck? *Stop looking at your watch. Keep your mind on the swimmers.* They frolicked, dived and played like porpoises, barely visible in the early darkness. Colored lanterns strung around the deck cast a soft glow, tinting the bodies of the swimmers in rainbow colors.

Suddenly she realized most of them were swimming in the nude. It didn't especially offend her, but skinny-dipping with a bunch of strangers wasn't her cup of tea. Two of the girls climbed on deck and came over to her.

"Come join us. The water's fine," one said, and took her arm.

"Sorry. I don't swim well," Holly said firmly.

"You're kidding! Never mind, we'll keep you afloat," the other girl said as they both pulled her against the low railing.

"Listen, I mean it!" Holly cried, terror escalating.

The girls laughed. "So why are you wearing a bathing suit then?" They jerked her hard, and she screamed, exerting all her strength to retain a foothold.

"Damn it, get lost, you two. Can't you hear? The lady can't swim," Chris yelled angrily, and pulled her safely back into his arms. Laughing, the two girls dived back in, oblivious to the crisis they had caused.

His embrace was warm and sheltering, and she snuggled against him, trying to stop shaking, wanting to stay there forever.

"Thanks for the rescue," she murmured at last.

He held her close for a moment longer, then released her. "Drunken fools," he muttered.

"You're late."

"Engine trouble with the plane I rented. I almost didn't come, but I'd promised." He looked down at the swimmers and raised an eyebrow. "Some party!"

"You approve of skinny-dipping?"

"One-to-one with the right person."

"We never did."

"Our loss. There were a lot of things we missed out on. Are you having fun at this bash?"

"It's not my kind of party, really. I don't know anyone but Paul, and everyone is drinking too much. Makes for dull conversation."

"Well, you never cared much for parties."

"Not true. I love having good friends around. But this?" She hunched her shoulders in a gesture that indicated her boredom. "I admit that solitude nourishes me a lot more than crowds do, but I'm improving. In my next life I promise to come back as a professional party giver. And just what are you doing?" she asked suddenly.

"Measuring," he said, spanning his hands around her waist. "Still the smallest in town."

He rested his cheek against her hair, and she heard his swift intake of breath. The outward Chris held her as of old. But what had happened to the other Chris, the one who had loved her? Was he still there, or had he disappeared forever? Holly wondered. Perhaps she was better off not knowing.

The accordionist finished his beer and struck up a lazy tune. Chris gestured toward the dance area. "How brave are you?"

"Tops when it comes to dancing," she said.

They had the deck to themselves. Chris was no accomplished dancer, but he had a keen sense of rhythm and was able to get inside the music and become part of it. She felt it in his quick coordination and the electric feel of their bodies moving precisely together as if they were one. No fancy turns, no elegant whirls or complicated steps. Just a steady, smooth, dependable progression. It was heavenly.

His cheek touched her forehead, and she caught the faint fragrance of soap, the kind he always used. The remembered intimacy brought a lump to her throat, and she hid her head against his shoulder. He drew her closer as if he sensed her need of him and continued to hold her firmly, even after the music stopped.

"Let's get out of here," he said.

"You mean leave, just like that?"

"They won't miss us. Besides, I'm starved. It seems that I arrived here too late to get in on the food. Let's go find something to eat."

They went to say goodbye to Paul, but he was snoring loudly in his cabin. Chris found a pen and paper on the desk, scribbled a note and propped it on the rising and falling chest, where it wallowed like a small boat in a storm.

"Thanks for everything," Holly read. "Sorry to leave early, but Holly had an attack of bronkocytonitis. Happy sailing! Chris."

Outside he signaled with a flashlight to the boys on the shore, and Holly hurriedly changed back into her clothing. Minutes later they heard the lift of oars as the little boat coasted into view. They climbed in, and at once slid swiftly through the water.

"What on earth is bronkocytonitis? Sounds ominous," Holly asked when they docked.

"I hope so. I just made it up," Chris said as he tipped the boy generously. He then asked him to recommend a place nearby where they could eat.

"Señor, my uncle has the best seafood place around. It's on your way back toward town." He locked his lips to accentuate his recommendation. *"¡Maravilloso!"* He gave them directions, and they started along the wooded path that paralleled the beach.

"Food," Chris moaned. "I've had nothing since breakfast. I'm going to gorge myself on a whole lobster."

"I'm not hungry. I'll steal a bite or two from your plate."

"Oh, no, you won't. I'll order you a virtuous little salad."

The winding, shadowy path was sheltered by trees and tropical vines. Chris reached for Holly's hand and sensed the trusting curl of her fingers. The gesture warmed him. He was always surprised at how vulnerable she felt when he touched her.

"So old Paul is finally in the money. I'll wager he's spent plenty over the years on no-wins. Well, he'll have a ball blowing it," Chris said.

"I know what you'd do with a million dollars."

"Tell me."

"You'd take off for the Andes to make your dream documentary."

He grinned. "And I know exactly how you'd spend yours."

"Interesting. I don't."

"You'd buy an old Victorian house with gingerbread trim and three-generation magnolia trees. Right?"

"That old Victorian house was a symbol, Chris. House, castle or cabin, it doesn't matter. My dream is to put down roots somewhere, anywhere, so that my family can have a stable life. I want a father who comes home at night for my children."

"We were at opposite poles on that score."

"Too bad we didn't find that out before we married."

"But it looks as if you've found the end of the rainbow here in Oaxaca."

"Do you mind explaining?"

"It's not like you to be coy, Holly. You know what I mean. Avalon. I saw exactly how he felt about you that night during the regional dancing. He fulfills all the requirements, doesn't he? A charming old family estate, a highly respectable place in the community, and as if that weren't enough, he's damned good-looking and a hell of a dancer."

She laughed at his bitter tone. "Miguel and I are good friends, nothing more."

"Oh, sure. Has he proposed yet?"

"I think he and Juana are an item these days."

"So that's why he paints *your* portrait and escorts *you* all over town?"

"At least he doesn't desert me in the middle of some performance."

"If you're talking about the symphony, I can explain that."

"Please do. I'd be interested."

But before he could respond, they came abruptly upon one of the coastal lagoons common to the area. Surely the vision before them was a mirage, Chris thought. It was unreal, like a splendid stage set. He heard Holly catch her breath. She was as awestricken as he was.

They heard the whisper of the water as it gently lapped against the sand. The air was warm and humid and still. A veritable jungle almost surrounded the place. It was too dark to identify the flowers, but something akin to jasmine perfumed the night, and a few flamingos stood resolutely along the edge. Chris hesitated to speak in the event that the intrusion might cause the scene to vanish. Kicking off his shoes and socks, he dabbled a foot in the water.

"Perfect. How about a dip to cool off before we eat?"

"Not me. I can only float, remember?"

He hurled a pebble out toward the center. "It's shallow, barely waist-deep, I should judge."

"You're certain?"

"I'm certain."

"Well . . . it's awfully dark."

He placed his hands on her shoulders. "I know. So are you thinking what I'm thinking?" he asked softly.

Warning bells clanged all around her, but she refused to listen. "One-to-one?" she asked. He heard the tremor in her voice.

"And no strangers. We missed out when we had the chance years ago. Shall we make up for lost time?" Carefully watching for an denial, he slowly pulled her knit blouse over her head, brushed his lips on her shoulder and breasts, then unzipped her full, embroidered floral skirt so that it fell in a pile of blossoms about her feet. His heart pounded. How beautiful she was, and how long it had been since he'd seen her like this.

Unhesitatingly she stepped out of her lacy underthings and waded into the water. He shed his own clothes and followed. Moonlight sparsely penetrated the shadows, but his heart raced as he caught glimpses of her perfectly rounded hips, her lovely breasts and graceful legs and arms.

The pounding in his chest became a high, singing melody. The water was not even thigh-high when he caught up with her. For a while she floated on her back while he swam at a leisurely pace nearby. Then, he broke into a churning butterfly stroke and swam to the mouth of the lagoon and back again—in order to check for depth, he told himself—but knew it was an action designed to give him time to gather his composure.

A little later he floated alongside her and reached for her hand. She didn't pull away, and together they looked up at the stars, their hands locked together. His heartbeat swelled until it almost stopped his breathing. She had been totally his, and he'd been foolish enough to lose her, causing her terrible hurt and leaving her to erect a formidable hedge around herself. Could he break through again? Tonight? So far his timing had been notably imperfect. He wanted to hold her close, wanted the sweet taste of her flesh, wanted her to want him again. The silence could not have been improved by words, yet he felt some fragile cord of communication between them.

"It's a curious and wonderful feeling, isn't it?" she said finally. "So free. I can't explain it."

"How many other wonderful experiences do you suppose we missed? Think how much richer our lives would have been had our marriage lasted."

She sighed and stood up. "We'd better end this before you die of hunger." They waded toward shore. When they were just steps away from it, she stepped on a rock and almost lost her footing. He caught her and lifted her to her feet, then drew away at the intensity of the electricity that shot through him. For a long moment they stood motionless, simply trying to read each other's expression. Although it was dark, he could see her dark-fringed eyes widen. With apprehension? Or permission? Did he dare believe he saw love there? Or was it madness brought on by this magic place that made her light-headed and reckless?

Standing close, still not touching, he felt fire leap inside and, like a drug, it completely wiped out all the bitterness he'd harbored, all reason. This was the woman he'd loved deeply, and in spite of all denials, loved still.

His hand rested on her cheek for a moment, and then, with a compulsion he couldn't have resisted had his life depended on it, he took her in his arms. *Don't rush her,* he warned himself, but he knew he'd be doing well if he exercised even minimum restraint.

Gently he nuzzled her ear with his lips, then kissed her. His pulse quickened when she didn't pull away. *Caution. Remember her actions at the monastery.* But surely the way she responded now indicated a core of feeling for him. Or did the moonlight work false magic?

With a kind of desperation, he pulled her hard against him. Oh, God! Sweet-tasting fire! Flesh on flesh, hardness blending with softness, moving and fitting. His lips parted hers in a deep, gentle kiss. His fingers explored her satiny breast and the silk of her hair, then moved delicately over the arc of her hip and down her thigh.

She rested her head in the hollow of his neck and held very still, as if listening to the rapid pulse beating there. He felt a wild longing and he hoped she would reach up and kiss him, taste his skin and feel his pounding heart. He sensed that she too wanted to abandon herself to her feelings.

"I want to make love to you," he whispered, immediately feeling a change in her body that was almost imperceptible.

He saw the glitter of tears in her eyes. "I'll be honest, Chris. I want it, too. You're an incredibly wonderful lover. I can't think straight around you, even after all these years."

"So what's the problem?"

She pulled out of his arms, ran toward the heap of clothing and almost frantically pulled her outfit on over her wet body. "I have this thing about sex without commitment," she said so softly that he had to strain to catch her words.

"I'm asking you to consider commitment again."

"You don't mean that. It's just this place that's getting to you. Anyway, we know it's impossible. We've gone over the reasons often enough. We'd only destroy each other as we did before."

Frustration, anger and rising bitterness overcame him, and he lashed out at her. "You're a cheat. Do you realize that?"

"Considering my actions tonight, you have every right to believe that. But deep down, I'm against the kind of thing that will leave only regrets tomorrow. I don't know what came over me. All I'm sure of is that it can't go any further."

"You've a damnable way of communicating that."

"I know. I seem to lose control. I've missed the kind of tenderness you offer. It was one of the best parts of our marriage. Maybe you missed something about me, too. We both admit to a lingering physical attraction for each other, but we found out the hard way that marriage is a lot more than that."

"I see," he snapped, his voice still husky with fury. "In a saner moment we agreed not to meet again. We should have stuck by that."

"Since neither of us seems to be able to control our impulses, I think that's best."

"Obviously I'm a slow learner," he said curtly as he jerked his clothes on. "But I finally get the picture. Come along. I'm not hungry anymore. Since it's against the law to fly private planes at night, we'd better head for town. It's peak tourist season, and there are only a few places to stay in around here. We may have a hell of a time trying to find two rooms. The boat boys have probably all gone home, so we can't get back on the yacht. Failing all else, we may have to spend the night in the cockpit of the plane. Under the circumstances, that could pose a problem neither of us would care to face."

CHAPTER THIRTEEN

HOLLY RUSHED HOME from her ceramics session with Doña Elena in order to dress for Lee's exhibition at El Presidente. She'd worked hard all afternoon on some platters. Trying to satisfy Paul's voracious demands for her work kept her busy. At least he'd stopped pressing for the animal whistles that she'd steadfastly refused to copy.

She'd told Doña Elena about Paul's request, and the serene lady had merely hunched her shoulders. "No matter. Others have copied them. Why not you?" But Holly refused. Everything from Holly's Selecciónes had to be original.

She'd thought a lot about the previous week's incident at the lagoon. The compulsion she'd felt had been too real to ignore. Under the law, irreconcilable differences was an accepted reason for divorce. Irreconcilable differences still remained, yet she felt driven to involve herself in the relationship again.

They'd found rooms that night after their quarrel, but she'd hardly slept. There'd been no problem taking off from the short dirt runway the next morning. The place had been deserted except for a sleepy attendant at the gas pump.

Instead of the painful silence she'd expected on the way home, Chris had talked about everything except the purely personal. He'd discussed the plane they'd flown, which he called a tail dragger—it had lots of power, and with its fat tires, landing on or taking off from the dirt runways was a breeze. Then he'd talked about his documentary and some of the changes he intended to make in the script.

The conversation had been pleasant, but it had left her frustrated. *Here we go again,* she'd thought. *Instead of hiding our feelings behind this impersonal smoke screen, we should be examining them.* But was it possible to do that without getting into another hassle? She'd doubted it. Besides, expressing feelings had never been easy for her, and apparently Chris didn't want to talk about his either.

All during the past week she'd tried to detach herself from what had happened at the lagoon and concentrate on ordinary things: sketching designs for the fruit bowl she planned to make soon, listening to the mysterious whoosh of the jacaranda as it brushed against her window, trying to locate the rabbit in the moon that Mexicans saw there instead of the man. All seemed inconsequential. All that mattered to her these days was the remembered touch of Chris's hand on her cheek, the saltwater taste of his lips and the way he'd said her name over and over.

She'd invited Miguel to go with her to the exhibition this evening. He was an avid supporter of the arts, and Lee's teacher, Señor Hamilton, was his longtime friend.

Lee had come by or called a half-dozen times to make certain she would be there. "Remember, the other kid has about a jillion aunts and uncles, and I hardly have anyone," he'd said.

His face had been a study in anxiety. She could empathize. Often as a child she had been the only pupil at a school function whose parents weren't present.

She'd tried to reassure him. "Don't worry. I wouldn't miss it for anything. Miguel and some of the Casa Avalon guests are coming too. And, of course, Chris will be there."

"Yeah; he promised. Señor Hamilton says I'm really improving. Do you think *he* will notice?"

"I do," she'd said, hoping she was right. Chris at times had a curious insensitivity about complimenting the work of others. It was as if he already knew and appreciated the abilities of the individual and considered superlatives redundant.

Miguel drove her to the early evening reception in his handsome Rolls-Royce. He always seemed like a boy with his first car, thoroughly enjoying the handling of the vehicle as well as the looks of admiration it received when he passed. She found the trait endearing in the otherwise suave and sophisticated man.

About twenty-five people had already gathered at the reception. Her eyes swept the room, but Chris wasn't there. Both relief and disappointment welled up within her. She knew it would be best if she and Miguel left before he arrived. Regardless of how serene her facade, the canny Lee would most certainly sense the climate between them. She and Chris represented the only family he could claim, and he'd tried so hard to bring them together. She wouldn't spoil this heady time for him tonight.

Miguel immediately buttonholed his old friend, Señor Hamilton, and Holly meandered among the carvings, each displayed on a separate pedestal. The styles of the two students were radically different. Lee sculptured boldly, catching a likeness through a strong line or a simple curve. The other student's work was so true to life, each piece could have been a dimensional photograph.

She marveled at the talent of the two youngsters and wondered if someday they would become names in the art world.

She caught Lee's eyes on her as she studied his work. Did her opinion mean so much to him? At the end of the room a life-sized head was dramatically spotlighted. She strolled over to look at it, and her hand flew to her mouth to stifle surprise.

The head was of Chris! But what a contrast to the mean, cantankerous little carving Lee had made in anger almost two months ago! Here was the Chris she'd known. How had a mere boy captured the separate parts of him: the leprechaun with the gleam in his eye; the workaholic who took off overseas at the drop of a hat because he needed an interview; the dreamer; the perfectionist? All were there. The sensitive likeness spoke volumes about Lee's depth of perception and his feelings about Chris.

He appeared at her side, a wide grin spreading across his face in spite of an obvious effort to sustain a nonchalant air. "What do you think?"

"It's absolutely wonderful, the best thing you've done." She gave him a hug. "I'm so proud of you. Does Chris know about it?"

"No, I wanted it to be a surprise, to kind of make up for that rotten one I did a long time ago. I sure hope he likes it." The raw longing in his face made her throat constrict.

"He'll be thrilled," she said.

"All my pieces are for sale but this one. I made it for you. Hey," he said with concern. "You're supposed to be happy when you get a present."

She wiped her eyes. "I'm really touched." How could she live with this likeness, a continual reminder of her ill-fated love? But she would never refuse it.

Lee was darting anxious looks toward the door and Holly was nervous, too. What was keeping Chris? Surely he was aware how much it meant to Lee for him to be here.

She worked her way through the crowd toward Miguel, hoping she could suggest some diplomatic way to leave, but he looked as if he were there for the entire evening, happily visiting with friends. He always seemed to run into acquaintances, no matter where they went.

Waiters now served small sandwiches and cookies, wine and punch. Lee, contrary to his usual habit, barely touched the food, but kept his attention riveted on both clock and door. Finally he came over and introduced her to his teacher and the other boy whose works were exhibited tonight. He made a great show of indifference when the student asked if his father had come yet. *Father? Had Lee really told people Chris was his father? Oh, Chris, get here, damn you!*

The minutes scampered by rapidly until only five remained before closing time. The showing would be open to the public during the coming week and Chris could see it then, but it would be too late for Lee.

Miguel walked around with her once more, making perceptive comments on the various pieces. "Time to leave?" he asked finally. "Before we go home I'd like to take you to hear a singer at Rafael's, a little piano bar near the university. I hear she's causing quite a sensation. She's from Barcelona and does authentic ballads from the region. You know how fond I am of those."

Worriedly Holly looked around for Lee, but he wasn't in the room. "Yes, I'd enjoy that, but could you spare a few minutes more? I think I'd better talk to Lee. He's upset because Chris didn't arrive.''

Miguel told her to take all the time she needed and then wandered back to chat with Lee's teacher again. Holly raced down the hall and into the foyer of the hotel. No Lee. Then she spotted him, a forlorn figure standing in the entryway, peering up and down the street.

She put a hand on his shoulder. "I'm sorry, Lee, but there has to be an explanation. Chris always keeps a promise."

"Right. With people that count, and I'm not one of those," he said bitterly. Then he jerked away from her and headed down the street. She ran to catch up with him.

"Please don't make any judgments until you know what happened."

He faced her, his expression contorted with hurt and anger. "I hate his guts. To hell with him. I'm sick of trying to please him. I'll bet he stopped off for a beer with some guy and forgot all about me."

"You're wrong! Trust him until you find out."

"*You* did and look what happened."

She swallowed hard. Oh, no, what had Chris told him? Did he have to be so precocious? "This is different."

"I'm going to take off as soon as we go back to the States next month. I'd go now, but I'd never make it across the border. Take off, that's what he really wants me to do, isn't it?"

"Not true. He's been trying as hard as you have. All you lack is a little communication."

"Oh, sure. He isn't interested in people. All he cares about is filming them. He'd probably like to stick pins in them and put them in a display case like a bunch of insect specimens. He doesn't care how they feel...." His voice broke.

Holly put a hand on his shoulder. "How are you getting home? Miguel and I will be glad to take you. We're going to a piano bar. Rafael's, I believe."

He shook his head. "Thanks, but Señor Hamilton is treating us to some ice cream. I wish I didn't have to go, but he's an all-right guy, and I wouldn't want to hurt his feelings."

"Good thinking. And I'll make you a bet that Chris has a perfectly logical explanation."

He turned his head away, and she knew he was hiding tears. She gave his shoulder a squeeze and felt almost ill as she walked back into the hotel to find Miguel.

THE PIANO BAR was on the other side of town. Miguel showed a passionate interest in anything Spanish, and a new singer who hailed from Barcelona intrigued him.

"I should think Juana would be interested. The singer is from her part of the country," Holly said.

"Apparently the *señora* has already heard her. Unfortunately she didn't think much of her. 'She doesn't sing well, and her costumes are more theatrical than authentic. Don't waste your time,' Juana told me. Surprising that she is so hard on a fellow countrywoman, isn't it? Juana is rarely critical. Ordinarily I'd take her advice, but a musician friend of mine highly recommended the singer. Let's drop by for a little while anyway. We can always leave if Juana proves right."

The place was a sophisticated, intimate little bar that looked more like New York than Oaxaca. A handsome gray-haired man played dreamy, romantic melodies on an electric piano. Unobtrusive rhythms by a drummer accompanied him. They were on a raised platform in front of the tiny dance floor. Two couples swayed to the music, but everyone else sat in the darkened room sipping drinks, some quietly holding hands, some engrossed in quiet conversation.

After an intermission, the pianist came out with a guitar, and in the middle of a spirited flamenco tune the singer, billed as Señorita De La O, made a dazzling entrance, whirling her full, ruffled red skirts like flames. The crowd burst into applause as she began the exuberant song. Her staccato words pelted the room like firecrackers. Such vitality! The audience was caught up in her energy and roared approval at the conclusion. The singer had a mellow contralto voice, obviously trained. "She's marvelous!" Miguel said, and Holly agreed.

With a lightning change of mood, Señorita De La O launched into a ballad that expressed the pain of unfulfilled dreams, a popular Latin theme. Her emotional delivery was so genuine, so poignant, it seemed to come straight from the heart. The room grew hushed. The song was familiar to Miguel, for he mouthed the words along with her.

"*¡Dios mío!*" he suddenly gasped.

He looked at Holly as they both said at once: "Juana!"

Under all that makeup and the elaborate hairstyle, she looked very different. No wonder she hadn't wanted Miguel to come here. She'd kept her theatrical talent very secret. *Señorita De La O?* Was she leading some kind of double life? And why?

"We'd better go," Holly whispered. "I'm afraid she'll be upset when she sees us."

Miguel didn't move. "Ah, now many things make sense to me concerning this lady," he said. He watched intently, almost hungrily, while the beauteous Juana fin-

ished her program. As the applause died down, Miguel
rose and walked the few steps to the platform. He bowed,
then offered his arm. Mixed emotions crossed Juana's
face as she recognized him, but her savoir faire remained
intact. She tucked her hand in his arm and flashed him a
brilliant smile. He brought her to the table where Holly
sat, motioned to the waiter and ordered three Pedro Do-
mecq cream sherries.

She settled herself in the chair with much flouncing of
skirts and jangling of bracelets. "So the masquerade is
over! You should have taken my advice, dear Miguel.
Now you must listen to unhappy explanations."

He laid a hand on hers, quieting her drumming fingers. "Not unless you wish to tell us, *querida* Juana."

"Why do I work all day in La Tienda, and at night in
a piano bar? I tell you. It is because of necessity."

How could that be? Holly wondered. The woman had
only herself to support, and the way she'd saved she had
to have a comfortable nest egg by now.

Juana nodded knowingly. "I know what you think.
Juana is greedy. Juana wants her dream house at once.
Not so. There can be no house. Only the dream." Her
chin rose firmly and her eyes were brilliant with unshed
tears.

"If you are in trouble, I want to help," Miguel said
earnestly.

"And surely all those relatives of yours will be glad to
come to your assistance," Holly added.

Juana laughed mirthlessly. "No cousins. No aunts or
uncles either. I always yearned for a family. In Mexico I
have no one, so I invent them. My invisible support system."

"You mean no relatives in Acapulco? No Uncle Tomás in Tampico? No cousins at all in Laredo?"

"Fiction, every one of them."

"Do you mind explaining?" Miguel asked kindly.

"Not a pretty tale. I've told no one. Maybe the burden will lighten if I share it," she said finally, perhaps encouraged by Miguel's comforting hand. She told her story then. "I ran off and married a well-to-do Mexican businessman who heard me sing at a Barcelona music festival. Oh, my parents tried to stop us, but I was in love," she said wistfully at the memory. "He was too old for me, they said, too worldly, too glib, and a foreigner! I turned a deaf ear and broke their hearts. I haven't heard a word from them since.

"He brought me to Mexico City where we made our home. A year later he was found in his car with a bullet in his heart. More shock followed when I learned he was connected with the underworld, smuggling drugs, illegal aliens. It was all over the newspapers. I hadn't the slightest suspicion. I was devastated. *¡Dios mío!* How naive I was! Whenever I questioned him about his work, he always laughed and told me to stick to my music—it wasn't necessary to bother my pretty head about the intricacies of business. We lived exceedingly well in a lovely home with servants, but not a single asset was found. I was left virtually penniless.

"I was too ashamed to go back to my parents and lived in terror that they might find out about the man I'd married. My father is a respected and well-known judge in Barcelona. He would have suffered terribly if it were revealed that his daughter had married a criminal.

"Then came the telephone calls and letters demanding repayment of a loan supposedly made to my husband by one of his associates. When I denied any knowledge of the loan and explained my situation, he only laughed and said it was no concern of his and said I could plan on the same fate as my husband if I contacted the police.

"When he threatened to go to Spain and extract the money from my father, I agreed to pay him. Every month a courier comes to La Tienda to collect, always posing as a tourist." She shook her head in a hopeless gesture. "For six long years this has been going on! I haven't been able to save a penny until recently when, during evenings, I turn into Señorita De la O. Thus far he doesn't know about that lady."

"*Madre de Dios*, Juana! Are you saying you've been giving your money to that *bandido* all these years?" Miguel cried.

"*Señor*, what else can I do?"

"The man is a blackmailer. We must put a stop to it *immediatamente*!"

"But he's dangerous. He's threatened murder, and I couldn't bear it if he contacted my father."

"Don't worry. I'll take the matter up with the police at once, and the next time this criminal appears at La Tienda they'll host a warm reception for him. Relax, *querida* Juana, your long travail has ended. The chief of police is one of my closest friends. Allow me to take care of everything."

For a moment Juana put her head in her hands, then she took a deep breath and locked her fingers in Miguel's again. She seemed unable to speak.

With an apology, a waiter interrupted them. "Pardon, but is Señorita Jones at this table? There is an urgent telephone call for her."

Heart pounding, Holly followed him to a small office. Only Lee knew where she was. In his frustration had he done something terrible? *Please, God, don't let it be trouble!*

"Holly?" There was a tremor in Lee's voice, and it sounded strained and unnatural. "Someone called from a hospital and said Chris was in an accident. I couldn't understand the person's Spanish very well, and she only knew a little English. I don't know what happened or where he is. Could you come?"

CHAPTER FOURTEEN

HOLLY SAT in the taxi clutching her fists so tightly that the nails dug into her flesh. Fear pounded at her in giant waves. What kind of accident had Chris been in? It had to be serious, didn't it? Otherwise Chris would have called instead of a staff member at the hospital. It was taking forever to get to Chris's house where she knew Lee was keeping an agonizing wait. Most taxi drivers in Oaxaca seemed to consider themselves competitors in the Grand Prix. This one surely was half asleep. *Live, Chris, live,* she prayed over and over.

Somehow she'd managed to convince Miguel not to come with her. She'd merely told him Lee was having problems and that she wanted to stay with him for a while. Holly had noticed what had happened between Juana and Miguel tonight. They needed time, just the two of them, without the disturbance of someone else's troubles. A pang of loneliness had stabbed her when she'd watched them together. She'd return tonight to an empty room.

The taxi eased to the curb. She let herself out, handed the driver a bill and ran to the door where Lee stood waiting.

"Thanks for coming. Hope you don't mind," he said. His eyes were red as if he'd been crying.

"Tell me exactly what happened."

"All I know is that some lady called from a hospital and jabbered so fast that I understood only a word or two."

"I'll start telephoning." She stopped short as she spotted a suitcase by the door and a soccer ball in a mesh bag. "What's this all about?"

He ducked his head for a moment, then resolutely met her eyes. "I was going to split. Of course I had no idea where I was going, and hardly any money." His mouth twisted. "Really smart, right?" He choked back a sob. "I feel terrible, Holly. Those things I said about him, and all the time he was lying hurt in some hospital."

"Don't worry about that now. Find me the telephone book."

She dialed the first hospital listed. No patient by the name of Brooke there, but they gave her the number of the hospital that accepted most emergency cases.

"Yes, Señor Brooke was brought in late this afternoon," someone said in Spanish at the admissions desk. "*Momento*, I'll refer your call to the attending nurse."

It seemed that Holly waited ages. Lee stood next to her, his body bent forward, every muscle tensed as if willing the news to be positive. Finally someone answered. "Nurse Ramirez speaking. Señor Brooke has a concussion."

"Concussion!" She was falling, spinning endlessly. Head injuries could be fatal. "Is it serious?"

"Concussion is always serious. Luckily there is no skull fracture or intracranical hemorrhage. Nevertheless, he must remain in the hospital for a day or two until it is determined that no neurological symptoms are present," the nurse said in a weary monotone. She might as well have been measuring out spoons of Pablum.

"What happened? Do you know?"

"A witness said Señor Brooke was leaving the village of Teotitlán when he swerved to avoid hitting a cyclist, skidded into a ditch and turned over. He was thrown from the vehicle."

"When can we see him?"

"He's still unconscious. Not until he's out of intensive care. We can't predict at this time. *Perdóneme*, I must go."

"Thank you, Nurse," she mumbled, and turned to the waiting Lee, her wrist so weak she could barely replace the receiver in its cradle.

"He's unconscious. Concussion," she said, and repeated the facts to the anxious boy.

"What can we do?"

She shook her head and tried to keep her voice steady. "We can only wait."

He sat in silence as he took in the information. Suddenly he leaped up. "Oh, no!" he cried. "What happened to his camera? Do you think it got left at the site? If something happened to it, he'll be totally wiped out. He bought it just before we came down here."

Yes, it would devastate Chris if his expensive camera were ruined, especially now when he was under so much pressure to complete his filming. "We can check with the hospital, or perhaps the police have it."

"Hurry. We have to know." Two more calls verified their worst fears. The hospital knew nothing, and the police were holding it but said it was smashed beyond repair.

"But surely Chris has other cameras at home?"

"Yeah, but they're sixteen millimeter. He wanted to try this documentary in Super-8 as an experiment," Lee said glumly.

Double adversity. Not only would valuable time be lost because Chris was incapacitated, but who knew how long it would take to replace his gear? "It's probably insured, but the paperwork could take weeks."

"I remember the dealer who sold him his Super-8. Les something or other, an all-right guy, real friendly. Maybe we could call and ask him to send another camera."

"Unless he knows Chris well, I doubt he'd send it without payment."

"What are we waiting for? Call. I have thirty-five dollars I've been saving to buy some rosewood. Will that help?"

"Of course," she said only half believing. She knew nothing about cameras, but was certain they were expensive. "We'll work out something, but maybe we shouldn't interfere. Chris may have other ideas."

Lee's expression grew stern. "Listen, Holly," he said in the manner of a kindly father reproving a daughter. "He's in a jam. He's in a foreign country with no one to depend on except us. I think we ought to do something."

Chastened, Holly agreed. "It's too late to call tonight. Come by La Tienda in the morning, and we'll call the hospital before we do anything. I'm going home now."

"Okay. I'll stop by on my way to my lesson. Hey," he said, and then hesitated, turning shy. "Could you stay a minute longer? I want to show you something. You'll see why I feel like such a heel." He led her to Chris's desk in the cluttered den. "He keeps all his film stuff in this room. It's off-limits to everyone. I couldn't find the telephone book tonight so I came looking in here."

Lee pointed to the life-sized ironwood tern done in simple, sparse lines, its forked tail saucily tilted and its neck arched as if it were ready to snap up some hapless victim. "See what I mean? You know how I always yell about how he doesn't give a darn about my work? All the time he must have had this on his desk. It was one of the first sculptures I made, and it earned me ten dollars. He probably bought it at the market where Señor Hamilton sends some of our work on consignment."

But her attention had suddenly turned elsewhere. On the far wall hung a portrait. Hers. Miguel had talked as if it would be hung in the library at Casa Avalon, but it had never appeared, and she'd forgotten all about it. She recalled Miguel's remarks about how he sensed something between her and Chris. He must have given the portrait to him, and Chris naturally felt he had to hang it.

Holly glanced at the glass display case that had held her own ceramics. She'd assumed he'd sold them to Hugo's, but they were all still there. So he hadn't tossed her out of his life completely after all. Why? "We all make mistakes," she said bleakly to Lee, knowing hers were the greater ones. "Don't waste your energy on regrets. Concentrate on how to convince the dealer to send a new camera."

She called a taxi, and all the way home tried to deal with the continual vision of Chris, pale and still as death in the hospital bed. What if he never regained consciousness? A concussion was potentially dangerous. There could be internal bleeding, destruction of brain tissue, infection... *Oh, God, let him live!*

WHEN SHE ARRIVED at work the next morning, a Señor Rodriguez had opened up and explained he was replacing Juana for the coming week while she dealt with some legal matters. With the blackmailer? Holly had read of such criminal goings-on, but things like that had always seemed to occur in remote worlds inhabited by gangsters, never in ingenuous places like Oaxaca. Miguel would be in his element, fighting far more than windmills this time in order to come to the rescue of his lady love.

Holly looked at her watch frequently, aching to call the hospital, but she'd promised to wait for Lee since he couldn't cope with the language. When he at last arrived, she asked him to take her place at the counter while she used the telephone. She reached the nurse's station promptly.

"Yes, Señor Brooke regained consciousness early this morning. He's recovering well, but absolutely no visitors are permitted until tomorrow," a nurse said.

"He's awake!" Holly cried. Elation shot through her like adrenaline.

"All right!" Lee cried, and gave a whistle of joy. "When can we see him?"

"Visiting hours tomorrow evening."

"Great! Now let's see if we can get him a new camera so we'll have some good news for him."

After a considerable hassle with the operator, Holly finally managed to get the dealer's number and put through the call. When the dealer came on, she handed the phone to the impatient boy.

A few minutes later a smiling Lee announced that the store had a complete record of Chris's original purchase and would duplicate the order and ship it airmail as soon as a two-hundred-dollar deposit was sent. The camera should arrive within two or three days after that.

"I'll see to it," Holly said, and was grateful her checking account would cover it.

"Be sure to add my pesos," he said, pulling bills from his pocket. She started to refuse, then realized she shouldn't.

"I'll take care of it when the bank opens after siesta," she promised. They planned to meet at the hospital tomorrow evening for the seven o'clock visiting hour, and Lee took off for his wood-sculpturing class.

The hours dragged. It was almost two entire days until she could see Chris. The nurse said he was doing as well as could be expected, but what did that mean? No complications? Anxiety racked her like a fever.

She dressed with care the next evening, choosing a two-piece knit dress of the violet shade Chris had once told her she ought to wear more often. Its classic lines gently molded her figure, and the color made her complexion glow softly, like the pearls she clasped around her neck, the pearls he'd given her so long ago.

Hospitals always depressed Holly, and the moment she entered she became aware of the antiseptic smell, the impersonal staff and the ominous hush that told of lives in limbo. Lee had already arrived. He jumped up to greet her. They stopped at the reception desk for Chris's room number, then walked down the long hall to find it.

They stood for a moment at his doorway and peered at the prone form on the bed, then tiptoed in. Chris's head was swathed in bandages, and his eyes were closed. His pallor took her breath away, and his stillness fed her fears. Emotion choked her. It was hard to imagine the intense, vibrant Chris in that inert body. His vulnerability was almost more than she could bear.

Chris moved slightly and stirred. "Marissa," he mumbled. "Nurse, get me Marissa." He must have touched the call button. A nurse appeared at once.

"Sorry," she said. "Only one visitor at a time."

Lee looked so downcast that Holly moved into the hall. "I'll wait in the lobby. You go first."

"You're sure?"

"Of course. It doesnt matter." She knew he was anxious to reassure Chris concerning the camera. Besides, she'd begun to have second thoughts about staying. She walked to the waiting room, found a chair and picked up a magazine, but she thumbed through the pages without reading a word.

The worst was over. Chris was going to be okay. She felt weak with relief, but another truth pounded away at her. *I'm breaking all the rules by coming here. He doesn't really want to see me. I'll do all I can for him, but I don't want to force myself on him. So leave. Now. Walking away builds character. Oh, sure. Damn.*

She and Chris had made a pact not to see each other again. Every word of their last quarrel was still etched in her brain. Did that rule out a visit like this? It hurt desperately to see him, even briefly. It made her ache for a time when she could talk with him, hear his laughter, revel in his vitality. But those were the very things she'd vowed to forget.

And wasn't that Marissa's name she'd heard him mutter? In spite of everything was Marissa the woman he turned to when he was in need? Not her. Not even Lee. She'd better think things through carefully. Could she trust herself to be objective?

CHRIS STIRRED and sighed, but his eyes remained closed. Every time he opened them a strange kind of blurring expanded the room so that it floated dimly around him as though he were swimming underwater in some deep, shadowy grotto. It made him nauseous. He didn't need that in addition to the savage ache in his head.

He had no idea how long he'd been in the place. Nurses wouldn't tell him anything…straightened the blanket and told him to rest. Bicycle…yes. Now he remembered. Old man on a bicycle. Swerved in front of him. Jeep skidded, rolled over…couldn't remember anything else. Too fast…yes, he'd driven too fast…had to get to Lee's exhibition. Damn the luck…film schedule shot to hell. What about deadline? Must get out of this place. Now.

Tried to get in touch with Bill. Nurse called for him earlier, but no answer. Turn the scriptwriting over to Bill. That would help. Where the devil was he? Get Marissa to track him down. Hell, he didn't want to call *her*. Maybe he'd have to. Wouldn't tell her the real reason, or she'd head down here. God, what a mess! He felt for the nurse's call button and missed. "Marissa," he mumbled. Yes, call Marissa, but be cagey.

"Can I help?" a voice asked. Not the nurse's.

Chris opened his leaden lids slowly and saw an anxious, boyish face peering down at him. Things were clearer now. Good. "Lee, is that you?"

"Sure is. How do you feel?"

"Well enough to go home," he growled.

"At the desk they said another week."

"No way. Sorry I didn't get to your wingding. Something happened to me on the way to the gallery."

"Well, I guess! We missed you."

"So how did it go?"

"It was a blast! Totally terrific!"

"I talked to Señor Hamilton a while back. He's excited about your work. I'm proud of you."

"Thanks," Lee said, his voice skidding around several levels. "Hey, did you know the old Jeep fared a lot better than you did? I went to the garage where it's located, and they've just about got it fixed up as good as new. There were only a few dents and a broken bumper."

"Good. What say I try to arrange for them to release the Jeep to you and you can pick me up and take me home?"

"Say, I'd like that. When?"

"Soon as I talk the doctor into dismissing me. You can go pick up my camera, too. Understand the police are holding it for me."

"It won't do any good. I already checked. Your camera got totaled."

Chris felt as if someone had landed a hard punch in his stomach. "I should have known. Might as well give up. I suppose that means the film inside is shot to hell."

"If it isn't exposed, you could send it to that Film Life place that you used once, the one that restores damaged film. Hey, don't worry about it. We'll handle it."

"Oh, you're into sleight of hand now?"

"No, just telephoning. I talked to the dealer where you bought your Super-8, and he's sending another. Holly and I mailed the deposit yesterday. The camera should be here by the time you get home," Lee said in the manner of an efficient administrative assistant.

Chris closed his eyes for a moment. Holly had done this for him? His heart stood still. The mention of her name had hit him hard. "Sounds like you and Holly have been busy."

"Yeah, well, we figured you'd be real upset about not finishing up on time, so we wanted to help. My adopted dad always said when a person was in trouble, his family should rally around."

"I see."

"Of course, you and Holly and I aren't exactly related, but we rallied anyway. We're the only family you have, right?"

"Holly said that?"

"Well not really, but she helped with the phoning and tended to sending the deposit and all. That proves something."

"It sure does, and I appreciate it. I suppose Holly didn't mention whether or not she might drop by to see me?"

Lee looked at him oddly. "She came with me. Didn't you see her?"

"Came with you!" He raised himself then fell back with a groan. "Where is she?"

"In the waiting room. The nurse said only one visitor at a time."

"Well, go get her. On the double!"

Lee scurried out of the room. Chris waited impatiently. Damn hospital rules. What was wrong with having only two visitors? Minutes passed. Where was she? d she wandered out of the waiting room? Breathless, Lee finally returned.

"She left. Said something about how too many visitors weren't good for you. I kinda got the idea she thought you didn't care to see her." He shuffled his feet uncomfortably. "I'd better go, too. The nurse said I shouldn't stay long."

"Go after her. I want to see her."

"She's long gone. I walked all the way to the foyer with her trying to persuade her to come."

"What got into her? Tell her to call me tonight. Doctor's orders." He indicated the phone at his bedside.

Lee grinned broadly. "Count on me!"

"Thanks, Lee. You're a good man."

Lee's olive complexion took on a rosy hue, but his eyes never wavered. He reached a hand down on the coverlet, a hair breadth from Chris's. His lips moved silently as if trying out one unsuitable word after another. "Sir," he said finally. "I sure hope you get well soon." He turned away abruptly and left.

Chris brushed a hand across his eyes. *Sir.* No impersonal "you" or "he" this time? Lee had called him "sir" once before, but tonight it somehow sounded different. The tone of his voice had expanded the word, made it sound almost as comfortable and familiar as a name. He'd heard concern, respect, and yes, even a little affection. He closed his eyes and smiled. Actually, "sir" sounded okay. Yes, "sir" wasn't bad at all.

He felt the bedside table to make sure the nurse hadn't moved the telephone. Holly would probably call any minute. Holly and Lee were the only family he had, Lee had said.

The empty spaces of his life loomed sharply. He had no home filled with the sound of children's voices and laughter, with life rocketing around in every room. No feminine sounds, home sounds, encircling him with support and caring. Instead, he'd had to ad-lib a blundering adult role with an enigmatic teenager. Would he be able to change that?

CHAPTER FIFTEEN

HOLLY HAD BEEN UP since five in the morning. She'd gone to the huge new market at the edge of town to look for the handwoven table linen Juana wanted to use at her wedding reception. The pieces were made by a family in Santo Tomás and were often snapped up by discerning tourists before they ever got to the market. Holly had offered to see if any came in this weekend.

Juana was walking on air these days. The police had apprehended the blackmailer the next time he had come to collect, and his permanent address had been established at the city jail. During that tense time Miguel had remained firmly at Juana's side, guiding her through the tedious legal procedures, and offering continual strength and support. Apparently it didn't take long for him to decide they were made for each other, and the wedding was coming up soon.

Holly wholeheartedly agreed that it was a perfect match. Juana would be the kind of sparkling, effervescent hostess Miguel would be proud to have at his side in his active social life. She would pamper him with her herbs as well as with her sweet talk, and he would love every minute of it. Juana adored Miguel's courtliness and let him know it, but her own common sense, wit and complete lack of snobbery would keep him on an even keel.

Bowing to Miguel's wishes, Juana no longer worked at La Tienda Artesanías. She was having the time of her life planning the wedding. Miguel had called Juana's parents and had given them a warm invitation to be his houseguests during their stay for the festivities. After the long estrangement, Juana was ecstatic about the coming reunion. Holly was truly happy for this valiant little woman who, after so many troubled years, had at last achieved her "impossible dream." At the same time she lived with an almost unbearable ache that her own situation remained hopeless.

Holly had chosen to go to the market early in order to see the farmers arrive with their produce. What a sight it had been! They came by ox cart, donkey cart, horse drawn wagon, ancient truck, bicycle and foot, all laden with things to sell. Many waded across the nearby Atoyac River, balancing goods on their heads.

She gauged that the market itself sprawled over about fifteen to twenty acres, some stalls housed under canvas and some in several large buildings. At that early morning hour it became a blending of vigorous humanity, conversation, laughter, and people frantically arranging their produce. Each vendor vied with his neighbor in making ornamental displays of his wares: towers of tomatoes, little pyramids of herbs and spices on mats, shining heaps of maize, mosaics of green chilies. Vegetables were larger than any she'd ever seen: basketball-sized cabbages, huge red radishes, emerald cucumbers that looked like melons. The soil of the Oaxaca valley was rich indeed.

Wistfully Holly thought how much fun it would have been if she and Chris could have visited the market together. She knew he would have bought her a bunch of violets at one of the colorful flower stands where the vendors' faces mingled among the blooms like bronze chrysanthemums. He'd have asked to photograph some of the pretty girls who wore large bunches of green onions pressed down on their heads, and he would never have been able to resist the yeasty fragrance of the bread counters, piled high with loaves of all shapes and sizes. Holly could imagine them coming home with an armload.

Customers, mainly men, joked and chatted among the stalls while they consumed their inevitable tortillas filled with beans and chilies. Juana had pointed out that the food was actually very nutritious. The small black beans were full of protein, and the maize in the tortillas provided calcium. Chilies were rich in vitamin C. Hot chocolate flavored with cinnamon seemed to be a favorite drink, and Holly noticed that many of the vendors sipped colored liquids tied in plastic bags with straws poking out of them.

Women sat behind their produce, ready to bargain at the least show of interest and, between times, exchanged lively bits of gossip with their neighbors. One woman had a drowsy baby strapped to her back with the ever useful rebozo. Other small children played nearby and sucked on bits of fruit.

In the crafts section Holly found the tablecloths Juana wanted, just as the weaver unpacked them. Looking at the man's tired eyes and threadbare coat, she didn't have the heart to bargain. The price seemed infinitely fair as quoted.

It was an earthy market that in no way catered to tourists, but was actually the best tourist attraction in town, she decided as she walked back to the Casa.

She showered quickly and dressed. At noon she was to meet Lee with his soccer team. They were going on an outing and picnic to Monte Albán and she'd promised to act as a chaperone. Although they'd spoken on the phone, she hadn't seen him since the night the two of them had visited Chris in the hospital. He'd called her the next morning.

"Hey, where did you go last night? I tried to reach you?" he'd asked her.

"I went to a movie," she'd said, hoping to forestall any more questions.

"A movie! Why would you do that? He was disappointed because you didn't stay."

"To tell you the truth, I saw right away it was a mistake to come. We had made an agreement not to see each other again, and I realized I was breaking it."

"But this was different. He was hurt. I never thought you'd act like that, Holly." He'd sounded upset.

Well, she was upset, too. Sadly, the mistakes of adults affected others besides themselves, namely innocents such as Lee.

She put the finishing touches on her makeup and picked up her bagged lunch. She hadn't yet visited the ancient archaeological ruins so she was looking forward to the day.

The boys were nearly all Americans, Canadians and Australians who were involved in a summer program for foreign youngsters. Holly had no sooner arrived at the meeting place when Lee rushed up to her, greeting her with a wide grin and telling her how much he appreciated her coming. He introduced her to his coach and hurried her into a van with a half dozen of the boys. Lee, apparently in charge of transportation, told the father who was driving to go ahead and the other cars would follow as soon as they were filled.

The ruins of Monte Albán were only about six miles from town up a narrow, winding road that reached a plateau two thousand feet above the valley. Cars were parked in a special area, and they trod a dusty path to the ruins. She was glad she could help Lee out today. He'd been so eager to have someone there to act as family for him that even had there been a conflict she would have canceled it in favor of the expedition. She knew Chris was too involved with his documentary to give up an entire day. It would have meant a lot to Lee, but he was becoming far more understanding of Chris's work.

Watching the bright-eyed, exuberant boy as he organized the group, she couldn't help but wonder how it would be if she and Chris married again and the three of them became a family. *Stop indulging in fairy tales!* She'd pointed out often enough to Chris that it would be folly to allow their hearts to rule their heads, that their very real differences had separated them once and were bound to do so again. No matter how much they belabored the question, they were wrong for each other. He'd finally agreed almost too emphatically.

They rounded a bend and Holly gazed in wonder at the ancient buildings spread out before them: temples, an observatory, great plazas, a ball court, patios, platforms, sacrificial altars, an abundance of stairways and much more. Most of the walls were half standing, some weathered down almost to their foundations, but the beauty remained. No wonder Monte Albán was considered one of the greatest works by ancient man; they had no wheels or metal tools two thousand years ago. How had they moved and fit together the massive stones and constructed the tall, grand pillars with only crude implements? Awe filled her at the beauty and mystery of it.

The ball court was one structure that had remained almost intact, and they walked over to it now. It was an open T-shaped building with a playing field in the center and stone bleachers on either side where the boys now perched like a flock of chattering pigeons. The narrow ledges offered scant room to sit. The ancient Indians must have been even smaller than their present tiny descendants, Holly reflected.

She looked around. Her services as a chaperone were scarcely needed. There seemed to be two sets of parents, and the last stragglers included two other men who strode along with Lee between them. Her attention was caught by a familiar gesture as one man ran a hand through wheat-colored hair. Chris! No doubt about it. Something inside her caught fire. She felt it instantly in her quickened breathing and racing pulse.

As they climbed up into the section across from her, she noted that Lee was monitoring her closely, and was also keeping tabs on Chris. The scalawag! He'd probably worked this all out with the strategy of a general plotting a critical maneuver. She recalled his pitch asking her to act as chaperone. She had thought he'd come on pretty strong. How hard he worked for happy endings, not realizing the problems he caused. Well, she'd try to be a model of calm and poise in this ticklish situation.

One of the mothers asked for quiet and launched into a few facts about the site and the ball court in particular. The boys listened attentively. So did Chris. Sunlight washed over his fair hair and intent expression so that he seemed to stand out from the group. But then he'd always stood head and shoulders above most men, not only in looks but in ability.

He affected her equilibrium just by sitting there. She hated how he could subject her to ravaging highs and lows and destroy any chance of objectivity. Was it a privilege or a curse to love such a man? What would he do when he spotted her? Ignore her? Leave? She grew almost unbearably tense awaiting the moment.

Everyone rose to follow the guide to the next point of interest. Holly guiltily realized that the only thing she recalled from the spiel about the ball court was the ancient custom of the losing team's captain having to give up his life. Apparently that fact had had a sobering effect on the boys. They spoke in hushed tones as they walked to the central plaza.

She stopped for a moment to remove her shoe in order to find the pebble or whatever it was that was biting into her foot. An errant breeze ruffled her hair.

"Smell the wind. It has September in it," Chris said, coming up behind her. Memories washed over her. The lines were from a poem they had both loved.

She whirled around and scanned his face. He was grinning. She curbed a barely resistible urge to reach out and smooth his collar down. "Well, what do you know, another chaperone," she said.

"You, too? I'd say our boy is an expert recruiter." They looked at each other, weighing response and reaction, and suddenly broke out laughing. His laugh was open and generous and still touched off an inner excitement in her.

"Recruiter? I'd say more a peacemaker," she said. "His intentions were good, so please don't scold him."

"On the contrary, I complimented him on his excellent logistics. He organized the entire expedition, you know. But all that aside, and considering our recent discussions, do you want me to make myself scarce?"

She felt as if someone had just flipped a wet towel in her face. "Let's not disappoint him. Why don't we just relax and enjoy the day."

"My sentiments exactly. Here, let me fix that." He took her shoe and pulled out a tack that had somehow worked its way into the sole. "Practicing walking on nails, are you?" he said as he knelt, held her ankle and slipped on her shoe. His hand lingered, and she pretended not to notice as warmth traveled up her leg and thigh.

"Where to now?" she asked as he stood up. The boys were far ahead.

"Aha. You didn't pay very good attention to the lecturer. The famous Tomb Seven is next. Discovered by an archaeologist in 1932."

"I've seen some of the artifacts from it in the museum—a fabulous collection."

Everyone took turns descending the steps into the dark two-room tomb where the ancient monarch had been buried with his worldly treasures. Afterward they followed the guide to the other structures.

Chris had wandered off with Lee, and they seemed to be having a lively conversation. Holly wondered if Chris felt uncomfortable with her unexpected company. He didn't look or act it, but he was much better at masking his moods than he used to be. She watched Lee's dark head and Chris's fair one bent to examine some indecipherable Zapotec glyphs and felt her throat constrict. How good it was to see them like this, no longer strangers.

In the sun's uncompromising glare, she saw the changes that seven years had brought to Chris's familiar features. The determined set of his jaw had not lessened, but maturity had added a kind of tolerance that made him infinitely more attractive.

Two hours later the hot, tired group straggled back to the parking lot where there was a small refreshment stand. After buying cold soft drinks, they found a clump of trees that offered adequate shade and sat down to enjoy their picnic.

Chris came over and sat next to her. "*Señorita*, would you have a little extra to share with a poor, starving peasant? I came without any food, and knowing Lee, he'll wolf down every crumb in that lunch bag of his."

"It just so happens the cook had her antennae pointed in the right direction," she said, and pulled out bananas, peaches, a papaya, several tortillas wrapped around chicken and beans, a package of cookies and a thermos of coffee. "I recall that depriving you of lunch was something akin to relieving you of your citizenship."

"You'd better believe it," he said hungrily, eyeing the treats spread before him.

They sat among the other adults who seemed to assume they were members of Lee's family. Their eyes met in agreement to offer no explanation.

"That boy of yours is quite an athlete," one of the men said to them.

"I'm glad to hear that," Chris replied. "Unfortunately I've never been able to get to the games. They're played when I'm working."

"I expect you're proud of him, too, Mrs. Brooke."

"Oh yes! I gather he's a great quarterback," she said with enthusiasm, and hoped she wouldn't have to admit she'd not seen any games either.

The man looked at her oddly, and Chris rolled his eyes.

"Get your games straight, lady. Quarterbacks play football." Chris muttered in her ear.

"That's what I get for dissembling," she said later when they were alone. "I never was any good at covering up anything."

"I know. It's one of your most endearing qualities." Chris gave her a look that made her heart turn over.

It was late afternoon when the last of the group walked back to the parking lot. Several cars had already left, and Lee directed the rest of the boys into the remaining van. He came running up to Holly and Chris.

"Say, I don't know how it happened, but the rides are all taken care of. No one's left to go back with you, Sir, except Holly. Why don't you stay awhile longer and do some more exploring. Most of the adults have already been here before. You might not get another chance like this."

"I see what you mean. Thanks a lot. You're an expert planner. Do you work on the strategy for your team plays?"

"Sure do. I'm really good at it. And one more thing, you don't have to worry about getting home early on my account. Mike's mom invited me to see a soccer game with them and stay all night afterward. The game will be played by real pros. It's okay, isn't it?"

Chris agreed it would be a treat. "What time can I expect you home?"

"Well, tomorrow is Sunday. How about noon?" He barely waited for Chris's assent, then took off like an Olympic runner.

"I can see it now," Chris said. "He'll soon be selecting the clothes I wear, choosing the food I eat and scheduling the time I brush my teeth!"

Holly laughed. "I love it."

"Well, come along, we'd better get moving if we want to accomplish our game plan."

And what was the game plan? she wondered. She decided she was having too good a time to find out.

"Would you be interested in listening to the first draft of the script for my documentary?" he asked. "I'd appreciate any input you might have." She thought she detected a little anxiety in the asking.

"I'm no expert, but I'd love to hear it."

"Just a minute then. It's in the Jeep because I want to run off a copy on a friend's machine on the way home. Haven't been ready to do that until now." He brought out a bulky notebook, and they walked back to the temple constructed over Tomb Seven. They sat down in the shade of one of the pillars. "I'd hoped Bill Delaplane would do the script for me, but he's tied up on another project. I have to sweat it out by myself."

Bill? So it wasn't Marissa. "You're an excellent writer, Chris. I always wondered why you turned that part over to other people."

"Never enough time. Seems as if I'm always trying to make a deadline. Like now. The accident fixed me but good."

"I know. I'm sorry."

"Incidentally, why did you run away that night at the hospital?"

"I realized I'd broken my promise. You probably felt the same the night of the sympnony."

"Purely unintentional. I ran into Colonel Hidalgo, and I waited too long to get back to my seat. I couldn't find you afterward. As for visiting me, couldn't you have made an exception considering I was practically on my deathbed?"

"Well, if I heard correctly, you weren't exactly climbing the walls in hopes of my visit. I gathered Marissa was the woman of the hour."

"That's what I get for thinking out loud. Marissa was the only person I knew who could get in touch with Bill for me. I was disappointed when you didn't return."

"Keep a promise, it says in my rule book."

"The gospel according to Holly! Do you always follow the rules?"

"Almost always." But with Chris sitting so close beside her, she wanted to forget every one of them. *Dangerous territory. Change the subject.* "With all you have to do, how were you able to get away today?"

"I shouldn't have, but Lee and I have been doing so much better lately, I didn't want to lose ground. Would you believe he's finally calling me something?"

"I've noticed. It's 'Sir,' isn't it? You two have come a long way. I'm proud of both of you."

"Lord, I couldn't take failing again!"

"Failing?"

"Human relationships. I failed with you."

"I contributed to our failure, too. I know that now," she said softly. She twisted her fingers together. Where was this conversation headed? This wasn't the time to go over the whole miserable aftermath of their divorce. He gave her a searching look and waited for her to continue. She shrugged. "Best to skip confessions. I'm anxious to hear your script." He appeared to want her to continue talking, but she picked up the heavy notebook and handed it to him.

For almost two hours he read, stopping to describe the visual portions so the dialogue and commentary made sense. His mobile expression ranged from despair at a poignant scene during a child's funeral to excitement at the skill of a master weaver. When he finished, she sat for a long time. The words had touched her deeply, and her throat ached almost too much to speak. "It's beautiful. Don't change a word of it."

"Well, it will have to do. Bill can't help me out this time."

Nor Marissa either, apparently. "I've never realized before that screenwriting was such a difficult craft, but you've done it! Your story comes alive. Your people are real, and they relate to one another. Even without seeing the film, the words made me cry as well as smile. It's human and durable, Chris. It has to be a winner."

He leaned over and took her hand, then released it as if he'd acted before thinking. "Do you realize how much it means to have someone believe in you?"

She nodded. "Yes, I do know."

His expression turned rueful. "You and I weren't very supportive of each other, were we?"

"On a scale of one to ten, about zero. But..."

"But?" he prodded, and his eyes glowed so eagerly she had to look away.

She jumped up and brushed the dust from her clothing. "Come on, it's getting cloudy. Let's take a quick look at the observatory, and then I'd better go home."

He tucked the heavy notebook under his arm, then decided to stuff it into a crevice above the doorway of the tomb. "I'll pick it up on the way back to the Jeep."

"Will it be safe?"

"Who'd want a beat-up old manuscript? Besides, it's getting late. Everybody's gone home. Come on, I'll race you. We need to get the kinks out of our limbs after sitting so long."

They ran across the field and up the steep stairway of the odd arrow-shaped building. Laughing and breathless, they chased each other through the structure, darting in and out of the several doorways.

Once, they ran into each other, and for a moment they stood, his hands on her shoulders, their bodies so close she couldn't tell whether it was her heart or his beating so wildly. He leaned down as if to kiss her. She willed the moment to continue, but he suddenly drew away. *He's remembering,* she thought, *and he's not about to get burned again.*

"Come on," he said, looking up at the dark clouds that were moving in fast. "It's starting to rain. Let's run for it."

The shower pelted them as they hurried back to the Jeep. When she slipped, he helped her up and set her back on her feet, but let go as they started running again. The break in their physical contact became a nebulous pain. If only she knew what he was thinking. It seemed they were always on the edge of things—on the edge of intimacy, the edge of communication, the edge of being truly themselves.

By the time they reached the Jeep, the rain had become a downpour. He opened the door for her and helped her in. "We'd better get out of here fast. The road will be a mess if this keeps up. Are you soaked?"

"Damp, but the temperature is warm so no matter." They had become two strangers discussing the weather. She was actually a woman in love, trying not to show it. She wondered what he was really feeling.

Chris concentrated on the slippery road as they zigzagged down the steep hill. She hated for the day to end, but any sensible person would avoid more togetherness.

"Care to stop for a cup of coffee?" he said when they reached the city limits.

I want to do that more than anything else in the whole world right now. She pointed to her wrinkled, damp slacks and blouse. "I'd better get home," she said firmly. What if it were possible, she thought idly, to record their conversation, inserting the simultaneous thoughts that went on in their heads? That would surely be interesting. At any rate, it would prove how poor they were at communicating.

A few minutes later he dropped her off at Casa Avalon. If he had asked her out for coffee again, she knew she would have gone with him. But they were wrong for each other, in spite of the chemistry that invariably erupted between them. One of them had to be strong.

Feeling virtuous but thoroughly miserable, she went to her room, undressed, climbed into a hot bath, then went to bed. Two hours later she woke with a start.

Wind howled outside, and rain pounded at the skylight. The showers had escalated into a wild storm. She rubbed her eyes. Something was bothering her... something screamed away in her head. My God! Chris had forgotten his script! It would be ruined!

Chris was always losing or misplacing things, but usually he found them in time to avoid serious repercussions. This time it looked as if his habit would bring real devastation. She put on a robe and ran to the patio phone to call him. It rang endlessly. Where had he gone at this time of night? It was after ten. Now she remembered. Chris slept so soundly the roof could cave in and he'd never know it.

He'd mentioned the notebook was his only copy. It had been typed but was marked with insertions and changes so only he could read it. He'd stuffed it into a niche of the outer wall, but by now the rain and wind could have de-

stroyed it. Losing his script could be the final straw that
would prevent him from meeting his deadline.

Without hesitation, she called a taxi, then ran back to
the room and got dressed.

CHAPTER SIXTEEN

THE TAXI DROVE up as the night watchman let Holly out of the front gate. "Monte Albán as quickly as possible," she said in Spanish. The driver looked at her aghast.

"No, *señorita.* Too stormy. No lights there. Why do you want to go at this hour?"

"Please, hurry. I left something valuable there this afternoon, and I must get it before it's completely ruined."

The driver shook his head. "Too dark. You'd never find it."

"I have a flashlight."

"And the grave robbers. They work at night, you know." His hands moved agitatedly on the steering wheel.

"Not this night, *amigo.* They don't like to get wet."

"I charge triple for such a trip." His voice escalated to a shrill screech.

"Here," she said, and thrust a handful of pesos at him. The man muttered curses to himself.

As they began the ascent, she almost told the driver to turn around and take her home. The rain was coming down in sheets, so that they couldn't even see a car length ahead. The taxi skidded every time they rounded a curve, even though the driver was being extra careful. Any minute they might hurtle over the edge into the dark canyon below. It was only a few miles to the site, but it seemed like a hundred.

Miraculously they at last turned into the area reserved for buses and cars. A dim night lantern from the refreshment stand shone weakly.

"I'll wait here and keep the engine running, so hurry! I don't like tombs," the driver said. He hunched over the wheel as if he would take off at any minute. No Sir Walter Raleigh, this one!

She got out of the car, raised her umbrella, turned on her flashlight and headed for Tomb Seven. She hoped she could find it. She wasn't afraid. No one would be demented enough to come here on a night like this. But what if her reluctant driver got edgy and left without her? *Don't think about it.*

She trudged into the darkness and at once felt mud ooze into shoes. The downpour had lessened a little, but even so, the beam from her flashlight penetrated only a few feet. Her eyes ached with strain. She must be completely out of her mind!

"Keep going. It isn't far." She mumbled encouragement to herself as she sloshed through the mud. The tomb was on the other side of the parking lot, away from the main group of buildings. It would have been a hopeless search without the flashlight, but it seemed to her the beam was getting dimmer. She didn't even want to think about how long the batteries might last.

She swung the light from side to side as she walked, and at last the rays caught the pillars, bleak and ghostly. Slipping and sliding, she ran up the steps and felt inside the shallow niche. It was there. Thank God! Carefully she drew it out. It was soaked. Clutching it to her breast, she started back to the lot. If she were able to pry the saturated pages apart and dry them individually, the manuscript might be saved.

Managing a foothold wasn't easy. It was only a few hundred feet back to the parking lot, but it was taking forever in this quagmire. As she finally staggered into the area, she watched in horror as the taxi backed up and tore past her.

"Wait!" she screamed, running after it, stumbling. Then she saw the Jeep. Chris, raincoat flapping like some clumsy black angel, ran to her and picked her up.

"You idiot! What are you doing here?" he cried, and gathered her close.

"Your manuscript. I called you. No answer. It would have been ruined." Wearily she sagged against him.

He swung her up in his arms, carried her back to the Jeep, lifted her in and tucked a robe around her drenched, shivering body. He set his manuscript in the back seat, then for a few minutes warmed her hands in his. There was something exquisite about the entwining grip of fingers, the warm contact of skin.

"What a woman! If you'd brave a storm like this to rescue my manuscript, how could I have believed for even a minute that you'd destroyed my research all those years ago?" She was too exhausted to reply. It didn't seem to matter now. He shoved the Jeep into gear, and they were both silent while he concentrated on his driving. The Jeep held the slippery road far better than the taxi. Occasionally he darted concerned glances at her, and once he reached over and touched her cheek. The intimacy of the moment sent waves of warmth through her. Tears of relief burst from under her lids, but she stared straight ahead. She no longer felt apprehensive. The script had been rescued, and Chris was beside her.

He breathed a deep sigh as they reached level country again. "Your phone call must have wakened me after all. I thought it was the storm. Like you, I was frantic when I realized we'd left my manuscript, so I took off as soon as I got dressed."

"How could we have forgotten?"

"Who knows? The sudden rain. I guess my mind was on other things." He looked at her in a way that left no doubt as to what had caused his lapse of memory.

"What happened to the taxi? I was sure he'd abandoned me."

"When I arrived and saw it waiting, I thought I must be hallucinating. I questioned the driver, and he said a crazy wild-eyed American girl was visiting one of the tombs. I knew right away it was you."

"Thanks a lot."

"You're welcome. So I paid him off and sent the poor guy along his way. He'd suffered enough."

"I had already paid him. No matter. Anyone who would cart a wild-eyed American girl to Monte Albán in the middle of the night deserves a bonus."

"You forgot *crazy*. Actually, you look like a drowned rat."

"You're full of compliments, aren't you?"

"I tell it like it is, and if you don't get into something dry very soon, you'll probably come down with pneumonia."

A few minutes later he coasted into his garage. "I'm still dripping," she said as they got out and walked to the front door.

"Head for the shower. Make it a hot one. I'll find something for you to wear."

She closed the bathroom door, peeled off her soggy, muddy clothes and stood under the hot spray until her skin tingled. She rinsed out her clothes as best she could in the bathtub, then wrapped a towel around herself. Chris knocked. She opened the door. Without touching her, he laid his velour robe across her shoulders and handed her a pair of Lee's slippers.

"Give me your clothing," he said. "Unfortunately this house didn't come with a washer or dryer. I'll see what I can do." His hand just missed brushing hers, but she felt a strong current linking them anyway. Neither of them had said a word about taking her to Casa Avalon. It was as if fate had catapulted them into this situation. She would try not to think about it until she composed herself enough to sort out emotions and feelings.

She found a brush in her purse and got rid of the tangles in her hair and eventually coaxed the curly ends up into a ponytail, which she fastened with a rubber band she found on the door knob. A few minutes later she joined him in the kitchen.

"Some outfit. You'd better find a new tailor," he said, smiling at the way she was swallowed up in the generous robe. He'd hung her clothes over a chair in front of the oven. He reached into the cupboard for a can of coffee and measured some into a pot.

She watched, suddenly ravenous. "You wouldn't have a can of soup, would you? I'm starved."

He looked at her narrowly. "Skipped *cena*, did you? I didn't feel like it either." Had they been hounded by the same gremlins?

He rummaged in the pantry. "I'm afraid Ramona scorns canned goods. There are plenty of tortillas, eggs and cheese, though."

"Scrambled eggs and quesadillas would be heaven," she said.

"*Momento*, my girl. Heaven was never so close." He found a beater, whipped the eggs, added milk and dumped them into a pan while she spread grated cheese on the tortillas and put them in the oven. She recalled the Sunday mornings they'd fixed breakfast together. The homey, intimate time had been a treasured part of the early months of their marriage. The same, satisifed glow seemed to encircle them now. She felt secure in the warm room, locked away from the storm. Coffee perked merrily, and steam coated the windows. Together they carefully separated the pages of his script and laid them on the floor to dry, then sat down to eat.

Once Holly looked up to see Chris watching her with an amused gleam in his eyes. "You look about sixteen with that ponytail, not to mention your appetite," he said.

"A lot of years have passed since sixteen-year-olds wore ponytails, and as for appetite, speak for yourself," she said, motioning toward his empty plate.

He grinned and lifted a bottle of sherry. "Care for a glass?" Before she could answer, he set the bottle back down. "Later. I have some things to say to you, and I want to do it with a clear head."

"We'd better do the dishes," she said abruptly, and Chris didn't protest. They cleaned up with businesslike efficiency. Then, Holly checked the clothes drying in front of the oven.

He came up behind her, nuzzled her neck and kissed it, an endearing habit that she'd once cherished. "Damn it, come and sit down. We need to talk," he said. She turned around, amazed at the action after he'd been so careful most of the day not to touch her. He dropped his arms away from her in a helpless gesture. "Your fault. Those wispy black curls on that lovely neck of yours create an irresistible attraction. Besides, you need your daily dose of hemoglobin."

"Hemoglobin! That's some excuse for a kiss!" she said, unable to suppress a smile.

"Don't knock it, my girl. I read somewhere that a doctor handed out a prescription to each of his patients that required them to give at least four hugs a day. It seems when someone is touched by a caring person, hemoglobin in the blood increases significantly. It carries vital supplies of oxygen to all parts of the body, toning it and even speeding recovery if illness is present."

"Wow! That's some line, Dr. Brooke." She planted her feet wide apart and deepened her voice. "Pardon me, ma'am, may I have a few hugs? I wish to improve my hemoglobin." Her laugh pealed out heartily, and he joined in at her antics.

Suddenly they stopped and looked at each other for a few long, quiet seconds, each trying to read the other's expression. He reached down and cupped her face in his hands. "Tell me something. Why did you do it?" he asked softly.

"Do what?"

"Climb that mountain tonight. You didn't have to."

"I'm not sure. I just knew I had to. I couldn't bear for you to lose your script."

"People don't do things like that for no reason. It usually means you care pretty deeply."

She leaned her head against his chest. "I care pretty deeply," she whispered.

He went rigid, and his hands tightened around her shoulders. "I need to know. Do you mean that?" The words crackled harshly.

"I can't deny it any longer, Chris."

His arms went around her then, and she stood, chin upturned, longing for his kiss, willing to wait until it came.

"You're sure, dearest girl? No running away this time?"

"Certain, Chris. And you?"

"I've never stopped loving you. Surely you could tell that. I've tried, Lord knows, but I couldn't." His eyes gleamed, emphasizing his words. She reached up and stroked the planes of his face, then leaned her head against his chest and listened to his speeding heartbeat.

"I guess we're in the same boat, Chris. What on earth are we going to do about it?"

"We'll work it out."

"No word pills this time—take ten and recover—it's not that simple."

"I'm sure of my love for you, but if you're questioning your own and wondering whether it's strong enough to cope with our differences, what about tonight? The way you went out on a limb for me. That tells me all I need to know."

She dismissed the argument with a frown. "I'm more concerned about our lack of commmunication. That's mainly what destroyed us. Not Marissa. I rarely could bring myself to say what I really felt, and you'd turn into a stranger."

He took her hand and held it between both of his. "We'll start practicing. We're not doing badly now. Anyway, we'll never retreat if one of us remembers to say, I love you."

She smiled. "And work on the hemoglobin? But surely you have concerns too, Chris?"

"Yes, I do, and I'm not sure I can explain it. I want our individual pursuits to bring us closer, not to split us apart as they did last time. What can I say? I believe if we truly love, we'll know when to let go. I guess that means we'll have to respect each other's need for space. In the end, that's a lot more nourishing than too much togetherness. I failed you completely in that respect."

"Oh, Chris, and I, you."

He stood a little away from her, and his eyes turned anxious for a moment. "You've forgiven me Marissa?"

"A long time ago."

"You see? If one truly loves, one can forgive."

"Talk is easy, Chris, and we've covered a lot of ground. Action can be a different story. Do you think we'll remember?"

"Darling, we know now how much it hurt to be apart all these long years. We're two reasonably intelligent people. Surely we've learned something if only that sharing our bodies is easy compared to sharing ourselves." He reached for her hand and laid it against his cheek, his fingers light and gentle. "I want to touch you. I need to. I want to love you, and I want you to love me. I'm not saying let's go to bed just for the fun of it. In spite of my one indiscretion, I'm all for commitment, and I do love you, Holly, darling. I need to say if often. It's been held inside me for too long."

"For me, too," she whispered.

"You're sure? No running away this time?" he asked.

"I'm sure."

He picked her up and carried her into his shadowy bedroom, lighted only from the hallway. He laid her gently on the bed and began removing his clothing. She watched, savoring the glimpse of his fit, well-muscled body, a sight she'd long hoarded in her memory. Anticipating the feel of him, the entwining of his long legs with her slim ones, she knew she wanted him beyond all reason.

Soon he lay down beside her. Even in the shadows his eyes seemed to shine with a special brilliance. He smelled subtly of soap, clean and masculine. Their arms locked around each other in a loving embrace. They kissed, and it was as if they'd quenched a long thirst.

They moved in slow motion then, as if needing more time to look at each other, to caress each feature with their eyes as well as their fingers, savoring sensations to the fullest. She stored away the exquisiteness of his touch, memorized each word that he said.

Gradually he slipped the robe from her shoulders as if he were unveiling a treasure. He brushed the rounded contours of her hips and waist with his lips, then tenderly held her breasts, kissing them until he coaxed response. All the while he spoke of how lovely she was and how much he loved her. Something rich and radiantly alive invested his words with a sincerity that was as real as the blazing fire between them.

His gentle hands and quiet voice turned her deliciously compliant, and she yearned to surrender heart and mind to his passionate care. Her body flamed as she felt her breasts harden against him.

His urgency fanned her own desire so that her body grew as insistent as his. His lips covered hers, sweet and demanding, destroying every barrier she'd put between them. Her limbs tightened around him. There was no turning back now. Filled with the joy of wanting him, knowing he wanted her, too, desire at last found its own answering, and flesh melted into flesh. The room blurred into vague outlines, and the hunger inside them suddenly exploded, sending ecstasy to every nerve ending.

THEY LAY QUIETLY for a long time afterward, kissing gently, saying tender things. She relaxed in the sweet aftermath of her euphoria, wanting it to last forever. She hadn't expected such happiness again. It was almost too great for one body to contain.

Everything was going to be all right after all. This time she wasn't allowing passion to minimize their problems, was she? They'd brought them out into the open, acknowledged them and vowed to overcome them. Oh, things wouldn't be perfect, but it wouldn't matter as long as they kept trying, kept talking to each other. They would start again, this time with their eyes wide open. Of course, nothing had been said about a wedding, but that would come soon, wouldn't it?

CHAPTER SEVENTEEN

HOLLY HAD NEITHER SEEN nor talked with Chris for over a week, but it didn't matter. The night they had spent together after the storm would nourish her for days to come. Never before had they shared their innermost concerns and feelings so openly. They'd come a long way. For the first time she'd come to believe that love really could enable them to handle their differences. She moved through the days, her mind busy with planning their new life together and remembering, remembering the comfort of his arms around her, the sweetness of his kiss, the meaningful things he'd said to her.

She caught herself smiling and humming at inappropriate moments and finally gave up her efforts to isolate herself from her feelings. For several days she allowed herself to revel in a kind of wonderful delirium.

Chris was holing up in his makeshift lab for two weeks, endeavoring to complete the editing of his film. He'd given strict orders to Lee to take all his phone calls and keep away all visitors. He was at home to no one.

"Darling, bear with me for a couple of weeks until I get the editing off my back. Then I want you with me every minute," he'd said the next morning when he'd taken her home. She recalled his workaholic periods when they'd been married, and how much she'd resented them. But now she knew better. *Give our love space,* they'd agreed. Let go when it matters. In the end it would bring them closer.

To help pass the time without Chris, she'd spent hours deciphering and typing his barely legible manuscript. Only two pages turned out to be completely unreadable. Last evening she'd made herself climb out of her romantic haze and concentrate on something earthy and practical. The cook had offered to teach her how to make tortillas, the staff of life in Mexico.

She soon found it was a laborious process that occupied long hours. First she took kernels of corn that had been soaked in lime water. She then put them in a metate and ground them into dough, an arduous task. Shaping the dough into small balls proved easy enough, but she found that it would take a lot of practice to pat the balls evenly and quickly into the perfect circles accomplished so readily by the native women, keeping them of uniform thickness and diameter. Finally she cooked them on an earthenware griddle.

She doubted that she'd make them again but was glad for the experience and decided women had time for little else after making enough for the family needs. She recalled that Chris had filmed the process in his documentary. ''The rhythmic pat-a-pat of hands shaping dough into tortillas has been called Mexico's heartbeat,'' he'd written in the script.

Juana and Miguel planned to be married soon; it looked as if the Avalon wedding would be Oaxaca's social event of the year. Holly looked forward to attending it with Chris. Meanwhile, her head was filled with visions of their own ceremony. They hadn't even had time to talk about that yet.

She wanted something simple, maybe in a small chapel somewhere with only Juana, Miguel and Lee in attendance. Chris would surely want that, too. He was not one for great ceremony.

Paul Dalton arrived the next morning with a large check for her, full of enthusiasm about the success of her ceramics. She still couldn't believe her good fortune. This was the fourth check she'd received since they'd started doing business together.

"I have some of the black pottery for you this time," she said, and saw his eyes light up with excitement. She'd used the pre-Hispanic method of overfiring. Afterward, the pieces were cleaned of soot and rubbed by hand until they displayed a soft, gunmetal-like gloss. Such pottery remained one of the true folk art expressions of Mexico.

"Marvelous. Just wait until you see what that brings!"

"I still can't believe this. You must be some salesman, Paul. How do you do it?"

He shrugged off the compliment. "I pick the posh galleries, ones with moneyed clientele willing and eager to pay for fine art. Don't ask questions, love. Relax and enjoy."

"'Relax,' he says, as he cracks the whip. I feel like I'm on a treadmill!"

"Want to invest a little of your take in a lottery ticket? I'm off to buy a lucky number. Hope it will win another million. Got to keep supporting myself in the style to which I've become accustomed. Yachts are the cheapest things about a yacht, you know. There's my two-man crew, fuel bills, and something always needs fixing."

"Better not risk any of your bank account then."

"You know the old bromide, nothing ventured, nothing gained. Besides, I had a dream last night that told me where and when to pick lucky numbers."

"So long, Paul. I like to see something tangible in exchange for my money." *Like a wedding dress.*

He picked up the carton of pottery with a grin. "You'll be sorry. After I buy my winning tickets, I'm flying to Puerto Escondido to spend a week or two on my yacht, then I'll head for the States and deliver your pottery. If you want a little R and R, come join me. Bring Chris along if you like. Are you still seeing him?"

"I'm afraid he's tied up working to meet a deadline for his documentary. Maybe later." Paul left then, admonishing her to keep her kiln filled and waving a handful of pesos to remind her of the rewards she could expect.

Later that afternoon as she worked at the studio, she overheard Doña Elena discussing some matters with her accountant. Holly thought about her own little business, Holly's Selecciónes, and realized she hadn't been keeping accurate records of her dealings with Paul. She'd probably need to do so for tax purposes.

She'd merely banked the checks Paul had made out to her. They'd always been so generous that she hadn't thought to ask for an itemized account. Elena had a stack of invoices from the galleries that featured her work, which showed the price paid for each item less the commission received by her agent. Paul had never given her anything like that. It worried her.

After Holly left Doña Elena's, she walked to Paul's Oaxaca office located on the second floor of a building near the *zócalo*. Introducing herself to the young woman at the desk, she explained her business arrangement with Paul. "I'm setting up a better system of accounting, and I need to go over the invoices. Mr. Dalton hasn't given me copies."

"He left for the coast this morning," the secretary said. "Best to wait for the bookkeeper. I don't know anything about it."

Holly spotted several blue ledgers stacked neatly on an adjoining counter. Holly's Selecciónes showed plainly on the label of one of them. She pointed to it. "I'm sure the information I want is in that one. It will only take me a few minutes to find what I need."

The secretary shrugged. "Why not? Don't tell the bookkeeper, though." The girl rolled her eyes. "She's a *bruja*, a witch! Use my desk. I need a break anyway. I'll go for a cup of coffee."

Holly thanked her, opened the ledger and started copying out figures. With relief, she saw that each ceramic piece was listed with the price paid, less the commission. It added up exactly to the money given to her. She'd get busy right away and set up her own accounts. Odd that he hadn't given her duplicate invoices. On the other hand, it was such a small operation that he probably thought it was unnecessary.

She checked the figures once more, closed the ledger and put it back exactly as she found it. She wanted no dealings with witches. As she rose, her purse fell behind the desk against a low glass-covered case that held a dozen other ledgers. How many clients did Paul have? Then her eye caught her name. Holly's Selecciónes? Did people keep duplicate books? She realized she was appallingly ignorant concerning business practices. A key was in the lock. She was interested only in her own business records, so she had no compunction about turning it. She drew the ledger from the shelf, glanced at the figures and froze. What was going on here?

Her candelabra were listed as earning five hundred dollars each. He'd paid her fifty dollars. The tree of life had sold to one gallery for seven hundred, and he'd paid her one hundred. And so it went. Each item had brought many times what was listed in the other ledger. Was this some kind of joke? Her ceramics would never bring such prices. In fact, she had felt almost guilty taking as much as he'd given her.

She closed the book, put it back and locked the case again. For a few minutes she wrestled with the conundrum. What did this mean? She simply couldn't believe that her things would bring so much money. As a potter, she was unknown in the U.S. except to her students.

Even if her pieces had earned such prices, she couldn't imagine Paul cheating her. He was her friend. Suddenly an idea washed over her like a blanket of ice. *Oh, no! Don't jump to conclusions!* But the thought ballooned, overcoming other answers. Paul had been unusually taken with his assessment that her work resembled Doña Elena's. What if Elena's signature had been forged on her works? It would not be hard to do on most of the pieces. The famous lady readily commanded those kinds of prices. Not Holly.

Was that why Paul was so insistent that she make the animal whistles? Anyone contracting for Doña Elena's ceramics would surely want these popular examples of her art. She felt numb. Was her imagination running riot? How could she find out?

The secretary returned, and Holly thanked her. "Don't you feel well?" the girl asked, looking at her oddly. Holly mumbled something and walked out of the office as if in a trance.

The implications were too frightening to consider. My God, if her suspicions were true, she could be prosecuted for selling forged goods! There had to be some explanation. Paul would never do such a thing to her.

If only she could call Chris. He knew Paul well. No doubt he'd have some suggestions on how to handle the situation, but he'd made it clear he was out to everyone until he finished editing his film. Perhaps the next step was to discuss the problem with Doña Elena. That wise lady would know what to do. Yes, she would call the minute she arrived back at the Casa.

LEE SET THE TELEPHONE RECEIVER back in its cradle with a feeling of uncertainty. Marissa Levesque made everything sound so right and reasonable, but he remembered how she had got him to drive her to the village where Sir was filming, even though he knew he shouldn't have taken her. That had almost turned into a disaster.

"May I speak with Chris? He's still in Oaxaca, isn't he?" she'd asked when she'd called.

At least Lee had known how to handle that question. "Sorry, he won't be available for another week."

"Where is he?"

"Editing his documentary, and he'll skin me alive if I let anyone interrupt him."

She gave one of her hearty, throaty laughs. "What a watchdog! I wish you could work for me. He's right there, isn't he? Okay, I know what he's like when he's working. Another week you say? How about next Saturday?"

"I'm sure you could call him by then."

"Not call, I'm coming, Lee."

"Oh?" He didn't like the sound of that.

"Yes, and I have a wonderful surprise for him. I want to deliver it in person."

"Surprise? Well, I don't know. Maybe we ought to wait awhile. He's pretty preoccupied now with his deadline."

"Oh, he'll be ready for a break. I know him. Call up some of his friends and tell them you're having a surprise party for Chris to celebrate the completion of his documentary. I'll furnish the champagne."

"Honest, Miss Levesque, I'm not sure I ought to do that. I don't think he likes surprises much."

"Lee, darling, believe me, he'll like this one. It's very special. I swear he'll be ecstatic."

"Well, can't you just give it to him? I don't know anything about parties, which people to invite or even how many."

"You can arrange it. Ramona will help. I'm depending on you. You're practically an adult now, and you have more pizzazz than any young man I know."

Pizzazz? He had the feeling she was pulling a snow job. "Well, okay. Maybe I can get Holly to help me."

There was a pause. "Holly Jones? Don't tell me they're still seeing each other?"

"They sure are. In fact—" He stopped suddenly. He wasn't certain that what he'd worked and hoped for was yet an actuality. All he knew was that Holly had seemed mighty happy for the past week. Something good must have happened that day at Monte Albán.

"In fact, what, Lee?" Mss Levesque said.

Why did she sound so snappish all of a sudden? "In fact, I know she will help me," he said, improvising quickly. He hadn't proof of anything yet. Only wishful thinking.

"Good. Tell her to make hors d'oeuvres, loads of them, and be certain to include something luscious with avocados."

"She's pretty busy."

"Don't worry. She'll do it." They talked a little more about the plans. "Invite everyone he knows. We want a real celebration. Remember, not a word to him that I'm coming. Goodbye, Lee. You and I are going to throw the party of the year. Wait and see!''

It looked as if he was going to do most of the ''throwing,'' but then she was bringing the big surprise. That counted for a lot. He hoped everything would turn out as great as she said, but for some reason he felt uneasy. Miss Levesque always sounded so positive, so reasonable, then afterward he had all these doubts. Like now.

What if Sir didn't want a big party, especially with Miss Levesque in charge? He had got out of sorts when she had come the previous June. Maybe it would be different this time. He hoped so. He'd talk to Holly. With her help everything was bound to turn out right. He began to feel enthused about the affair after all.

HOLLY HAD JUST ARRIVED back at Casa Avalon when Lee came pedaling up on his ten-speed, hot and breathless.

''Hi! Hope you can spare a few minutes. I have some important business to talk over with you,'' he said in the deep voice he'd settled into lately.

''Let's sit on the patio. I'll get us some soft drinks.'' She brought Cokes and a plateful of toasted tortilla strips, and they sat down at a little round table. ''What's on your mind?''

''Well, there's going to be a big party next Saturday to celebrate the completion of Sir's documentary. He'll be going back to Texas a few days after that. It will probably be the last time he can get together with his Oaxaca friends.''

''You say Chris is leaving next week?''

''Right. That's what he said.''

The fact jolted her. She hadn't realized he was leaving so soon. Didn't they have a lot of talking yet to do before he left? ''I see. Are you going with him?''

"Not this trip. He's meeting a friend to dub in the sound on his film."

"So who's giving the party?"

"Miss Levesque and I."

"Marissa Levesque! Is she here?" The name dropped on her like a ton of bricks.

"Not yet. She's coming in time for the party. Said she's bringing a big surprise."

"What kind of surprise?"

"I don't know. She said it would be announced after everyone gets there."

The words chilled her to the bone. Marissa had a way of disrupting her life whenever she appeared on the scene. "It sounds very mysterious." Ominous was the more accurate description.

"Yeah, she said it would make everyone really happy, especially Sir."

What did the woman have in her Pandora's box now? Nothing uncomplicated, Holly decided. She hadn't seen Chris for over a week. Had Marissa been in touch with him? Holly had been conscientious about not interrupting him. Apparently it was okay to do so if one's name was Marissa. "Well, what time is this affair? I assume I'm invited."

He looked at her, instant hurt showing at her caustic tone. "You're number one on my list, Holly. Actually, I hoped you'd help me out some, like making hors d'oeuvres and helping me decide which people to invite. He might get suspicious if he sees Ramona fixing a lot of food."

"It's thoughtful of you to plan this party for Chris," she said, contrite at her sharpness.

"Oh, I can't take the credit. Miss Levesque told me what to do. I'm just following orders."

"She's a great executive."

"You'd better believe it, but so far all I've done is ask Colonel Hidalgo to invite Sir to take a ride in his new car. They'll come back after everyone has arrived so he'll be surprised at all the people. I sure hope it's okay with him. He's been working around the clock and really looks tired. He deserves something special."

She looked at Lee's anxious face. "Yes, he does, and I'd be happy to help you. I'll bring the hors d'oeuvres and come a little early to arrange some flowers and help Ramona set up the buffet. Now, shall we get to the guest list?"

An hour later they wrapped up the plans. Lee got up to leave, grinning at her a little shyly, but his eyes sparkled. "Thanks. I knew you'd fix everything."

"Anytime, teach," she said with affection, and suddenly realized how much she cared about him and how much she wanted him to be a part of her and Chris's family. Family? Fears buzzed around her like killer bees. She wouldn't draw a comfortable breath until Marissa opened her Pandora's box.

She thought about the night she and Chris had spent together—the tender words, how much he'd said he loved her. But, she realized now, not once had he mentioned marriage. "We'll work it out," was what he'd said. What did that mean? At the moment it sounded vague and full of questions.

Chilly apprehension pelted her like hail. She wanted desperately to talk to him, to feel his arms around her and listen to his reassurances. Their recent commitment was newly born and it would need a lot of tender loving care to sustain it.

CHAPTER EIGHTEEN

THE SURPRISE PARTY for Chris loomed like a dark cloud that seemed to grow more menacing as the hours passed. It didn't make sense. Holly knew she was perfectly capable of handling Marissa, as lethal as she was. Perhaps it was the woman's unerring timing. Why did she have to arrive now to snatch away the few hours she and Chris had left to spend together before he left for San Antonio? Past resentments as well as present ones swarmed like gnats.

She'd arranged to use the Casa's kitchen to prepare the hors d'oeuvres she'd promised, and she'd worked all afternoon making a variety of tasty *antojitos*: seviche, chopped raw fish with chilies and lime juice; slices of jicama sprinkled with lime and chili powder; and the always popular avocado dip—guacamole. She'd also fixed several dozen *gorditas*, time-consuming but delicious and a favorite of Chris's. The word meant "little fatties," and no wonder. Rich pastry was wrapped around an even richer sausage mixture, then deep-fried.

She'd no sooner than completed the task when she received a call from Chris, the first since he'd holed up to complete his editing. Her pulse leaped at the sound of his voice.

"Would you believe I've finally finished?" he said without preamble.

"So you're right on schedule?"

"Afraid not. The other company pulled out a week ago, so they have a head start on the lab work."

"They spent so little time here, I can't believe their treatment will be as in-depth as yours or as creative."

"Thanks for your confidence. I can use it at this point."

"Still worried about your deadline?"

"That's what I'm calling about. Some important things have come up that I need to discuss with you. I've been doing a lot of thinking." His sober tone hit her like a hammer. About what? Oh, God, about what?

"Yes, we do need to talk, don't we?" They certainly did. Nothing had been said about marriage or other arrangements.

"And even worse, I thought we'd have a few days together before I met Sam for the sound editing, but in order to fit into his schedule I have to fly to San Antonio first thing in the morning."

Chris's schedules were always frantic. That was one of the things she'd vowed to accept.

"So what about tonight?" he asked. "Are you free? Sorry for not calling earlier, but I wasn't sure I would be able to wrap everything up in time. Ramona said she'd be happy to fix something special. Lee has plans with a friend. So there will be just the two of us. How about it?" His tone hinted of candlelight and wine and an intimate ambience.

Her eyes filled, and her throat ached bitterly. Damn Marissa, arranging the surprise party for this evening! It was clear that Chris suspected nothing. What to do? She was tempted to figure out a way for the two of them to escape the entire affair, but Lee had worked hard to bring it off, and Chris always enjoyed having good friends around. She wouldn't stoop to sabotage. "I can hardly wait," she said, hoping she sounded upbeat and sexy. She pictured the eagerness in his eyes, the faint questioning smile and the way it would spread across his lean face at her reply.

"I'm seeing Colonel Hidalgo at seven," Chris continued. "He insists on taking me for a spin in his new Ferrari. Why don't I pick you up around eight?"

That wouldn't work. All those trays of hors d'oeuvres would be an absolute giveaway. She improvised quickly. "As it happens, I have an errand I have to do in your neighborhood around that time. I'll go on to your house after that." She told him then about her discovery of the double set of books in Paul's office and her concerns about the possibility of a forgery.

"Paul means well," Chris said. "But he has a champagne appetite. If he was pressed hard enough, I suspect dollars would win over integrity."

"But what shall I do in the meantime? I've just given him another batch of ceramics. What if Elena's name is being forged on my things? Big trouble with the law, right? Besides, Elena is my dear friend."

"Maybe we're jumping to conclusions. I don't think we should say anything until we find out for certain what's really happening, if anything. I'll check the San Antonio galleries next week. Paul's U.S. office is there, so I'll feel out his partner, too. You have to consider that one of the associates could be involved in the dirty work. Or maybe Paul concocted the second set of books merely to boost the appearance of his income on a financial statement so that he could arrange for a loan. Don't worry. We'll follow through on it."

They discussed the matter for a while, then hung up. Holly wistfully contemplated the evening that might have been.

THE TAXI ARRIVED to pick her up at the Casa promptly at six that evening, and Holly stacked a half-dozen trays of food carefully in the trunk and gave the driver Chris's address. She wore an apricot silk gown, its full skirt trimmed in handmade lace. The modestly scooped neckline only hinted at the curves clearly outlined by the bodice. She'd chosen it for its color, which complemented her dark hair and fair complexion. The dress was graceful and feminine. She felt good in it. She wanted to be entirely herself tonight, the whole self that too often remained unexpressed, the woman she'd learned Chris loved best.

About a dozen guests were already there. She recognized a few of the same people who had attended that long-ago party when she'd first arrived in Oaxaca. She hoped they'd forgotten the incident in the pool. Lee exclaimed over the bountiful array of edibles and helped her carry the trays into the kitchen. The two of them arranged plates and set them on the patio buffet. Marissa bore down on Holly at once.

"Felicity, my dear, so good of you to come," she said in ringing tones, leaving no doubt who was hostess for the evening. Her dress, a startling poppy color, had an overblouse of sequins. The long pencil skirt hugged slim hips. A provocative slit up one side revealed a generous eyeful of a calf and thigh. It was the kind of dress that could turn a woman into either a Las Vegas showgirl or a blue-blooded patrician. Holly reluctantly admitted Marissa looked like a queen. No matter where she stood, the spot became front and center stage.

Marissa put her arm around Lee's shoulder and turned to Holly. "What do you think of the bash this young man and I arranged?"

Lee grinned. "Don't forget Holly. She made most of the food," he said generously.

"Really? How nice," Marissa said, and looked at her watch. "It's almost time for Colonel Hidalgo to arrive with our guest of honor. I hope Chris doesn't suspect anything."

"I spoke with him this afternoon. I'm positive he had no inkling."

Marissa's eyebrows lifted. "How could you possibly tell?"

"He invited me over for dinner. It worked out well, didn't it?"

Marissa's smile hardened as if in cement. "Amazing! Incidentally, Felicity—oh, pardon. Really, you shouldn't have changed your name. I can never picture you as Holly. Odd how our names suit us. Do we grow into them, or do our mothers have a sixth sense when they name us?"

"I'm afraid my mother's sixth sense deserted her when I was born. I never was able to mold myself into the person for whom I was named," Holly said.

"And I can never see you as anyone but sweet little Felicity in one of those quaint outfits you used to wear."

Holly shrugged. "I guess that will have to be your problem."

Marissa sent Lee to the gate to watch for the Ferrari, then expertly directed Holly to a corner of the patio. "Lee tells me you and Chris have been seeing each other again. My dear, do you think that's wise?"

Holly stiffened. "I think that's for Chris and me to determine."

"Of course, but I hope you give it a lot of thought before considering anything serious. But perhaps I'm reading more into Lee's comment than was intended."

"I've never imagined you as a mother confessor, Marissa."

"Good heavens, I'm hardly old enough to be your mother."

"Merely a figure of speech," Holly said.

Marissa's mouth was a grim line, and her eyes shone with steely light. *She's a shark*, Holly thought, *and she's planning to devour me*. Marissa took a firm hold on Holly's arm. "I suspect Chris won't arrive for a few minutes yet. That should give us a little time together, but we need privacy. Her grip was so unyielding that Holly couldn't have pulled away without making a scene. *Be a good girl, Holly. Sit, speak, roll over*. She was swept inside the house and into the den. Marissa closed the door and released her arm.

"I'll make this brief," she said, her voice flinty.

"Like an execution?"

"My, my, what happened to sweet little Felicity?"

"As I said, she never existed. But we'd better get to the point. I feel you have a very sharp scalpel and are about to dissect me. You may as well get on with it."

Marissa stiffened. "This is nothing to joke about. If you truly understood Chris and cared for him, you'd never have showed up tonight." *Dispose of the body. No littering, please. Keep the place clean.*

"And you do?"

"Absolutely. I know him better than he knows himself. He's a genius with a potential he's barely explored."

"I'm aware of that now."

"Then you realize he must be free of emotional entanglements."

"I thought such involvement came with being human. Do you have to be one-dimensional in order to be creative?"

"Marriage imposes commitment," she continued, ignoring Holly's comment. "He's a responsible man. If you drag him into marriage again, he'll go all out to fill the bill as a good husband and father. You'll smother his talent as surely as if you locked him in a closet and turned out the light."

"Odd that you weren't averse to a little emotional entanglement with him, or does coaxing errant husbands into adultery pose an irresistible challenge?"

Marissa flicked her fingers in a gesture of impatience. "I'll do anything to further his talent—anything. I was able to accomplish that once and, if necessary, I'll do it again. I won't ever marry him. I care about him too much for that. And I care about the contributions he's going to make to the world of cinematography."

"And you think I don't?"

"No, my dear, you do not. Take my advice and go home now. That's the greatest gift you could give him. Don't chain him to a white picket fence and a family!"

Outraged and trembling, Holly stared at the woman. "Don't play the noble female with me, Marissa. Say what you mean. *You* want to work with Chris again, and you'll stop at nothing to do so. *You're* the lady with the chains, and you're trying to chain him to you. You managed to destroy our marriage, and he's since refused to work with you. Doesn't that tell you something?"

For a moment Marissa looked startled, but she quickly recovered. "You still don't understand, do you?" she said, and sighed as if striving to tolerate Holly's appalling lack of insight.

Holly's breath came quickly, and her cheeks burned. Fury made her almost inarticulate. Fury against this barracuda, fury for allowing her arguments to wound. "Butt out of our lives, Marissa. You're not God, although I'm sure you've informed Him often enough that you're an able replacement!" Brave talk, but could it prevent the deadly virus of Marissa's words from invading her system?

Marissa opened the door. Her smile was cool and superior. "Let your conscience be your guide, Felicity," she said, and left the room.

What did that mean? Holly wondered as she walked back to join the party. In spite of a determined resolve, she suspected she'd begun to react precisely as Marissa had intended. She felt shaken and vulnerable. *A matter of conscience?* Hers was formidable, passed along from a long line of ancestors, with at least a couple of Puritans peering over each shoulder.

Lee frantically waved an arm from his position at the gate. "He's coming," he cried. Guests quickly assembled into a group. Chris entered the gate and moved onto the patio.

"Surprise!" everyone chorused.

Looking completely bewildered, Chris stepped back as if he'd been hit by a blast of hot air.

Marissa linked her arm through his and drew him into the center of the group. "Darling, welcome back to the world!"

Everyone talked at once. Someone poured margaritas, and Lee heaped a plate of food for him. Holly watched at a distance. Chris hadn't seen her yet. Frowning slightly, he was in serious conversation with Lee, who looked anxious and flushed. If only she could lip-read.

She picked up some empty bowls from the buffet and went to replenish them in the kitchen. Chris entered a moment later and came up behind her. He kissed the back of her neck and nuzzled her ear. "Did you know about all this, and if so, how could you allow it to blow our evening?"

"Yes to the first, and to the second, too late to do anything. Lee and Marissa are a formidable combination."

He turned her around to face him. "I know, but damn it, I was really looking forward to tonight. Wouldn't you know Marissa would gum up the works?"

Oh, bless you, Chris. That's what I wanted to hear. "Maybe tomorrow?" she asked.

He groaned. "I'm leaving early, remember? I'll be gone at least a couple of weeks."

"Well, after doing without you for seven years, I guess I can stand waiting fourteen more days." He cupped her face in his hands and gave her another kiss, firm and sweet and frankly sensuous. *Everything is going to be all right,* she thought shakily. *He's letting me know.*

At that moment Marissa poked her head into the room, wearing her tight, prearranged smile. "Felicity! It's a no-no to steal away the honoree. Come quickly, dears, there's going to be a little presentation." Holly and Chris gave each other a knowing look and followed Marissa outside. *Now comes the real surprise,* Holly thought, and felt a qualm in the pit of her stomach. What did the woman have up her sleeve this time? No matter. Chris was still holding her hand. There was something reassuring about the warm contact of palms.

Marissa stood on a stool and held up a beautifully manicured hand. The guests snapped to attention at once. Reflections from her sequinned dress bathed the guests in a shower of shooting stars. She allowed the hush to lengthen before she spoke.

"Dramatic situation number ninety-nine, page ten," Chris whispered. Holly smothered a giggle.

Marissa spoke then. "Friends, as you know, we're here tonight to celebrate Chris's successful completion of his latest documentary."

There was a chorus of "Right! Hear, hear! Congratulations!"

"And I have a special presentation to honor the occasion. Many of you know that there is a place Chris has always wanted to film, but it has somehow remained out of reach." Every eye was riveted on her now. Holly felt Chris stiffen. He dropped her hand. Ice crept into her veins.

"So," Marissa continued, "I have the happy privilege of presenting a year's funding from the Peregrin Foundation to film the remote villages of the Andes, a documentary he's wanted to do all of his professional life. I'm proud to say that Chris and I will be a team again on this venture." She handed him a legal-looking document and kissed him firmly on the lips.

Chris looked stunned. Holly felt herself shriveling inside. Any minute she'd slip through a crack in the tiles at her feet. A year, even longer, wouldn't matter... But another project with Marissa! The woman held the trump card after all. She knew full well what that project would mean to Chris. How many strings had she pulled? How many people had she manipulated to snag the plum assignment? The night seemed to turn chilly, and the stars blurred.

People crowded around offering congratulations and asking questions about the venture. Marissa supplied ready answers. It was apparent she'd worked out every detail. Holly eased over to the buffet and nibbled on one of the *gorditas*. It tasted like straw.

A few minutes later she looked up to see Chris watching her. She forced a smile and joined her hands in a victory gesture, trying vainly to find something reassuring in his expression. Words were what she needed at a time like this.

Marissa chatted on about how they must meet in Dallas in a couple of weeks to sign the contract, but Holly heard only bits and pieces of Chris's response. Something about other considerations, meeting with Sam, checking some business at some galleries. At least he'd remembered that.

A young woman asked Chris why, of all places, the remote Andes intrigued him. His eyes shone as he explained. Oh, God, how he wanted that assignment!

"When do you start?" one of the young women asked.

"As soon as Chris wraps up his Oaxaca documentary and can get his crew and gear together," Marissa answered for him.

Holly spotted Lee perched on the diving board looking as desolate as she felt. Could the two of them send Chris off for a year with Marissa without making him feel guilty about leaving them? Marissa's words pounded in her head. "Don't chain him to a white picket fence and a family."

"This calls for a toast!" Colonel Hidalgo said. Marissa designated someone to pour champagne, and glasses were lifted again and again as everyone joined in the good wishes. Oddly, except for an occasional nod or grin, Chris barely responded. He was obviously stunned by his good fortune. Who wouldn't be when one's life dream was suddenly handed to him on a silver platter?

"Felicity, we haven't heard from you, my dear, and we know how happy you are for him," Marissa said with languid malice.

All eyes turned toward Holly. She stepped forward without hesitation. "I'd like to paraphrase a traditional Mexican toast. *Salud, amor y libertad y el tiempo para gozarlos*! Health, love and freedom and the time to enjoy them." Freedom to reach one's potential required letting go. Wasn't that what they'd promised each other on that rainy night? It was a far more unselfish act than Marissa's self-serving maneuver. But Holly hadn't realized the scope of the promise, nor that she'd be challenged so soon. For a long moment her eyes met Chris's. His expression was enigmatic.

Somehow she managed to smile and maintain a reasonable facade of sociability for the rest of the evening. She felt as if she'd programmed amenity and put it on automatic pilot. Guests were beginning to leave now. Would Marissa take herself off soon, too? Holly doubted it. There had been no more time to be alone with Chris. People continually surrounded him. A word or two with him would tell her all she need to know.

She started clearing away the leftover food and dirty dishes, carrying a stack to the kitchen. Lee leaped down from his perch and followed to help. She rinsed and stacked the plates, then washed the champagne glasses, Lee drying them. They could do that much for Ramona, who would finish up later.

"Man, did you see Sir's face? That Andes stuff really knocked him for a loop!"

"Well, I guess if you suddenly got something you'd wanted all your life, you'd be bowled over, too."

"Really great, right?"

"Oh, yes."

"And super of Miss Levesque to arrange it."

"Indeed."

He slammed a fist on the counter. "It's rotten! Especially now, just when we were getting it together. I wished I'd never heard of this stupid party!"

Holly poured two cups of hot chocolate from the pot on the stove, and they sat down at the table and sipped the fragrant drink.

"It wouldn't have made any difference," Holly said.

"So, what do we do now?"

"Smile and wave goodbye, it says in the book," she said flippantly to cover the sudden tremor in her voice. At once she felt contrite at Lee's bleak expression. She laid a hand on his arm. "Don't worry, if he can't take you with him, I want you to stay with me. I need a brother around."

He gripped her hand and clung with something like desperation. "I counted on our being a family by the end of the summer. I tried real hard to make it happen."

"Do you realize what we're doing, Lee? Chris has got a fabulous opportunity, and we're sitting here holding a wake."

"Yeah, I thought of that, too, but it doesn't make me feel any different."

"Look at it this way. If we want to be a family, a year won't make any difference." She really didn't believe that. Not if Marissa went along.

"So the next step is thumbs-up and a jolly ho-de-ho?"

"You're not old enough to be cynical, young man. The next step for me is to go home. It's after midnight, and I have to get up at five in the morning to help arrange flowers for Juana and Miguel's wedding reception."

She picked up the phone and dialed a taxi, then joined the few remaining guests still in earnest conversation with

Chris and Marissa on the patio. Holly went up without hesitation and laid a hand on his arm. She could never be accused of being a poor loser.

"Good night, Chris. I can imagine the thrill you must be feeling."

He looked startled. "You're not leaving now?"

"I've already called a taxi. It should be here in a minute. I'm helping to decorate for Juana's wedding reception tomorrow. If I don't go now, I'll meet myself getting up."

Chris looked around at his lingering guests with something like desperation. "I'll call you. My God, Holly, we have things to settle." He followed her out to the street where the taxi already waited. "And give my regrets and regards to Juana and Miguel. I'm sorry to miss their wedding." Holly knew he'd forgotten all about it. The pattern was all too familiar.

He gave her a swift kiss and held her close for a moment. She made a gesture to the taxi that had just pulled up, and Chris walked her over to it. He spoke through the open window. "Damn it, a lot of things have suddenly changed in my life, and I need to talk them over with you. Sometimes I wish I'd never chosen this business. I'll call you as soon as I visit the galleries."

"Goodbye, Chris, and good luck." She closed the door, glad for the darkness so he couldn't see her brimming eyes.

She could have outwaited Marissa tonight. The challenge might even have been interesting, but she didn't want to hear how his life had suddenly changed. That was all too plain. Nor did she want to hear all the rationalizations that would accompany the telling.

Back home in her room at the Casa, she stretched out on the bed and went over the evening's events in her head. Déjà vu almost choked her. Marissa, the home wrecker, had arrived on cue. Life repeated itself. The pain was even worse the second time. And for Chris, another far-flung challenge. She'd seen the radiance on his face. How could she have ever convinced herself that he wanted to include a family in his life?

Marissa's words flashed in psychedelic colors. "Let your actions be a matter of conscience." Holly suspected that even now, if she and Lee insisted, Chris would refuse the assignment. Clip his wings? There was no way she could do it.

Unable to sleep, she got up and put a cassette in her tape recorder. Maybe music would shut out the memory of Marissa's triumphant smile, shut out the excited sparkle in Chris's eyes as he explained why he wanted to film those Andes villages. But even her favorite Beethoven string quartet couldn't erase the images.

For a short span of time here in Oaxaca, windows had opened wide, allowing brilliance beyond all expectation, but tonight those windows had slammed shut, and something exciting and precious had drained away into the night.

CHAPTER NINETEEN

INSTEAD OF ANSWERING the breakfast bell Monday morning, Holly sat in her room and planned her day. She felt as if she were in limbo, and needed something to hang on to even if it were only a list on a piece of paper.

She'd left her job at La Tienda Artesanías the previous Friday, having given notice earlier. Regardless of the precarious state of her future, she had unfinished business to attend to, notably the enigma concerning her pottery sales in Texas.

Chris hadn't called yesterday. The few words they'd spoken to each other at the party now seemed vague and lacking in substance. She considered the devastating possibility that he would take off for the Andes with an open-ended kind of message such as a quick goodbye and "See you next year!" She needed something substantial such as "I love you, and I intend to make you part of my life regardless of all obstacles." No doubt he was fighting his own private demons. Well, she'd bow out of his life and do it gracefully this time—no quarrels, no bitter recriminations. Yes, she had a conscience.

Juana and Miguel's wedding yesterday had lifted her spirits for a few hours. It had been held in the magnificent Santo Domingo Cathedral, and all through the ceremony she'd fantasized that she and Chris were standing on that altar.

The gala reception afterward had taken place in the spacious patio and courtyard of Casa Avalon, and every notable in the city had been present. The radiant Juana had presided over the affair with her usual wit and exuberance, charming everyone from the highest official to the Casa's cooks who'd toiled for hours preparing the food.

Miguel had had eyes for no one but his bride, and no wonder. In the delicate Spanish lace mantilla and her period gown, she had looked like a member of some royal family that might have lived a century ago—the romantic ideal of the portraits he painted. The arrival of Juana's parents had made the day complete, and Holly rejoiced that Juana's family was again united.

Family. Would Holly never have one? Throughout the festivities, she had hovered near the patio telephone hoping for the call that had never come. Couldn't Chris have found a minute to telephone just to say, "I love you. Everything's going to be okay"? Obviously everything wasn't going to be okay. She had better start getting used to the inevitable right now. As much as she hated to admit Marissa was right, it seemed obvious that someone with nesting instincts as strong as hers would be wrong for Chris.

She tucked the list in her purse and by noon had accomplished very little of it. Doña Elena was charming, unperturbed and completely exasperating in her diffidence.

She merely shrugged. "*Que será, será*, what will be, will be," she said when Holly explained the possibility of the forgery.

"But it isn't fair to the people who buy," Holly insisted.

"Do you have definite proof that this is actually happening?"

"Not really. Only the figures I saw in Paul's books. What other explanation is there?"

"My dear girl, people have double sets of books for many reasons. Maybe the second set was in pesos. That would account for the enormous difference."

Holly tried to recall the figures. "It's possible, but I don't think so."

Elena shrugged. "Don't line your pretty face with worry. If there is a rascal, he will be caught, maybe *mañana*, maybe later. No matter." With deft fingers, she whirled a lump of clay on a saucer and sculpted out the graceful form she saw there. As she worked she hummed a vague little tune. Clearly the subject was dismissed. But not for Holly. She could be prosecuted—even jailed if she couldn't prove she hadn't forged Elena's signature on her work—couldn't she?

Next she called two of the San Antonio galleries whose addresses she'd copied from Paul's ledgers. The first said they carried very few items from Holly's Selecciónes, but their prices matched the money she'd been given. The second said the only Mexican pottery they carried was by Doña Elena. What was going on?

She hurried to Paul's office. She'd ask the secretary to allow her to check the ledgers again. A different woman worked at the desk today. Holly introduced herself. "I would like to pick up several cartons of my pottery. Unfortunately I gave Señor Dalton the assortment meant for La Tienda Artesanías. I'll explain to him as soon as he returns from Puerto Escondido." A thin excuse, but maybe it would suffice.

"He took the shipment with him, *señorita*."

"May I check the ledger then? Señor Dalton neglected to give me any invoices before he left." Somewhat reluctantly, the woman handed her the original ledger.

"Sorry, this isn't the one I need. Let me see the other one."

The woman looked at her sharply. "What are you talking about?"

"A duplicate ledger. I've seen it."

"You're mistaken. There is one only for your business. I'll take time to go over the entries with you."

"I beg your pardon, but I've seen another one. I noted a number of discrepancies in the pricing. Perhaps you would be so good as to explain?"

"*Señorita!* I assure you, we keep one set of books only," she said, emphasizing each word.

Holly pointed to the cabinet in back of the desk. "It was stored in there."

The woman took a key from the desk, opened the cabinet and wearily ran a hand along the books that filled it. The ledger wasn't among them. The silence sizzled with her annoyance. Holly wondered. Either the woman was protecting Paul or she was truly unaware of the duplicate set. The situation looked hopeless. Obviously this was the "witch" the other secretary had mentioned, and she guarded the office as efficiently as a dozen Dobermans. Holly murmured a few amenities and left.

She'd trusted Paul and considered him a good friend. He'd paid her promptly and handsomely. At least one gallery had verified her own records, so why not forget the entire matter? She almost wished she'd never discovered the second ledger.

Well, she wouldn't pursue it further until she heard from Chris. She hoped he wouldn't get so engrossed in his work that he'd forget to check the galleries. She spent the rest of the day buying gifts to take home to friends and some silver-and-turquoise jewelry for her mother who, although widely traveled, had never visited Mexico.

Now happily married to another army officer, her mother still had no permanent home. All through the years Holly had attributed the breakup of her parents' marriage to their peripatetic life-style. Obviously style had had nothing to do with it. It gave her pause. Had she placed too much emphasis on establishing roots?

The next morning Lee came by to see her just as she finished breakfast. She brought him a cup of hot chocolate from the kitchen, and they sat down in a corner of the patio.

"Sir called yesterday and left a message for you. Said he tried to get you several times but no answer. He's in Dallas."

"Dallas!" Marissa's office was in Dallas. "But he said he was meeting his sound editor in San Antonio. What happened?"

"He said he had something real important to take care of there first. The film could wait."

It would have to be something of enormous significance to make him delay his work on the film. Signing the contract, of course. She felt as if a wave had just engulfed her, and she knew that underneath it all she'd nurtured a desperate hope that he would refuse the offer. "So what was the message?"

"He said under no circumstances were you to give any more of your pottery to Mr. Dalton."

So her fears had been justified. If only she could talk to him. "Did he give you a number where you could reach him in Dallas?"

"No. Just the number of the lab in San Antonio."

Who knew when he'd return there? "Listen, Lee, do you have the keys to the Jeep?"

"Sure do. Sir left a set for me. He gave me permission to drive to Señor Hamilton's for my lessons, and he said I could even drive my friends to the movie one night."

"Your friend, Mike?"

"My friend, Rosita." He grinned. "And her brother."

Her eyebrows lifted. "I see you've made progress."

"You bet. He trusts me."

"I'd like to borrow the Jeep today and maybe tomorrow. Would that interfere with your lesson?"

"Well, I'm on my way there now. I could stop afterward on my way home and pick you up. Where are you going?"

"Puerto Escondido to get my pottery back from Mr. Dalton. Unfortunately I gave him a lot this time."

"And Sir said not to give him any more."

"Right. So I'd better get it back before he leaves for the States. Puerto Escondido is at least a four-hour drive. If I can't make it back tonight, I'll stay in a hotel and return in the morning."

"Let me go along and drive you."

"I think you'd better stay here. If Chris calls and you're not there, he'll be worried. You can explain where I've gone and why. I hope to accomplish my errand and return long before he calls though." No doubt Marissa would arrange any number of diversions. Holly imagined the chic cocktail party she would give to celebrate the signing of the contract.

Lee left, promising to return by noon. Holly packed an overnight bag in case she had to stay. She might find Paul at the bar in the hotel where he sometimes hung out but more likely he was on his yacht, and if so, she hoped he wasn't off on a cruise.

On the long drive she would try to gather her wits and come up with a reasonable excuse to ask for the return of the cartons. Not having talked to Chris, she still had no concrete information. Maybe the long drive would also give her time to come to terms with a future that stretched bleakly ahead like an endless desert.

How had she ever convinced herself that she and Chris could find happiness together again? Well, she'd have to keep a stiff upper lip for Lee's sake. But how could she throw off depression when the love of her life sought joyously to put a continent between them?

CHRIS STOOD WAITING for the elevator that would take him to the suite on the top floor of the Huntsinger Building, a black glass monolith that dramatically thrust itself high above lesser and more conventional structures, a singularly appropriate choice for Marissa's office, he thought dryly.

He hadn't called ahead, but he wanted to get the whole thing over and done with now. Besides, he needed to check a certain gallery here in Dallas to confirm what he'd learned about Paul in San Antonio. He wasn't looking forward to this session with Marissa.

The padded elevator, complete with crystal chandelier and homogenized music, rose so silently and swiftly he barely had time to steel himself for the coming confrontation. A secretary announced him and escorted him into Marissa's office.

She smiled, her eyes warm and welcoming. "Darling, how marvelous! I didn't expect you until the fifth," she said, and rose to meet him, kissing him on the lips the moment the secretary closed the door.

"I thought I'd better clear things up before I get involved with Sam in the sound editing."

"So wise of you. We can move ahead all the sooner." She gestured toward the small bar. "Fix us a drink, the usual, and I'll get the contract. It's all ready to sign."

"I'm not signing, Marissa. That's what I came to tell you. You wouldn't listen to me last week after the party, and insisted that I think it over."

She whirled around, her expression incredulous. "Not signing! What do you mean?"

"I've made the decision. Can we let it go at that?"

Her eyes flashed fire. "Chris!" The cry jabbed him like an ice pick. "Do you have any idea how I've worked, connived, manipulated, yes, and even lied to bring this off for you? I'm handing you a completed deal, hassle free. My God! How can you turn it down?"

"For the very reasons you've just mentioned. I suspected from the start that in order to arrange this, you'd have me so tied up in obligations I'd have no say. I'd like to see the small print. True, isn't it?"

"Don't be ridiculous. Any big operation like this has its set of requirements. Good heavens, it's their money. What do you expect?"

"The driver's reins. I want to do my own negotiating, set my own conditions. I'm not interested in knuckling under to every individual with whom you've made a deal, and I'll bet there were plenty."

She walked over and looked out the window. He had to admire the animal grace with which she moved as well as the sway of her slim hips as she brushed past him. He wasn't moved. Chalk it up to her sense of drama.

Suddenly she whirled to face him. "Don't tell me Felicity or whatever her name is has finally got to you?

Don't sacrifice your future, Chris. The world needs a creative genius like you."

"My future is precisely what I'm concerned about, and I intend to arrange it myself. I love Holly. I've always loved her. I want her in my life again, so damn it, Marissa, back off. As for creative geniuses, they're a dime a dozen in the film industry. In less than ten minutes after you announce my decision, you'll have any number knocking at your door."

She took a quick intake of breath as if suddenly remembering something. "Oh, Lord, what will I tell Alex Bordessa?"

He grabbed her arms. "Bordessa! What's he have to do with this?" That power-hungry egomaniac was a menace to the industry.

"Well, actually, he's the producer. You'd be in complete charge of filming," she said hurriedly. "Don't look like that, Chris. Agreeing to Alex was the only way I could swing it."

He let her go as if she were too repulsive to touch. "So you'd knife me in the back before we even started! You know what he's like. He'd tie my hands at every turn and take credit for any original idea I was able to sneak past him. How could you stoop so low? I know what you think of him."

She sat down at the desk and put her head in her hands. Damn, he hoped she wouldn't cry. He'd never seen her do that, but she always made such a production of everything. At this point he imagined she'd resort to anything.

She looked up at him, her eyes still dry. "I knew how much you wanted to do that documentary, and more than anything in this world I hoped to make it possible. I did it the best way I could."

"You don't know me. You don't know me at all or you'd have realized I wouldn't have gone along with it. Listen, Marissa, the Andes isn't my only goal in life. As a matter of fact, the main reason I'm in Texas now is to tend to other options."

"Don't bore me with explanations," she said, wrinkling her nose as if she'd just smelled something unpleasant. "I thought you'd learned your lesson. Do you have to get burned twice? You'll be sorry, Chris."

"Dammit, can't you get it through your head? What do I have to say to convince you?"

She rose, walked over to the window and stood with her back to him, looking over the sprawling city. The silence lengthened. Finally she straightened her shoulders and turned to face him. "You're absolutely certain?" Her voice was low and more intense than he'd ever heard it. "Is there anything that will make you change your mind? Name it, darling, and I'll move heaven and earth to arrange it. I'll even see what I can do about Bordessa."

Damn the woman. He hated her verbal maneuvering, the way she kept at him, like a bird pecking at a crust of bread, tearing loose a crumb at a time.

"I won't change my mind," he said quietly.

Her posture changed subtly, and her thin, clever face showed lines he hadn't noticed before. She brushed a hand across her eyes. "Marissa Levesque on the losing side. That's a laugh, isn't it? You'd better go before I get sloppy. You and Holly will make it this time, Chris. I saw that. Perhaps that's why I've been so bitchy. You've got it all—Holly and that adorable Lee. I envy you your happiness. Goodbye, Chris. I wish you well."

Her words took him by surprise. She was far more gracious in defeat than she'd ever been in winning. He'd never have believed it. He bent down and kissed her on the cheek. "Thank you, Marissa," he said, and left.

CHAPTER TWENTY

CHRIS LOOKED UP the address of the Holtzen Gallery. "Dealer in quality handicrafts and art goods, the largest and most prestigious of its kind in Dallas," read the ad in the yellow pages. He would check it out, then call Holly with the dismal information he'd gathered in San Antonio. He expected nothing less than the same at Holtzen's.

If a man had wings on his feet, it was he. Even the depressing evidence he'd uncovered about Paul hadn't cooled his elation. Yesterday he'd signed a contract, one that he'd desperately wanted, but one for which he'd had faint hope. There had been at least fifty applicants from all over the world.

He could hardly wait to share the good news with Holly. He'd wanted to tell her the night of the party, but Marissa had fixed that. Anyway, he needed time to explain the potential of the job for them both, time to convince her to come with him. Yes, time. But everything had happened at once: that damn party, working with Sam, checking the galleries. He'd called her several times but hadn't been able to reach her.

He hadn't believed Marissa's offer for a minute and had been certain there was a catch somewhere. He'd remained noncommittal, not wanting to provoke a scene at the party. For a few minutes he'd allowed himself to relive his longtime dream of filming the ancient Andes villages. But not with Marissa.

When he had gone to her office today, his suspicions had been confirmed. No way would he have signed such a contract, even if he hadn't had the other job. With Marissa calling the plays, it would have been hell. With Alex Bordessa, it would have been impossible. And without Holly, it wouldn't have been worth it. If he hadn't promised to check the galleries, he would have hopped on a plane and flown back to her at once. He pictured her finely carved facial features, her trim body, her cloud of dark hair contrasting sharply with her white skin, and imagined the feel of her in his arms again. Love, need and hunger combined in a desperate longing.

Yesterday in San Antonio he'd found Paul's former partner and had discovered their business relationship had recently been severed. As Chris suspected, Paul was known as a big spender in Texas. Hoping week after week to strike it rich on the lottery again, he had found himself near bankruptcy.

"I hear he's trying to sell his yacht to satisfy his creditors," the former partner had said. "A hell of a guy when he isn't drunk. Generous as all get out. Always picked up the tab. Good for a loan anytime and not particular if you forgot to pay it back. I saw the handwriting on the wall, though. Lucky I got out when I did."

"Where is he now? Do you know?"

"Haven't the slightest. I know one thing, the man is desperate. Wouldn't put it past him to grab a hostage and hijack a plane to Africa, especially if he was drunk. He's really down, man."

"Africa?"

"Forget I said that. And don't count on me to squeal if the police are involved. Won't know a damn thing."

Yesterday Chris had also visited the San Antonio gallery that Holly had named and had recognized her ceramics at once. On the bottom of each piece was Doña Elena's forged signature, just as Holly had suspected, so it was no surprise when he found the same thing in the Dallas gallery. Apparently Paul's initial contact with one of the galleries had been honest enough, but when his financial condition had worsened, he had scrounged for any means to bring in money.

It took another two hours to go over the matter with the police. An entrapment was planned in both the San Antonio and Dallas galleries within the next week when Paul was due for a delivery. It gave Chris a miserable feeling to see a man wreck his life so foolishly.

At the Dallas airport he tried to call Holly before catching the plane back to San Antonio. She was away for a day or two, the maid said. Where was that girl keeping herself? She'd ended her job only last Friday. Apparently the free time was going to her head. A call to Lee was more successful. "How are you doing?" he asked.

"Okay, but it's kind of lonesome."

"Invite Holly over for dinner. Ramona will be thrilled to have one more person to appreciate her cooking. Did you give her my message?"

"Sure did. After you said not to let Mr. Dalton have any more of her pottery, she got real excited and took off to get her stuff back. She borrowed the Jeep."

"In heaven's name, where did she go?"

"Puerto Escondido."

"She drove there?" My God, she shouldn't drive that long, lonely road alone, much less get anywhere near Paul, given his present condition!"

"She said she might have to stay all night if she couldn't find Mr. Dalton right away."

Dalton was desperate. No telling what he'd do, the partner had said, especially if he was drunk. "We'll have to go after her, Lee. I'm afraid she might be in big trouble. I'll explain later. Now get this. Call Aviación Zapoteca. The number is scribbled on the first page of the telephone book. Reserve a Super Cub, the plane I usually rent for this afternoon. Don't take no for an answer. Tell them anything. The truth is best. Tell them that we have to rescue a lady."

"Wow! This is exciting!"

"I'm taking off for Mexico City, even if I have to hang on to a wing. I should make it in time to catch the flight home, which arrives in Oaxaca at five."

"I'll be there, sir."

IT HAD TAKEN Holly over five hours to drive the 263 kilometers. The road had been full of ruts, at least two-thirds of it dusty and unpaved. Hot and tired, she parked the Jeep on the main street and made the rounds of the little town's handful of hotels. Paul wasn't at any of them. Then she found a bartender, who told her that Paul had left for his yacht early that afternoon.

She hurried past the Esplanada Municipal and down the rough steps that led to the beach, then south to find the quiet cove where the yacht was anchored. She passed the little harbor where a fleet of fishing boats was docked. Farther on, colorful cabanas, like squat pumpkins, lined the beach. A few people still remained, although it was already after sunset. Surfers effortlessly rode giant breakers in a dynamic outdoor ballet. She was tempted to pause at one of the little open-air food stands and have a dish of the succulent-looking shrimp, but it was getting late. She'd tend to business first.

Twenty minutes later she arrived at the tranquil U-shaped cove, which offered shelter from the aggressive waves that pounded the more exposed beaches. The yacht rode anchor a few hundred yards offshore. No colored lights were strung on deck to welcome guests or announce some gala occasion as at the christening. In the early dusk it looked like a ghost ship. A feeling of desolation crept over her. Even a lone tern that swooped overhead had a furtive air. Maybe Paul hadn't gone out there after all.

She found a boy leaning against a beached rowboat and agreed to his price to row her out to the craft. They'd gone about halfway when she spotted Paul waving eagerly at them. As they drew alongside, Holly handed the boy his fee.

"I'll hang around onshore for the next hour," he said. "If you want me to come get you, signal with a flashlight."

"Holly, love, it's you! You came after all," Paul cried with surprise, and extended an unsteady hand to help her aboard. "Where's Christopher?"

"In San Antonio with his sound editor." She'd completely forgotten about the invitation. "I know you're leaving soon, and I have some business I want to discuss with you before you go," she said, feeling suddenly uncomfortable on the unlit deck. He set out a chair for her and went aft, looking toward shore for a minute, his stance so unsteady that she wondered if he was going to fall over the low railing, which was more decorative than practical. The sour smell of liquor trailed behind him.

She felt apprehensive. Maybe she shouldn't bring up the pottery. Paul didn't seem himself. His usual ebullience was missing, and he was very drunk. Oh, Lord, she hoped he wouldn't misinterpret her visit.

Eventually he ambled back and sat down, rubbing a hand across his forehead as if to clear his thinking. "Don't mind me. I thought at first you were the lady who was interested in buying my yacht. She promised to meet me here this afternoon. Can't imagine what happened. Can't imagine," he mumbled several times.

"You're selling your yacht? I thought you loved it."

He shook his head and gave a mirthless chuckle. "You've heard the old maxim? Happiest day in a man's life is when he buys his first boat. Second happiest day is when he sells it. Yeah, finished my yacht period. Dismissed my two-man crew this morning. Time for a change. Think I'll buy a plane and fly myself to Timbuktu. Good place, Timbuktu. Want to come along?"

She laughed, not certain what to say. He peered at her through the deepening twilight. "You need a drink. What'll you have? Plenty of Scotch. Not much else. Damn bar's depleted." He shook his head morosely. Where was the jolly self-confident man she knew? His voice was slurred and unnatural, and his countenance, eyes puffy and face bloated, was a caricature of his former self.

He handed her the drink. She took a sip and almost choked. Pure liquor. He hadn't used any mixer. She shuddered. "I can't stay long, Paul. Actually, I came to pick up my ceramics."

"No, must stay. Lonely these days. Need someone to talk to." He fumbled among some glasses and bottles by his chair and finally located a half-empty bottle of

Scotch. He filled his glass, spilling almost an equal amount on the deck, and gulped about half of it.

Holly stared in alarm. At this rate he'd surely pass out soon. She'd been a fool to come here alone. How would she cope with a drunk? Even his crew was gone. She pretended to sip the drink while he talked about the yacht and how expensive it was to keep it afloat. While he rambled on, frequently repeating himself, she managed to pour the liquor over the railing.

"Paul, really, I can't stay any longer. I want to drive home tonight, and it's already getting dark. I'd like to get the cartons of ceramics I gave you last week." He stared into space as if searching for some remote planet.

She reached over and nudged his arm. "Please, Paul, do you have them on board? The cartons, remember?"

He vaguely considered her question. "Around somewhere," he said finally, his words very slurred now.

"I didn't think you'd mind," she said, watching for a glimmer of suspicion at her request. "You see, I promised an order to La Tienda some time ago, but I haven't had time to fill it. Since you and I will be discontinuing our business when I leave Mexico in a couple of weeks, I thought it would be okay if I gave them this batch." The statement had enough truth in it to seem logical. She held her breath.

He nodded. "Right, love. Gotta keep promises. Important. Don't I know!"

Holly nervously gripped the arms of her chair trying to quell her impatience. "So, if you'll tell me where the cartons are, I'll pick them up and signal the boat boy to come get me."

He nodded. "Sure, anything to please the little lady."

"I appreciate that, Paul. Oaxaca is so full of fine potters. You'll have no trouble finding someone. Why not approach Doña Elena? You'd make a bundle if you could handle her things," she said, the words popping out in spite of herself. His head shot up sharply for a man in his condition, and for a moment their eyes caught and held. His were so knowing, she wondered if he'd somehow guessed her suspicions. The squarish, husky man seemed to crumple and shrivel. Even his chair seemed too large for him. He made an effort to rally.

"Not to worry, love. Getting out of exports. Too risky."

"Really?" she said impatiently. "If you'll tell me where I can find a flashlight..."

"Don't need one. I'll take you in the dinghy."

She took in his pathetic condition. There was no way he would be able to launch the little boat, nor could she, even though she was sober. But he didn't budge. Neither had he seemed upset concerning her request. Could it be that he had nothing to do with manipulating the figures in the ledger after all, that whatever skulduggery had been practiced, Paul had taken no part in it? She rose. "Well, then, if you'll tell me where you've stored my stuff, I'll get it."

"What's the hurry? Have another drink. Damn bar's a mess, but we'll find something."

His refusal to cooperate was infuriating. Was there no way to get through to him? She watched as he sorted through several glasses scattered untidily on the deck. He chose one, inspected its murky interior, filled it anyway and handed it to her.

She fingered the glass as if it were full of poison. "Thanks, but I'd better not drink any more. I've had nothing to eat since breakfast. Would you have the makings for a sandwich?" She was hungry, true enough, but maybe the excuse would give her a chance to look for a flashlight. She was ready to forget about the pottery.

He waggled his hand. It flopped back and forth like a spent fish on a hook. "Go ahead. Nothing for me, though. On a diet. Scotch and water." He laughed uproariously, but she noted the hysterical edge. Her hands grew clammy. She had to find some way to signal the boy onshore or she'd be stranded.

In the galley she searched for a lantern or flashlight, but none was there, nor did she locate one in any of the minuscule staterooms, although she found the cartons. They were the least of her worries at this point. She raced to the bridge and flung open cupboards and drawers, hoping Paul wouldn't become suspicious of her absence and come looking for her. Nothing there either.

They were too far from shore for her calls to be heard. Paul was in no condition to launch the dinghy, and she'd probably drown if she attempted it. What if she had to spend the night here? Her flesh crawled at the thought.

Back in the galley, she found little on the cupboard shelves except a box of crackers and a tin of coffee. The refrigerator yielded some stale french rolls and a package of cheddar. She made strong coffee, sliced the rolls and filled them with the cheese. Maybe a little food would sober him up.

She set the coffee and sandwiches on a tray and carefully carried it up on deck. Paul had moved to starboard and stood precariously near the edge, weaving almost rhythmically as he balanced himself against the gentle swells that nudged the craft. He stared blindly through the darkness as if still hoping for the prospective buyer to show up.

Holly held out the tray, and he reached over and patted her shoulder. "You're a great kid, really special.

Know that?'' He picked up the coffee, but the cup slipped out of his hand and smashed to bits on the deck. She set down the tray and ran for a towel to mop up the mess.

"No matter. Not hungry," he said as she completed the chore. "Could use a little T.L.C. though. Life has turned into a kick in the pants." With surprising strength, he suddenly pulled her into his arms. His sour breath nauseated her, and she cried out in alarm as she tried to writhe out of his embrace.

A look of surprise crossed his puffy face. "Sorry, love. Didn't mean to scare you. Don't know what got into me," he said, all penitence now, and released her so abruptly she stumbled backward and lost her balance. Frantically she reached for him, arms whipping the air, hands clutching at emptiness as she fell across the low railing and plunged into the dark water below.

CHAPTER TWENTY-ONE

CHRIS FASTENED the seat belt and closed his eyes. He'd been certain he was going to miss the connecting flight from Mexico City to Oaxaca, but he'd made it by seconds. There must have been an angel on his shoulder. If Lee had arranged for the Super Cub, they could take off for Puerto Escondido as soon as he landed. He didn't even want to consider the possibility that the rental plane wasn't available.

The more he thought about Holly going on her wild mission, the more uptight he became. If only he'd been able to talk with her before she'd left. He tried to reassure himself. Holly was intelligent. She'd take care. But would she? He recalled the way she'd charged off on that stormy night to rescue his manuscript. He grew so tense he ached all over.

The stewardess handed him a Coke and a small package of peanuts. He'd rather have had a stiff drink, but he was going to pilot the Super Cub. He'd need a clear head. It was vital to get to the seaside village by sunset, since it was against the law to fly at night. If he got caught landing after dark, he'd be arrested, and he was well aware of the complications that could ensue, not the least of which was the impounding of the plane. Resolutely he picked up a magazine and made himself read the articles. The one-hour flight seemed interminable. At last the seat belt sign flashed on. He glanced at his watch. Good. They were on time.

He looked out the window as the 727 reduced altitude in preparation for landing. The rounded, bare mountains were tawny in the sun and reminded him of sleeping lions. His time here in this fascinating area was nearly over, but it would always hold a special place in his heart.

The plane landed smoothly. With difficulty, he restrained impatience as tired passengers took their time pulling out bags from under the seats and lumbered down the aisle at a leisurely pace. He had carry-on luggage, so there was no waiting at the carousel. He spotted Lee's anxious face at once, then the infectious grin as he bounded up and grabbed Chris's bag.

"Everything's go. Super Cub's gassed up and ready, and a taxi's waiting," Lee said.

"Great! We haven't a minute to lose."

They strode to the waiting taxi. "Aviación Zapoteca. *¡Immediatamente!*" The driver obviously relished such an order. He slammed into low gear, revved the engine, popped the clutch and burned rubber as they careened onto the highway. The private aviation company was five miles out of town. Few cars were in sight. No delays there.

Lee cleared his throat. "Say, I'm kind of in the dark. What's the big rush? Could you put me in the picture?"

"The picture isn't pretty, I'm afraid. Holly may have got herself into a jam. That Dalton fellow who markets her ceramics has turned out to be a real stinker."

"Isn't he the guy who won all that money on the lottery?"

"Yes, but he's about to go broke and is desperate for money to stave off his creditors. Bit off more than he could chew with the yacht, I guess. My concern is that he likes his liquor a little too well and becomes a different person when he's drunk. His partner told me that he wouldn't put it past Paul to grab a hostage and skip the country. He mentioned Africa.''

"Africa! Do you think he'd take Holly?''

"Who knows? I'm plenty worried. We've got to get there as soon as possible. Holly is resourceful, but she's had no experience dealing with someone like Dalton.''

"How long to fly to Puerto Escondido?''

"Two hours unless there's a head wind.''

"That means she probably arrived a couple of hours ahead of us. Do you think...?''

"Keep your fingers crossed.''

"I've been doing that ever since you called, Sir.''

Chris glanced at the boy with warmth and affection. The feeling had come a lot recently. In fact, they'd become real friends. Maybe the time had come to bring up adoption. Three months ago he'd never have believed it would happen. He'd talk it over with Lee soon. Maybe the "Sir" would change to something more personal then. If not, it wasn't important. Feelings were what mattered.

The manager of Aviación Zapoteca wasn't at the airfield. Perhaps he'd already left. Good. There would be no questions. If the man believed Chris wouldn't arrive at his destination before dark, permission to take off would not be granted. Plane owners took no chances.

The five rental planes were lined up adjacent to the runway. The Super Cub was the smallest. It had no radio, and navigation relied on a compass. If darkness overtook them, would he be able to find the abandoned dirt runway near the cove? He wouldn't dare land at the municipal airport, but surveillance at private airstrips wasn't rigid. He looked at the wind sock. Damn! There would be a head wind, and worse luck, wasn't that the manager coming toward them?

HOLLY SCREAMED and at once the sea closed over her. She held her breath and tried to remain upright. Her lungs would surely burst before she reached the surface. Once there, she gulped and called again for help, flailing her arms in an effort to keep her head above water. Couldn't Paul hear her? If he didn't realize soon that she'd fallen overboard, it would be too late.

Then she heard his voice, faint and mournful. "Holly? Come back, love. Don't leave me!" The cry of a bewildered child. Oh, God, she was drowning, and that drunken fool thought she was hiding from him! Panic, raw terror, paralyzed her mind. *Remember! Try to remember what Lee taught you.* Nothing.

Maybe just as well. Knowing how to swim would only prolong the agony of drowning. . . .

Above, below, all around her the world had turned to water. Ears roaring . . . chest bursting . . . strength going fast. What had happened to the parade of one's life that was supposed to flash before a drowning person? All she saw was Chris's radiant face when Marissa announced the grant.

Float, you fool! At least you can do that! Great talons of exhaustion clutched at her limbs, but those were stars above her, real stars, and she was floating, not drowning. Some indestructible source inside her had finally come to her rescue. She lay in the water and willed her heart to slow its pace and tried to quiet the gasps that raked her raw throat. *The sea is calm, the water is not freezing, and the lanterns shining from the food stand on the beach provide a clear compass.* Thank God for a landmark. She'd drifted so far from the yacht that she could barely see it.

But she couldn't stay afloat forever. Firm ground looked far away. If she held out long enough, would the tide finally wash her ashore? She didn't think so.

A faint feeling of resolve rose inside her. *Think. Try to remember. Recall every last thing Lee taught you.* "Lie on your back and pretend the body is a boat," he'd said. Yes, and the arms are the oars. She'd managed three or four strokes for him on one occasion, but how many strokes did it take to reach land? Hundreds? Never mind. She'd count to three or four, then start over again.

A breathlessness kept seizing her. She seemed to be suffocating for lack of air. Her lungs felt as if they would explode. Why fight it? Drowning wasn't a bad death. No, you coward. Take charge! "Take charge!" she said, repeating the words aloud like a litany.

If only she could become one with the ocean for a while, a wave that lapped the shore. But her skirt had wrapped around her legs, binding them together. Slowly she eased the elastic down over her hips, and after an eternity she managed to kick the garment free.

She reached her arms high, pulled hard through the water and flexed her legs as Lee had taught. She felt herself glide. A miracle! *Again. Do it again. Two strokes, three. It's working!* But weariness soon overcame jubilation. Exhaustion would defeat her. She'd squandered all her strength at the start. Arms ached intolerably...lungs burned. Every breath was agony.

No matter. Keep going...getting closer. Don't panic. Face facts...fears are more awesome than the distance to shore. You can do it. One stroke, two, three. Now do it again.

Were the shore lights closer? It seemed so, but it could be a mirage to tantalize her weary body. And why did she feel so heavy? Surely she'd sink. How could anyone feel that heavy and still float? What matter? She couldn't manage one more stroke.

Damn it! Keep going! Now the wash of the tide teased her, thrust her ahead, then pulled her far back again. She must be close, though. Any minute she'd surely be able to touch bottom. Then she saw it coming, a wall of water rolling toward her, a rogue wave among gentler ones. It toyed with her, tumbling her like a cork, battering her with its force, dragging her over gravel, then angrily abandoning her on the beach.

Groggy and gasping for breath, she dug her fingers into the sand and clung with desperation. Summoning one last remnant of strength, she dragged herself a few feet farther up on the beach and wept at the glorious feel of it. It was solid and real! She'd made it to shore! Every muscle trembled with exhilaration.

She tried to stand, but her body was too weak to respond. Never mind. She'd taken charge of her life and she'd won. Euphoria filled her to bursting. Thoughts floated around her as if painted on banners in bright colors. She need never allow anything to defeat her. She could handle whatever came along.

Yes, she lived! Each remaining day of her life was a gift. She'd regard each one as a treasure to be dedicated to the things that mattered. She'd had her own blind spots, some values that were all wrong. Tonight's agony had washed away the debris. What remained was real and fundamental.

She'd go with Chris wherever he wanted. She could practice her own art anywhere. Places weren't what kept families together. Concern, love and understanding were what counted. She'd tell him the moment she got home. Soon. Yes, she'd fight hard for him, but if it didn't work out, she knew she could handle that, too.

Spasms of trembling racked her body. *Shock must have set in...too spent...too used up...too drained. Must rest.* She curled up against a piece of driftwood and collapsed into welcome unconsciousness.

THE SUN HAD SET some time ago. Chris was circling the little harbor of Puerto Escondido. A few lights twinkled around the square. The manager of Aviación Zapoteca had been accommodatingly naive about their itinerary. It seemed all one had to do in Mexico was mention a damsel in distress and doors opened. Chris had pushed the Super Cub for all she was worth, bucking a head wind the entire way. Even so it took a half hour longer than expected.

It was too late to land at the municipal airport, and he still hadn't found the abandoned runway he'd used before. He circled out over the cove and spotted the yacht, almost invisible except for the red and green lights on its bow and stern. Then he headed due east.

"Down there! See it?" Lee cried. "It doesn't look long enough. Can you make it?"

"Hang on. This baby can stop on a dime!" Chris said as he circled once more and prepared to land. He took the rough dirt like a pro, and the plane stopped within inches of a clump of trees.

Lee let out a deep breath. "Man!"

They jumped out. "Better head for town first. The yacht is dark. Holly's probably not there after all, thank God. Look for the Jeep. She's bound to be in the vicinity," Chris said.

They hiked across the field, reached a road and jogged toward the little seaside village. Meanwhile Chris drove himself to distraction imagining the dozens of intolerable situations in which Holly might find herself. He saw her bound and gagged in the back of a truck headed for some far destination... locked in a sleazy hotel room... fending off an insanely drunken Paul...

Oh, God! Let me find her in time!

They bore left on Avenida Alfonso Pérez Gasga and walked toward the beach. A few minutes later they spotted the Jeep in front of Hotel Las Palmas.

The bartender there knew Paul, but hadn't seen him all week, and, yes, a young woman matching Holly's description had come in earlier asking for him. The story was the same every place they went. Frustrated and anxious, Chris decided they'd better go back to the cove and try to find someone who'd row them out to the yacht. If Holly and Paul weren't there... He didn't want to think about the possibilities.

The only sign of life was the little *fonda*, food stand, on the beach. Several people were drinking beer at the outdoor tables. Only the pinpoint red and green lights told them the yacht was still anchored in the cove. They plowed through the sand to the *fonda*. *"¿Donde está Señor Dalton?"* Chris whipped out the words.

The man spoke a little English. He jerked a thumb in the direction of the yacht. "Went out there this afternoon. Fine man, Señor Dalton. *¡Muy generoso!*"

"Did you by any chance see a young woman go out there today, probably late afternoon?"

The man's eyes glazed. *"Señor*, are you her husband?" He shook his head and pulled a long face. "I think it's best you don't go."

Damn. The fellow had it all wrong. Nevertheless, it was apparent he'd seen Holly or he wouldn't be acting so evasively. The place had an excellent view of the beach. He couldn't have missed her.

Lee nudged Chris's arm. "I saw some rowboats near the water. Maybe we could rent one."

The man shook his head. "The boys have all gone home. Sit down and have a beer. Make you happy. For sure, *señor*."

Chris slammed pesos down on the counter. "This is an emergency. I'll do the rowing." The fellow stared open-mouthed as Chris took a flashlight from his pocket and beamed a pathway across the beach to the edge of the water where the boats were located. Lee ran on ahead. A few moments later Chris saw him stumble, then cry out.

"Sir! Hurry! Oh, no," he cried as he bent over the huddled form. "I think someone has drowned!"

Chris ran alongside, flashed the light across the body and froze.

"My God," he cried. "It's Holly!"

CHAPTER TWENTY-TWO

THE BEAM FROM THE FLASHLIGHT raked Holly's still form. Her hair was tangled and plastered against her head and cheek. Water still dripped into the sand. Her skirt was gone, and so were her shoes. A torn blouse and slip clung wetly, revealing every curve of her slender small-boned body. The tangy odor of seaweed and salt swirled around them. She made a pathetic little heap against the driftwood and seemed part of the flotsam that had washed ashore with her.

"She's drowned!" Stark terror filled Lee's cry.

Frantically Chris felt for a pulse. His hand shook so he couldn't tell if movement fluttered in the slim wrist or whether it was his own wild heartbeat throbbing against her. "She can't be dead! God, show me she isn't dead!" Dread turned his fingers stiff and awkward as he searched for a sign of life in the hollow of her throat.

"Try artificial respiration!" Lee cried. "I know how!"

But Chris had already straddled her body. He forced her jaw open and placed his mouth on her cold lips. Lee chanted the rhythm for him like some frenzied coxswain and kept the flashlight beamed on her while Chris forced in his life-giving breath. Almost at once a faint moan escaped her lips, and her eyelids fluttered. She tried to twist her head away and weakly thrashed her arms.

Relief wrenched Chris's entire body as he picked up Holly's limp form and held her close. "Darling, it's all right, it's all right." He rocked her against him, a sob escaping, his joy at her survival so great he could barely speak. She felt small in his arms, fragile and completely vulnerable. Had Paul done this to her? Enough fury burgeoned within him to rock a city.

She opened her eyes. "Who...? Why...? I'm okay... really...not drowned...just exhausted. I did it...swam all the way. Can you believe that?" she said weakly, and clung to him. In the revealing beam of the flashlight, she looked wan and disheveled, but her femininity was intact. She reached up and touched his cheek.

"Chris? Why are you here?"

His arms tightened, and he didn't answer at once. *I'm here because you are my life, because you are the heart of the home I need and want. Because you're a giver, not a taker, because you knocked some sense into a couple of bonehead guys and turned us into a caring family.* "Because you're a crazy, damn fool woman," he said.

She smiled as if she'd heard every word he'd thought. Odd how tranquil she felt. Was this what was meant by euphoria? The long nightmare was over. Her eyes strained through the darkness. Was that Lee hovering next to them? She put an arm around Chris's shoulders and reached out to Lee. They drew together. For a few moments, arms entwined, they held one another close, their hearts too full to speak.

"Got to get something warm into you," Chris said gruffly at last, and they broke apart. He carried her across the beach to the food stand, Lee dogging every step. *Bebidas y Bocadillos*, Drinks and Snacks, the sign under the hanging lanterns said.

A radio blared a raucous brass combo at odds with the night, but as far as she was concerned, the music couldn't have been more idyllic. The little outdoor café, hardly more than a counter and a few stools, was devoid of customers. The man who tended it washed some glasses.

"Café caliente, pronto!" Chris said, and waited impatiently while the man poured the steaming black brew into a mug and set it on the counter.

Lee reached over and shyly patted her hand, then studied the menu as if he understood every word of it.

Tears filled her eyes. What had Lee said? *One's family rallied around in time of trouble.* She breathed contentedly. They were her family. She knew it, was sure of it.

She nestled closer against Chris, and his strength seemed to flow into her, filling her with a sense of well-being. She felt safe, protected, as if she'd come home at last. "I still can't believe you're here. How did you know where to find me?" she asked with a catch in her voice. He set her down on one of the stools and held the cup to her lips.

"Drink this," he said sternly. "Then we'll get to the whys and wherefores."

She tasted the strong black coffee and drank it slowly, savoring the heat that warmed her, feeling her aching muscles begin to relax. The attendant hovered over them, solicitous about her condition, asking questions and setting out a plate of snacks for them. Meanwhile, she and Chris exchanged explanations concerning how they'd all found themselves at this unlikely spot, and Lee managed to consume a plate of tacos and two bottles of Coke.

"I'm sure Paul never realized I'd fallen overboard," she said after describing her battle to reach the beach. "He seemed to be at the end of his rope, lonely and desperate, wanting to reach out to someone. I'm certain he meant no harm. But he was drunk, and I was afraid."

"Well, he'll be having company soon, the minute he sets foot in one of those Texas galleries." Holly felt a deep sadness at Paul's fate.

"Our swimming lessons paid off after all," Lee said, coming up for air after all the hot food.

"The main reason I'm here," she said, smiling warmly at him.

"The reason you're here," Chris said, "is because you're the most hardheaded, stubborn, tenacious, obstinate woman in the country."

"You left out crazy," she said happily.

"That, too," he snapped.

Holly ran a hand through her wet hair. "Why is it that at times of crisis, I always manage to look like a drowned rat? Rescued ladies are supposed to look fragile and glamorous."

"Just like a woman, thinking first about her appearance."

"Well, I can't go home like this."

"We aren't going home. It's too late to fly, so we'll just have to stay here."

"What about the Jeep?" Lee asked hopefully.

"I know what you're thinking, and yes, you may drive it. Holly and I will fly home in a few days. We have some important business to tend to."

Lee's eyes sparkled, and he looked back and forth at the two of them. "You're talking about a vacation?"

Chris gave him a good-natured slap on the shoulder. "I'm talking about a wedding."

"Wow! Wait until I tell Ramona and Juana!"

"Never mind. We prefer to do our own advertising."

"For sure," he said with a mile-wide grin.

Holly wondered if some of the water had seeped into her brain. "Hey, no one consulted me."

Chris lookd at her fondly. "This is Mexico, *querida*. Men make the weighty decisions here."

"Yeah, Holly," Lee said, aping Chris's machismo. "This is Mexico. All you have to do is to say *sí*."

"*Sí, señores,*" she said obediently, then changed her tone. "But just you two wait until we get home!"

"Speaking of home, I have a soccer game tomorrow," Lee said. "Is it okay if I drive back tonight? Don't worry. I'll keep an eye on the speedometer, watch out for cattle on the road, all the right stuff."

Chris handed him some pesos for gas, snapped a key off a ring and gave it to him. "Be careful. We want to keep you in the family."

Lee's eyes glistened, and for a few seconds he seemed tongue-tied. "Yes, sir, Sir," he said finally. He twisted the key in his hands. "I hardly know what to say. Totally awesome! Just like I hoped." Holly gave him a quick hug and kissed his cheek.

"See you soon, teach," she said. He took off as usual, as though he had just heard the starting gun at a track meet.

Chris looked at his watch and then at Holly's bedraggled appearance. "I admit you'd hardly be a cover girl candidate. In fact, I'd probably get arrested if I took you into Puerto Escondido looking like this. We have twenty minutes before the boutiques close. I'll hotfoot it to the village and get you something to wear. Wait right here."

The man at the stand took charge at once. "Pedro will guard your lady with his life," he promised. He gave her a towel to dry her hair and served an enormous bowl of chili, asserting it contained restorative powers beyond that of any medication. After one mouthful, she was convinced the hot stuff would either cure or kill in at least five minutes.

Less than an hour later, Chris returned with a pair of sandals in one hand and a dress over his arm.

"I never shopped so fast in my life. The woman thought I was a madman. I found us a hotel room, too, right on the square."

Since the little café afforded no amenities, Holly borrowed Chris's comb, took the sandals and dress and walked over to a clump of hibiscus to change. She peeled off her wet garments and wadded them into a ball. Chris hadn't thought to buy any underthings, or perhaps there hadn't been enough time. It didn't matter. The heavy, crinkled turquoise cotton gave away no secrets. She plucked a red bloom from the bush, tucked it into her hair and went back to Chris.

His eyes brightened. "Some transformation!"

"¡Olé!" Pedro said heartily. Chris left some pesos on the counter, and they thanked the solicitous fellow, then started for town on the dirt road. The night was balmy, and the moon rose over their shoulders, laying a golden sheen on the tropical growth that lined their path. It lent a feeling of mystery. Occasionally the whir of birds' wings interrupted the silence, and once there was a cry from a high-flying gull. Chris squeezed her hand as if to let her know the beauty of the night touched him also. They didn't need to talk to communicate.

A little later they saw a small rustic chapel at the side of the road. Its doors stood open as if to welcome all comers. Holly was not a deeply religious person, but she felt tonight that she'd had a profound and mystical experience, one that would affect the rest of her life. She needed a little more time to wonder, to reflect on the way her world had suddenly turned around. Well, not quite turned around. There was that year-long absence to face while Chris was in the Andes, but she could deal with that now. She gestured toward the chapel. "Shall we go in for a minute?"

He nodded, and they entered. Shadows leaped and danced around the little sanctuary as moving air challenged the flickering candles. Holly linked her arm in his, feeling both joy and peace. They walked slowly down the aisle to the altar. It was abundantly banked with flowers, both real and artificial. A potpourri of fragrance eddied around them.

"There must have been a wedding here recently."

"Shall we have ours here tomorrow?"

"Miguel says that a church wedding alone doesn't constitute a legal marriage in Mexico. The requirement is first for a brief civil ceremony. The church wedding is usual but not necessary according to the law."

"Two weddings? Good! I'm all for anything that will tie the knot a little tighter."

So was she. *Don't think about the Andes. Don't think about Marissa. I'm the one he wants to marry.* "Well, as long as we're here, we could have a rehearsal. You know, practice our vows," she said half jokingly.

"Any vow I say here will be the real thing," he said. He faced her and took her hands in his, his expression so solemn her heart began to pound. This was no game. Candlelight touched his strong face. His steady gray eyes met hers, and she felt a surge of tenderness at the love she saw there.

His voice was firm as he began to speak. "First, I pledge all my love and commitment to our marriage through both the good and the bad times so that together we can handle whatever comes along. Next, I promise whatever it takes to help us unfold our truest and best selves so that we can leave something behind to justify the space we used." Holly's heart was so full that she wondered if she could utter a word. He nudged her arm. "Your turn."

"You know I'm not articulate when I get all choked up."

"Inarticulate will do just fine."

She spoke haltingly, wanting every word to say exactly what she meant. "I promise to love you with an understanding heart, to remember that letting go can bring us closer, not farther apart." He picked up her hand and brushed his lips across her ring finger.

"I'm not finished," she whispered, as if the ceremony were for real.

He grinned. "So finish."

"Well, I promise to keep tabs on our hemoglobin."

"Good. At least four hugs a day, remember? And I'm for starting right now."

They embraced and kissed, reinforcing their promises. As always, there was a surprising tenderness to his lips. Warmed by his pledges and the absolute certainty that they belonged together, Holly knew they'd never become strangers again. At last they turned and walked out of the chapel.

"I couldn't feel more married," Holly said.

"In the truest sense. We'll tend to the legalities tomorrow." They walked a little way down the road and paused by an open space to take in a view of the ocean. The amethyst sky had long since become jet black and was now star-filled. A cautious moon moved in and out of scattered clouds. The gravelly wash of waves on the beach was the only sound.

He turned her toward him so that intermittent moonlight touched her face and probed her expression for so long that she grew alarmed. "Chris, what's the matter? Are you having second thoughts?"

"On the contrary. I'm hoping that *you* have none."

Was he worried about leaving her for the Andes? She'd promised to let go. Didn't he remember? "I'm sure, Chris."

"Well, everything's happened so fast this past week, I haven't yet told you about a new job that's waiting for me in Toronto."

"Toronto and the Andes too?" She swallowed hard.

"I'm not going to the Andes, Holly."

"Not going! But Chris, you've wanted it for years!" Surely she hadn't heard right.

"I admit I was tempted. For all of thirty seconds. Chalk it up to sophomoric nostalgia. Anyway, I'd already accepted the Toronto offer to head up a new cinema-television school devoted entirely to documentaries. Now that's a real dream assignment! All summer I knew I was being considered for the post, but I didn't want to say anything until I knew for sure. I wanted that position more than I can say and I hoped that you'd consider coming with me if I went there. That's what I wanted to discuss with you the night of the party." Boyish anxiety showed in his face.

She thought for several moments. In the first flush of their renewed commitment was he doing this for her? Was she already winding those chains around him? "Chris, are you certain? I know very well how much that Andes project meant to you."

"Positive. There's no way I would enter into any more arrangements with Marissa. I'd be strung up like a puppet. Heading this new film school is the most exciting challenge I can imagine. I have full approval to work on every innovative idea I present. Do you realize what that means to me?" His eyes shone with excitement, and she knew he spoke the truth.

"But what about your Oaxaca documentary? Here I am delaying you even more."

"After reviewing it with Sam, I decided the film needed more editing, which meant there was no way I could meet the deadline. I don't know who got the contract," he said cheerfully.

"I'm sorry. All that work!"

"Not to worry. Sam took one look at the film and said no problem. Mexico is a hot topic now. Since the earthquake and the dramatic devaluation of the peso, everyone wants something on it. Sam lined up two TV executives who want to see it the minute it's completed."

Joy surged through her. There'd be no year's separation, no project with Marissa. All the uncertainties of the long summer months faded away. The past terrifying hours, when she'd fought to stay alive, had brought insight and perspective. She'd realized the fragility of human life and was now powerfully aware of the need to sort out the essential from the trivial. She was where she belonged, where she wanted to be. They'd be a family after all, she and Chris and Lee. They were all she needed or wanted.

"Would you believe they even have a house ready for us to move into? And I've already talked to someone about building a kiln for you in the backyard. I'm afraid the place isn't your dream home, but it's large. There's plenty of room for Lee, and even for more family if we want."

She squeezed his hand in answer.

His expression was still anxious. "So how does Toronto sound to you? It's a beautiful city. You can probably teach if you want, or maybe you'd like to open a small gallery to feature your works and those of other local artists. Holly, darling, it means everything to me for you to be happy there." His anxiety was palpable, and she hugged him.

"Chris, I'd love that!"

"I have to be there the first of the month. You'll come with me?"

"I'll come with you." She was never more certain of anything in her life. She reached up and smoothed away his frown. "Why do you still look so worried?"

"Well, I know how you feel about putting down roots and all that. And I keep thinking about those three-generation magnolia trees you admired. Most of all, I'm concerned about that Victorian house you set your heart on. The place in Toronto sounds a little avant-garde from what I was told."

"You dear man. Believe me, places and things aren't what count when it comes to stability and a feeling of belonging. I know now that that comes from inside."

"But what about roots? My contract is for four years. It could mean another move."

She put her arms around him again, drew his lips down to hers and kissed him. "My dearest, listen to what I'm trying to tell you. Wherever you go, that's where I want to be. You are my roots, Chris. You are my home. Take me with you."

Harlequin Superromance

COMING NEXT MONTH

#234 THE FOREVER PROMISE • Meg Hudson
Fourteen years ago Claire Parmeter left King Faraday at
the altar when she discovered that another woman was
carrying his child. Now King and Claire meet again.
Mutual desire draws them together, but the ghosts of
their past threaten to separate them once more....

#235 SWEET TOMORROWS • Francine Christopher
Valerie Wentworth thinks she's put Wall Street behind
her forever. But that is before an irate financial planner
waltzes into her antique-doll shop. Not only is Cutter
the most gorgeous man she's ever seen, but he has the
formidable wits to match her own, and their bodies,
well...they fit together perfectly.

#236 HALFWAY TO HEAVEN • Pamela Bauer
Designer Rachel Kincaid can't afford to fall in love with
sexy department store magnate Cole Braxton III. She is
still holding out hope that her missing fiancé will return
home. But Cole isn't about to wait around forever.
Faced with a barrage of difficult choices, Rachel finally
realizes the answers lie within her heart....

#237 CHILD'S PLAY • Peggy Nicholson
Snatching a small boy from under his bodyguard's nose
is no mean trick, even for Tey Kenyon. She can't let
Mac McAllister interfere with her plans, but interfering
with her heart is another matter!

WILLO DAVIS ROBERTS

To Share a Dream

A story of the passions, fears and hatreds of three sisters and the men they love

Well-known author Willo Davis Roberts captures the hearts of her readers in this passionate story of Christina, Roxanne and Megan. They fled England in 1691 in search of independence, only to find a harsh new life in Salem, Massachusetts.

Can you keep a secret?

You can keep this one plus 4 free novels

Janet Dailey
Americana

Don't miss a single title from this great collection. The first eight titles have already been published. Complete and mail this coupon today to order books you may have missed.

Harlequin Reader Service

In U.S.A.
901 Fuhrmann Blvd.
P.O. Box 1397
Buffalo, N.Y. 14140

In Canada
P.O. Box 2800
Postal Station A
5170 Yonge Street
Willowdale, Ont. M2N 6J3

Please send me the following titles from the Janet Dailey Americana Collection. I am enclosing a check or money order for $2.75 for each book ordered, plus 75¢ for postage and handling.

_____	ALABAMA	Dangerous Masquerade
_____	ALASKA	Northern Magic
_____	ARIZONA	Sonora Sundown
_____	ARKANSAS	Valley of the Vapours
_____	CALIFORNIA	Fire and Ice
_____	COLORADO	After the Storm
_____	CONNECTICUT	Difficult Decision
_____	DELAWARE	The Matchmakers

Number of titles checked @ $2.75 each = $_____

N.Y. RESIDENTS ADD
   APPROPRIATE SALES TAX $_____

Postage and Handling $____.75____

                            TOTAL $_____

I enclose _____

(Please send check or money order. We cannot be responsible for cash sent through the mail.)

PLEASE PRINT

NAME _____

ADDRESS _____

CITY _____

STATE/PROV. _____